1

IT MIGHT HAVE BEEN THE NUMEROUS SHOTS OF WHISKEY and the goading of his fellow drinkers down at The Empire Bar, but Brady Sheppard thought crashing his ex-fiancée's wedding was the best idea he'd had in years.

Too bad he wasn't drunk enough to believe he'd gone through the side entrance of the First Presbyterian Church undetected because of his stealth and military training. He'd caught a break, that was all. It'd been bound to happen eventually.

The sounds of a string quartet masked the soft click of him pulling the door shut. Bracing his weight on his crutches, he slanted forward. To his left, waning sunlight filtered through two stained-glass windows, breaking up the shadows of a long hallway. Glancing around the corner, he spied five women in identical dark purple gowns lined up in a haphazard row, flowers clasped loosely in their hands as they chatted in hushed whispers while waiting for their cue to walk down the aisle.

The door at the end of the hall opened and Brady's heart

rate picked up. Backing against the wall, he stayed hidden in the shadows as Jane Cleo Montgomery stepped into the hall. She, too, had on a purple dress and held flowers, her brown, corkscrew curls piled on top of her head. As she passed him unaware, she said something over her shoulder and laughed.

And that was when he saw her. Liz. *His* Liz.

He didn't move, barely breathed as the woman he was supposed to marry glided toward him, a serene smile on her beautiful face. His hands tightened on the crutches. Of course she was happy. She was getting what she'd always wanted. A fancy, summer wedding in her hometown, surrounded by family and friends. Except he wasn't the groom.

Ignoring the throbbing pain in his knee, he hobbled out into her path.

"Hello, Lizzie."

The color drained from her face as she pulled up short, stumbling over her long train. "Brady."

That was it. After everything they'd meant to each other, the years they'd been together, all she could give him was his name. He wanted to shake her. Demand that she take back everything in that goddamn letter she'd sent him over a year ago when she'd blown his life apart. Wanted to see more in her eyes than nerves. Something that told him she regretted what she'd lost. That she was hurting, even just a little.

And how pathetic was he that he'd take whatever scraps she tossed his way?

"I'll get Dad," J.C. said from behind him.

Swinging his crutches forward, he backed Liz down the hallway. Her familiar floral scent confused his already

A MARINE FOR CHRISTMAS

BETH ANDREWS

muddled brain. Her gown had a fitted, beaded bodice and puffy skirt that accentuated her hourglass figure. She'd swept her glossy, dark hair up and wore one of those tiara things attached to a veil that ended below her small waist.

She was the most beautiful thing he'd ever seen.

"Glad I'm not too late," he murmured.

She swallowed, her hazel eyes wide. "Too...too late?"

"For the ceremony."

"Brady, please..." She held out her hand only to curl her fingers into her palm and lower it back to her side. "Please don't do this."

He went hot, then cold, trembling with the effort to contain his anger. Those were the exact same words he'd said to her after he'd read that damn letter. He'd called her from his base in Afghanistan, begged her to give him another chance.

He moved even closer, crowding her. She gasped, her warm breath washing over his face. "What do you think I'm going to do, Lizzie?" he asked quietly.

"I...I'm not sure." Her voice was as quiet as his. And when she met his eyes, the strange intimacy of their conversation reminded him of how he used to hold her after they'd made love. How it seemed as if they were the only two people in the world. "Make a scene or...or interrupt the ceremony..."

He shook his head to clear it. The ceremony. Right. He stepped back, grimacing with the pressure on his left leg.

"Are you all right?" she asked. As if she cared about him. Dr. Elizabeth Montgomery, trying to heal the poor Jarhead's injuries.

He glared at her. "Afraid I'm going to stand up when the minister asks if anyone objects?"

Someone laid a heavy hand on Brady's shoulder. "Son, you need to leave." Brady glanced at Liz's father. Don Montgomery, tall and pudgy with intelligent brown eyes and thinning dark hair threaded heavily with gray. The physician's round face was red above his starched collar.

"I'm not your son," was all Brady said. Though, until recently, he'd considered Don to be like a second father.

Jane Cleo brushed past them to stand next to her sister, looking from him to Liz and back again.

"Go home," Don said, not unkindly. "Don't make this harder than it has to be." When Brady didn't so much as blink, the older man sighed and reached into the inside pocket of his dark suit jacket. "I'm afraid if you won't leave on your own, I'll have to call the police."

"No," J.C. and Liz said at the same time.

Liz pushed between them, facing her father. "Brady would never do anything to hurt me." Then she turned to him, pleading with her eyes. It just about cut him off at the knees. "Would you?"

Damn it. *Damn it!* She was right. No matter how much he'd had to drink, no matter how pissed he was, he'd rather die than hurt her.

He was as big of a fool for her as he'd always been.

"Goodbye, Brady," she said softly before linking her arm through her father's and tugging him down the hall, J.C. following.

He stood in that dark hallway while the music changed to a classical song he'd heard before but never in a million years would be able to name. All he knew was that as that song played, Liz was walking down the aisle toward the man she was going to marry.

He wiped a hand over his mouth. He wanted a drink. Needed it to dull his mind.

Instead, he found an empty spot in the back where he could stand unnoticed. And torture himself by watching the woman he'd loved for half of his life become someone else's wife.

"I NEED A FAVOR."

J.C. licked sweet buttercream icing off her fork. "I'm not holding your dress while you pee again," she told Liz quietly, hoping the other members of the bridal party seated next to her at the head table couldn't hear. "Once in a life-time is one time too many."

An elderly couple walked past, congratulating Liz. She thanked them

before turning back to J.C. "This is serious," she said in a harsh whisper.

"More serious than wedding cake?"

Liz had detached her veil but kept the tiara firmly in place. She always had liked to pretend she was a princess. Which left J.C. to play the role of lady-in-waiting.

Liz picked up J.C.'s plate and carried it with her as she pulled her sister to her feet. "Come on."

They made their way across the large room, weaving around the tables and chairs tied with wide, purple taffeta. The tables were topped with narrow glass jars of varying heights filled with water, lavender rose petals and lit, floating white candles.

Liz stepped behind a large column. "Get him to leave."

J.C. didn't need to be told who *him* was. Brady Sheppard. She peeked around the column. Yep. There he sat at the end of the bar, all scruffy and brooding in his rumpled T-shirt and faded jeans, his dark blond hair still military-short. He stared at the spot where she and Liz stood. No surprise, given he hadn't taken his eyes off the bride ever since he'd hobbled into Pine Hills Country Club a few hours ago.

Poor Brady. She should be ticked at him for crashing her sister's wedding —and she was. A little. But after everything he'd gone through, everything Liz had put him through, it was tough to work up a good mad. Especially when he seemed so...lost. So alone.

Taking her plate back from Liz, J.C. scooped up a small bite though she could no longer taste the delicious vanilla cake and milk chocolate ganache filling. "Ignore him. Don't let him ruin your special day."

It was a refrain she, the other bridesmaids and the mothers of both bride and groom had repeated numerous times already.

"I have ignored him and he's already ruined my day. And now it's time for him to leave." She nodded toward the other side of the room. "Before Carter's frat brothers talk him into doing something stupid."

J.C. looked over to where her new brother-in-law stood by the presents table. Pale blond hair, green eyes, chiseled features...Carter Messler—make that *Dr.* Carter Messler— was not only handsome, funny and smart, he was also the most easygoing guy J.C. had ever met. Usually. Surrounded by his groomsmen, though, they had one thing in common: they were all scowling at Brady. Carter's scowl was the darkest.

"But...Carter's a pediatrician," J.C. said. "Pediatricians don't go around getting into fistfights."

"I've never seen him so angry." Glancing nervously at her new husband, she lowered her voice. "Brady could get hurt."

J.C. smashed the remaining cake crumbs under her fork.

Brady had never backed down from a fight. Which was probably what had made him such a good Marine. And she doubted he'd let a bum knee and crutches stop him from taking a swing or two.

Liz was right. He had to go. And not just because J.C. didn't want to see him get his stubborn head bashed in. The disheveled, ex-Marine partaking in the open bar was preventing Liz and Carter from enjoying their day.

"What do you want me to do?"

Liz squeezed J.C.'s hand. "Whatever you have to. He'll listen to you," she said desperately, as if willing it to be true. "He's always liked you. He used to tell me you were like the little sister he never had."

And wasn't that enough to make her ego take a serious nosedive.

"I'm not making any promises" she said, handing her plate to Liz. "But I'll do my best."

J.C. resolutely kept her gaze forward instead of glancing at her reflection as she passed the mirror behind the polished bar. She didn't need visual confirmation that her hair was rebelling against the dozens of bobby pins the stylist had used. Unlike Liz, ignoring problems usually worked pretty well for J.C.

She stopped in front of him. "Hello, Brady."

"Janie." He sipped from a squat glass of amber liquid. "You look different."

She'd heard a variation of that statement all day from numerous friends and relatives who hadn't seen her in the past two years. And while it usually pleased her to have people notice the sixty-five pounds she'd dropped, she could've sworn she'd run into Brady since then. "I lost some weight."

His narrowed eyes roamed from her head to her feet and

back up again. "I was talking about the dress." Her skin prickled.

"Oh," she said breathlessly as she wiped a damp palm down the front of the simple, halter-style gown. "Is there someone I can call to come get you?"

Resting one arm against the bar, he leaned back. "Am I going somewhere?"

"I think it's for the best if you did."

His light blue eyes sharpened. "You do? Or Lizzie does?"

"Me. Liz. Carter. My parents. The other bridesmaids... I'd say it's unanimous."

"What if I'm not ready to leave?"

She fisted her hands around the material of her skirt. She felt for him.

Honest, she did. But just because Liz had moved on with her life didn't give Brady the right to act like an ass. It wasn't as if he was the only person in the world to be in love with someone who didn't love him back.

Moving to his side, she was careful not to touch him. "I get it. You're upset and you want to hurt her back. Well, congratulations, you succeeded. But enough's enough."

Other than a momentary twitch of his left eye, he remained expressionless.

After a moment, he raised his glass to her, downed the remaining drink, then set the glass on the bar. "Don't bother calling anyone on my account. I'll see myself home."

Positioning the crutches under his arms, he stood, gazing somewhere over her left shoulder. She glanced back to see Liz and Carter, arms around each other as they swayed to the band's version of "Unchained Melody." When she turned back, Brady was already halfway to the door.

What she wouldn't give to have Brady look at her with even a fraction of the longing she'd seen in his eyes when he stared at Liz. To have him see her as Jane Cleo instead of just Liz's little sister.

Lips pressed together, she watched him until he went out the side door of the clubhouse. Could he drive with his injured knee? Would he? No. The Brady she'd known most of her life would never drink and then get behind the wheel. She pushed a loose bobby pin into her hair, jabbing her scalp in the process. Of course, the old Brady didn't have a permanent glower, would never crash a wedding or suck back whiskey as if it were the only thing getting him from one minute to the next.

She headed to the rear of the bar where the bridal party had stashed their personal items. No one would miss her if she slipped away for a little bit.

Long enough to make sure Brady got home safely.

Twenty minutes later, J.C. wondered which of them of them was the bigger idiot. Him for thinking he could walk the ten miles home on crutches. Or her for leaving her sister's wedding to give him a ride, all because she still hadn't gotten over her stupid, childhood crush.

Her. Definitely her. She'd not only driven him, but helped him inside and onto the couch and even made coffee.

She frowned as it dripped into the pot. Well, wasn't that what people did when they cared about someone?

Carrying a cup of coffee, she made her way to the living room where Brady was slumped on the couch, his head resting against the back of it, his left leg out straight.

"I thought you could use this," she said, holding the mug out as she sat next to him. When he made no move to take it, she put it on the coffee table and then clasped her hands together in her lap.

Other than to tell her he was staying at the cottage on

The Diamond Dust, the historic plantation the Sheppards called home, he'd remained silent on the drive over. So there she was, in the middle of the woods in a sparsely furnished living room with her sister's stoic, drunk ex.

Finally she cleared her throat and made a move to leave. "I'd better get going."

Nothing. No "Thanks for getting me home." The man didn't even blink. She'd taken one step toward the front door when his gravelly voice stopped her.

"I didn't want to hurt her."

"Excuse me?"

He finally sat up and took a long gulp of coffee. Stared down at the mug. "I didn't go there to hurt her."

Her heart racing, she retook her seat. "Why did you do it then?"

"I had to see."

"Had to see what?"

He set his coffee down then rolled his head from side to side. "I had to see it happen. Had to watch her marry someone else. So I'd know it was real. And that it really is over between us."

She laid her hand on his forearm. "Brady, I...I'm so sorry."

He looked down at her hand then up at her face, his gaze hooded. "You're still as sweet as you always were, aren't you, Jane?" he murmured.

His tone was low and dark. Dangerous. Gooseflesh rose on her bare arms. "I...I hate that you're..." In pain. Broken. Unable to see beyond Liz. "That you have to go through this."

He shifted, his knee bumping hers. She slid over several inches. But...was it her imagination, or did he keep getting closer?

"Like I said, sweet." He skimmed the tip of his forefinger down her cheek.

She sat motionless, her mouth dry as he cupped the back of her head. Then he tugged her head down and kissed her, his lips brushing hers once. Then again. The third time, he slowly deepened the kiss, his lips warm and firm, the rough pad of his thumb caressing her jaw. His tongue slipped between her lips, coaxing a response.

He eased back, his eyes searching hers. "Okay?" he asked softly.

She exhaled shakily. Was it okay? She'd dreamt of this, of him touching her, kissing her...wanting her...her entire life. Almost as long as she'd loved him.

Ignoring all the reasons why they couldn't do this, she pressed her mouth to his.

Brady groaned and speared his fingers into her hair, scattering bobby pins across the couch. When his other hand cupped her breast through the silk of her gown, she almost jumped out of her skin. But then he lightly pinched her nipple and she arched her back, fitting herself more fully into his palm.

Willing herself to relax, she tentatively smoothed her palms over the hard contours of his chest up to his shoulders. He lifted his head long enough to strip his shirt off, tossing it behind him before kissing her again. She couldn't stop touching him. Couldn't believe she really was touching him. He was so beautiful, his body lean but muscular. His skin soft. And hot.

Still kissing her, he grabbed hold of her underneath her thighs, tugging her down until she lay flat on her back. Lifting her dress, he swept his hand up to her hipbone, leaving trails of warmth in his wake. He parted her legs and lightly stroked her through her panties. She squirmed. Her thigh muscles clenched.

Before she could raise her hips in a silent demand for him to touch her harder, he pulled her panties down, leaving them around her ankles. Then he lifted his mouth from hers so he could unfasten and shove down his jeans. Her head was still spinning as Brady thrust her dress up around her waist. Cool air washed over her.

Slow down. She brought her legs together. And for the first time, she noticed Brady's features etched in pain.

"Your knee," she said. "Are you—"

He kissed her again and settled on top of her, keeping most of his weight on his right side. Spreading her legs slowly, he gave her a chance to stop him. She didn't.

He didn't return her feelings. But she couldn't refuse him. Didn't want to.

Then he was at her entrance. Hot, hard and insistent. Enticing.

He pushed into her, his thickness stretching her. Taking her hips in a viselike grip, he began to move.

Unlike her fantasies, there were no tender words. No lingering looks. None of the fireworks she'd imagined. There was no connection between them other than the joining of their bodies.

Oh, God. She'd made a huge mistake.

Her throat burning, she stared up into his handsome face, her hands clutching the cushion beneath her. His mouth was a thin line, the hair at his temples damp with sweat. And no matter how hard she silently willed him to, he never once opened his eyes.

Finally, after what seemed like an eternity, his pace quickened and his body grew taut. Emptying himself inside her, he gave a guttural growl.

And called out her sister's name.

2

THREE MONTHS LATER

SEVEN O'CLOCK in the morning—on Thanksgiving, no less—was way too early to start throwing up.

Bent over the porch rail, J.C. wiped a shaky, gloved hand over her mouth. Wrinkling her nose at the bushes below her, she straightened. At least she hadn't puked in her car. Again.

Her stomach still churning, she crossed Brady's porch and pounded on the door before digging into the pocket of her bulky coat for a mint. She would not freak out. She could handle this. And once Brady knew, he'd help her. He'd figure out what to do.

But first he had to answer the damn door.

Wrapping her arms around herself, she scanned the surrounding woods. A blanket of damp leaves covered the forest floor and not even the sun shining in a gorgeous blue sky could pierce the darkness of the trees. She'd parked behind Brady's silver pickup, so it stood to reason that if his truck was here, he was here.

She rattled the doorknob—only to have it turn easily in

14

her hand. She blinked, then slipped inside and shut the door. "Hello? Brady? It's me. J.C."

The living-room blinds were drawn, but she had no trouble making out the shape of the cream sofa. The sofa where what should've been her dream come true had turned into her greatest nightmare.

Sunlight shone through the tiny window above the kitchen sink. She crept through the small foyer toward it but stopped at the doorway.

The cottage had seemed sterile, just-moved-into, when she'd last been there three months ago. But now the kitchen was a mess. And not your ordinary, didn't-do-the-dishes-last-night-and-left-the-empty-milk-carton-on-the-counter mess she often made in her own apartment. Dirty dishes were piled high in both sides of the sink and took up half the counter space. Garbage overflowed from the bin in the corner and crumbs littered the hardwood floor. Cupboard doors hung open as if someone had ransacked the place. And it would take a jackhammer to chisel through the food on the stovetop.

And she didn't even want to know what that awful smell was. Covering her nose and mouth with her arm, she ducked her head and rushed down the hallway, careful not to brush up against anything lest she risk some sort of infectious disease.

"Brady," she called again as she passed the small bathroom, her eyes straight ahead. After the horror of that kitchen, you couldn't pay her to look in the man's bathroom. At least, not without some sort of Hazmat suit on. She stopped at the closed door to his bedroom and knocked. "Brady, are you up?"

No answer. She twisted the silver stud in her left earlobe. She'd already let herself into the house, no sense stopping now. She opened the door but couldn't see a thing. Did he have something against mornings? Or just sunlight in general? She found the light switch and flipped it on.

The bedroom was as messy as the kitchen, minus any decaying food or garbage. Clothes were tossed on top of and all around the three-drawer dresser. A sock hung from a hardback chair in the corner and a lamp lay on its side on the carpet next to the bed, where a large lump snuffled softly and then began to snore.

She stepped hesitantly into the room. "Brady," she whispered. He continued snoring. With the toe of her sneaker, she nudged a white T-shirt out of her way, then stepped over a pair of dark boxer briefs to the head of the bed.

She picked up an open bottle of whiskey from the nightstand and wasn't sure if she should be relieved it was still half-full. Finding the cap behind a digital clock that blinked twelve, she screwed it on.

Brady slept on his stomach, his long body stretched diagonally across the bed. A sheet covered him from the waist down, leaving his naked back and one bent leg exposed. His shoulders were broad, the lean muscles clearly defined. He had a black vine tattoo that started at his right hip, wound its way over his back and up to his shoulder before curling out of sight. His right arm hung limply off the side of the bed, his left held a pillow over his head.

Too bad or she might have poured the rest of the whiskey over his face.

"Brady." Nothing. If not for his soft snores, she'd think he was comatose.

"Wake up."

Other than a twitch of his toes, he didn't move. Holding the whiskey bottle by the neck, she nudged his shoulder with the bottom of it. "Wake—"

Brady's hand shot out and grabbed the bottle, tossing it onto the bed at the same time he wrenched her forward. Before she could so much as open her mouth to scream, he flipped her onto her back and pinned her to the mattress, his muscular thighs straddling her hips.

His large, strong hand was around her throat.

Panic shot through her as his fingers tightened, cutting off her airway. She bucked wildly underneath him, clawing at his wrists, but she may as well have been fighting a statue. The wild tangle of his shaggy, wheat-colored hair and the darker stubble on his cheeks and chin sharpened the already sharp lines of his handsome face. His blue eyes were like ice chips, cold and empty.

"Brady...stop...it's me," she managed to spit out, though it hurt to talk. To breathe. "Jane Cleo. Please..."

He blinked, and his hold on her loosened. Realization flashed across his face and he leapt off her to the other side of the room. She rolled onto her side as she gasped for breath.

"Damn it, J.C.! What the hell are you doing?" Brady demanded, the hint of Southern accent doing nothing to soften his harsh, sleep-roughened voice. "I could've killed you."

"I...I was trying to wake you," she rasped.

He pressed the heels of his hands against his eyes. "How did you even get in here?"

Her arms shaking, she pushed herself up into a sitting position, keeping her gaze off his naked body. "The door was unlocked."

"That didn't give you the right to come in."

"No. Of course not. But I wanted..."

"What? A repeat of the last time you were here?" he

asked, then gave one quick shake of his head. "Not interested."

Tears stung her eyes, made her already sore throat burn. "I didn't come here for a repeat of anything, you bastard," she said fiercely, her hands gripping the crumpled sheet. "I came to tell you I'm pregnant."

BRADY REARED BACK, hitting his already spinning head against the wall behind him with a dull thud and jolt of pain. "What?"

"I'm pregnant."

Oh, shit. He swallowed, but his tongue felt as if it were wearing a fur coat. "How?"

"The usual way."

"Who?"

She struggled to her feet, her arms crossed against a coat bright enough to burn his retinas. "A traveling salesman," she snapped. "Who do you think?"

That was the problem. He couldn't think. Not with his head pounding. And a panic unlike he'd ever felt crawling up his spine.

He stared at her stomach, but her coat was too bulky to discern any changes in her body. "Are you sure?"

She threw a sandwich bag at him, hitting him in the chest. "See for yourself."

Shoving his hand through his hair, he frowned down at the bag where it'd landed by his feet. "What are those?"

"The pregnancy test I took last night, along with the two I took this morning. You'll notice every last one of them has a stupid plus sign."

He dropped his hand, hitting his bare thigh. And realized she'd literally caught him with his pants down. Searching for and finding a pair of gym shorts, he jerked them on, ignoring the throbbing in his bad knee. He took a deep breath and held it for the count of five.

"No," he growled. "Are you sure it's mine?"

She bristled, reminding him of some mortally offended, overgrown Shirley Temple impersonator with her round face and her frizzy curls smooshed down by an ugly, piss-colored hat. "Of course I am."

And with those words, any hope he might've had that he hadn't royally screwed up yet again flew out the window. Just proved how useless and cruel hope could be.

Instead of kicking a hole in the wall like he wanted to, he shrugged. With his bad leg, he probably couldn't do much damage anyway. "Can't blame me for asking."

But the look she gave him said she not only could blame him, but likely would for a hellishly long time.

He worked to not limp as he crossed to the bed. Told himself it didn't bother him when she darted away like a rabbit. His stomach roiled from not having anything in it other than the Jim Beam he'd downed last night.

The idea of having a kid should make him feel something besides disappointment. Even the angry red marks on J.C.'s slender throat, the marks he'd put there, should make him feel something. Guilt, at least. But to feel guilty about any of it would mean he'd have to have some semblance of conscience, of humanity, left.

Sitting on the bed, he reached back for the Jim Beam before picking up a spotted water glass with smudged lipstick on the rim from the floor.

"Do you think that's going to help?" J.C. asked, disgusted.

He flicked her a glance, then poured two healthy shots into the glass.

"Can't hurt."

She made a sound, sort of like his mother's teakettle right before it starting whistling. But thankfully, she kept her mouth shut. He gulped his drink, savoring the burn as it hit the back of his tongue.

He carefully stretched his left leg out in front of him. And noticed J.C.'s eyes lock on the webbing of scars. The raised, white welts were from the shrapnel when the roadside bomb had gone off. The thinner lines were from the two surgeries he'd endured only to be told his leg would never be one hundred percent.

His fingers tensed on his glass and he debated risking another death glare from J.C. to get a second shot. As if the pain and stiffness could let him forget he wasn't whole anymore, the scars reminded him.

As did the pity in people's eyes.

Wiping the back of his hand over his mouth, he worked to keep his expression bland.

She blew out an exasperated breath. "Well?"

"Well what?"

"Don't you have anything to say?"

He scratched the side of his head. Realized he never did make it to that barber appointment his mother had set up for him last week. Or had it been two weeks ago? "Can't think of anything."

Her mouth popped open. "You can't think of anything?" she repeated, her voice rising. "Don't you think we should discuss this?"

"Seems a little late for that."

"But what are we going to do?"

"That's up to you."

She stepped back, her hand to her heart. "Me? Don't you have an opinion?"

He turned his attention to pouring more whiskey into his glass. "Your body. Your decision."

"I am not having an abortion, if that's what you're getting at." Underneath the slight tremble in her voice was a determination that he'd never before heard from Jane Cleo.

"Like I said, your decision."

Whipping her hat off, she crushed it in her hand, her hair poofing out around her head as if it had a life of its own. "But what are we going to do now?"

He drained his glass as he stood. "I'm not sure about you, but I'm going to hit the head and then go back to sleep."

She blocked his exit. "That's it? You don't have any reaction to the fact that you're going to be a father?"

His skin grew clammy. "I'm not going to be a father."

"I told you," she said, speaking through her teeth, "I'm sure it's yours."

"I don't doubt that." His memory of what had happened between them was blurry at best, but he knew she was telling the truth. Even if he'd spent the past few months pretending that night had never happened. That he hadn't taken advantage of J.C. That he hadn't slept with Liz's sister.

That Liz hadn't married someone else.

But that didn't mean he was going to saddle some poor kid with him as a father. And he sure as hell didn't need the added responsibility of a child.

Especially when Liz wasn't the mother.

"What I mean is," he continued, "I don't plan on being a father. Not to your baby or any other kid."

"You want me to handle this alone?"

He slammed the bottle down on the nightstand. She flinched. "What do you want from me?" he growled. "You can't show up here, wake me up and throw something this huge in my face and expect me to take care of it. To take care of you. Because if that's what you expected, you're talking to the wrong man."

She shut her eyes. "This isn't happening. This isn't happening."

What was she doing? J.C. had always been a bit...eccentric. Which was fine when she'd been a teenager and had staged a one-person sit-in at the high school cafeteria to protest the school's refusal to offer meat-free lunches once a week. But this was just plain weird.

And if that one word didn't sum up Jane Cleo Montgomery, nothing did.

She opened her eyes and walked away. Finally, his torment was ending. Except, she whirled back around and threw her hat. It sailed over his head and hit the wall behind him.

"Do you have any idea what I've been going through?" she asked quietly, but his headache spiked just the same. "How scared I've been? For over a month I told myself that I couldn't really be pregnant. But now, well—" she gestured to the bag of pregnancy tests "—there's no more denying it. My worst fears are confirmed and now I get to deal with the joys of an unexpected pregnancy, which includes puking every morning, no matter what I eat or even if I eat."

Brady rubbed the back of his neck. "What do you want me to say, Jane? That I'm sorry? Okay, I'm sorry."

"I don't want an apology. I want you to get your head out of that bottle and help me. How am I going to tell my parents?" she asked, her voice breaking. "How am I supposed to face Liz?"

Grinding his back teeth together, he reached over for the whiskey bottle and added more to his glass. Ignored the unsteadiness of his hand as liquid splattered over his fingers. Damn it, did she think this was easy for him? Any of it? He wiped his hand on the sheet. He'd regretted what had happened between them the moment he'd come to. The last thing he wanted was for Liz —the woman he'd sworn to love for the rest of his life—to find out he'd slept with her kid sister.

"Your family's close," he said. And they'd coddled J.C. her entire life. They wouldn't let her go through this alone. "I'm sure once they get used to the idea, they'll help you out."

"Thank you for sharing that brilliant piece of logic," she said so coldly, so sarcastically, he raised his eyebrows. "Tell you what, when you figure out what, if any, part you want to play in this baby's life, let me know. In the meantime, you can go to hell."

He saluted her with his glass. "Already there."

With a low growl, sweet Jane Cleo Montgomery, the girl who was so bubbly and happy it was as if she'd swallowed a goddamn beam of sunshine, stormed out. A moment later, the front door slammed shut, followed by a dull thud. Which was probably one of the framed family photos his mother had hung in the living room falling.

Brady finished his drink and hung his head, his hands between his knees. Once she thought things through, she'd agree he shouldn't have any part of this kid's life. And he sure didn't want any part of it. Yeah, he used to think about having kids, of becoming the type of father his own dad had been, but that was before. Before his knee, and his life, had gone to hell. Before Liz decided he wasn't enough.

WHO SAID SHE DIDN'T have a backbone?

23

So what if Brady was no help to her at all? Or that he didn't want anything to do with the baby she was carrying? Or with her, J.C. thought late that afternoon as she ignored the heated debate her mother and grandmother were having next to her over whether to thicken the turkey gravy using cornstarch or flour. J.C. shut off the flame under the huge pot of boiling potatoes. She'd handled Brady's rejection. Not only handled it, but told him where to get off.

Too bad her backbone turned to Jell-O whenever she thought about telling her family she was pregnant. She sipped from her glass of ginger ale, but it did little to soothe her suddenly dry throat. Picking up two pot holders, she hauled the heavy pan of potatoes to the sink and dumped them into the waiting colander, leaning back from the steam in an effort to keep her hair frizz-free, if even for just an hour.

Well, she just had to suck it up and tell them. It wasn't as if she could hide it much longer anyway. When she'd put on her long suede skirt earlier, she hadn't been able to button it around her rapidly expanding middle. Which had resulted in a fifteen-minute crying jag and her rethinking her stance against elastic waistbands. A stance she'd taken up after she'd lost weight and had worn her first pair of size-six jeans.

Now she had a large safety pin holding the two edges of her skirt's waistband together and it still dug into her with every inhalation.

Would the indignities of this day ever end?

She poured the potatoes back into the pot and carried it over to the counter. Giving up this round of culinary battle, Grandma Rose carried a tray of her homemade angel biscuits to the living room, a pinched expression on her wrinkled face, her heavily shellacked blue-tinged hair bouncing with each step. J.C.'s mother, Nancy, stayed at the stove stirring the gravy. And humming.

"What did you do to Grandma?" Liz asked as she came into the room. "She's in there mumbling about the sad state of the world today and how the youth of America have no respect for the traditional way of doing things."

"Mom schooled Grandma in the art of gravy making," J.C. said.

"I didn't school anyone." Nancy adjusted the heat beneath the pan with one hand while stirring with the other. "I just pointed out that I've thickened my gravy with cornstarch for the past thirty-four years and that her son has never had any complaints about it."

"Ooh...burn," J.C. mouthed to Liz.

Liz's sleek chestnut hair swung as she nodded. "Second degree," she

mouthed back. They shared an easy smile.

Until J.C. remembered what she'd done. How she'd broken the number one rule of sisterhood: no going out with your sister's ex.

J.C. wiped the back of her hand across her damp fore-head. It had to be one hundred degrees in her sister's cramped kitchen. It didn't help that she'd had to wear her heaviest turtleneck sweater today, an oversize, soft cable-knit that covered her stomach. And hid the slight bruising from her encounter with Brady. And while she sweated in clothes that added at least ten pounds to her curvy frame, her mother and sister were both cool and stylish. Nancy in trim dark pants and a V-neck top, her short, layered hair was a shade darker than Liz's with only a few strands of gray. Liz had on skinny jeans and a gorgeous billowy mauve top with a wide band at the bottom that accentuated her tiny waist.

Not that J.C. was bitter or anything.

They usually had Thanksgiving dinner at their parents' spacious house, but Liz had wanted to host her first official holiday dinner in the house she and Carter were renting while their dream home was being built. And since

Carter's family was in Ohio, it was going to be him, Liz and J.C., their parents and Grandma Rose.

J.C. poured cream over the potatoes, then shook in salt and pepper. All the people she loved the most in this world, everyone she needed to tell about the baby, would soon be gathered around the table. She'd get to face them over plates filled with green bean casserole, sweet potatoes, turkey and stuffing, and then see their shock turn to disappointment when they heard about her latest screwup.

What better way to spend the holiday?

She threw a stick of butter into the pan. Then, seeing the amount of potatoes, added half of another stick before shoving her sleeves up to her elbows, picking up the masher and mixing it all together.

Her mother, obviously satisfied no lumps would dare appear in her gravy, poured it into a gravy boat and peered over at J.C. "Honey, are you feeling all right? You look a bit flushed."

"I'm fine," J.C. said. "Just...it's hot in here." Okay, so there was a definite edge of whining in her voice. Her life was falling apart and so far she'd had a really crappy day. She deserved a pout.

Nancy laid the back of her hand against J.C.'s forehead, the gesture bringing tears to J.C.'s eyes. "I don't think you have a fever," Nancy decided. "Are you sure you're over that stomach bug?"

She averted her gaze. "Definitely. It was probably something I ate," she said, referring to the lie she'd told her mother last Sunday when she'd gotten sick after they'd had brunch.

Nancy smiled and rubbed J.C.'s arm. "Good." She glanced at the potatoes. "You need to scrape the sides down or you'll miss lumps. Here, I can finish—"

"I've got it." J.C.'s grip tightened when her mother tried to take the masher from her. "Why don't you go on out and save Dad and Carter from Grandma's lecture about the merits of thickening with flour?"

"Be careful you don't over-mash them or they'll get gluey," her mother warned. "And remember, you can always add a little milk if they're too thick."

"I've got it, Mom. Really."

Though she seemed conflicted about leaving the fate of the potatoes in J.C.'s hands, Nancy nodded and then walked away.

Her mother's back disappeared around the corner and J.C. let go of the masher as if it had caught fire. God. As if she needed an advanced degree to mash potatoes. And considering it was the one task her family entrusted her to handle for family dinners, you'd think they could give her more credit. Picking up a large spoon, she scraped down the sides and then began pounding away in earnest.

By the time Liz came back into the kitchen, J.C.'s arms were aching from the effort and sweat was trickling between her shoulder blades.

"You can stop now," Liz said as she attempted to work a few potato pieces out of J.C.'s curls. "Those vicious potatoes are dead."

"Just making sure I got them all."

"I think that's a safe bet. Here," she added, handing J.C. a large blue serving bowl. "Put them in this."

"Did you have to cook the entire ten-pound bag?"

"I didn't want to run out."

"Who did you think was coming? The Jewell High School marching band?"

"If they do," Liz said, shutting off the oven, "we'll be covered."

J.C. scraped the last of the potatoes from the pan and added them to the mountain already in the bowl. "We could cover ourselves with mashed potatoes and still have enough to eat."

"Now I know what Carter and I can do with all the leftovers."

"Eww... Please. That's one visual I really don't need."

"Wait," Liz said, when J.C. picked up the heavy bowl. "I made something special for you."

J.C. set it back on the counter. "What?"

"Close your eyes." J.C. squeezed her eyes shut. She heard the oven door being opened and then shut.

"Ta-da!" Liz said.

"Uh..." J.C. studied the brown, football-shaped loaf in the baking pan. "I repeat, what is it?"

"Tofurkey."

"Is that like a contagious disease? Because that thing looks like a breeding ground for bacteria."

"It's not a science project, it's a tofu turkey." Setting the pan down, she used a large metal spatula to transfer the loaf onto a small serving platter. "Mom and I didn't think it was fair that you got left out of the biggest tradition of Thanksgiving, so we decided to make you a vegetarian turkey. I found the recipe online. It's basically tofu wrapped around stuffing—Mom made a special version of her bread stuffing using vegetable broth instead of chicken broth."

J.C. blinked and for some reason, the blob of browned tofu didn't look half as bad as she'd first thought. At that moment, it looked downright delicious. "You made that for me?"

"Well, I'm sure not going to eat it and I doubt anyone else here is, either." "I think it's beautiful," J.C. managed, unshed tears thickening her voice.

There were times, more than a few, when they were growing up when J.C. thought she hated her sister. Times when she'd wanted to hate her, if only to try to ease the jealousy that came with having an older sister who was smarter, prettier and more popular than J.C. could ever hope to be.

But the truth was, J.C. loved Liz. There was no way she could harbor any animosity toward the person who was not only her sister but also her best friend.

She threw herself at Liz, knocking her sister back a full step as she clung to her.

"Hey," Liz said, returning the hug, "what's this?"

And Liz's concern made J.C. feel even worse. "You made me a tofu turkey."

Liz smoothed J.C.'s curls away from her face. "It's tofu and stuffing, not a cure for cancer. Now come on, what's wrong? It's not like you to get emotional over a meat substitute."

God, how she wanted to tell Liz everything. And maybe if she told Liz about the baby, then Liz could break the news to their parents.

But while that had worked when J.C. had been fifteen and had gotten her belly button pierced, she doubted she could get Liz to bail her out of this situation.

J.C. stepped back. "I always get emotional at the holidays."

"Yes, but usually you reserve it for sappy commercials."

"That one where the college kid comes home to surprise his family and makes coffee to wake them gets me every time," she said lightly, picking up the potatoes again. "Now come on. Let's get these real potatoes and that fake turkey on the table."

And the sooner they all sat down, the sooner she could admit she'd had a one-night stand with her sister's ex-fiancé and was now pregnant. Pregnant and scared out of her mind.

3

J.C. PUT THE POTATOES ON THE TABLE AND SAT NEXT TO her mother. Even though they were eating at the picnic table Carter had brought inside, it somehow still looked like one of those fancy layouts in a home and garden magazine. Liz had covered it with a red tablecloth and then added a white runner down the middle. On the runner, gourds and a few pinecones were scattered around glass bowls filled with bright red and green apples, cranberries and mini-pumpkins.

J.C. unfolded her red-and-white cloth napkin onto her lap and tried not to think about how the last time she'd hosted a family dinner, they ate off paper plates. And her mother had provided most of the food.

Ten minutes later, grace had been said, dishes had been passed and her plate was piled high with food. J.C. nibbled at a flaky, buttery biscuit but couldn't seem to swallow properly. If she didn't come clean to her family right now, she'd never be able to eat her meal. And she was starving.

Setting her biscuit down, she brushed the crumbs off her fingers. "I have an announcement," she said but her voice was so reedy, no one heard her over their laughter and conversation. "I have some news," she yelled, blushing when everyone quieted and stared at her.

To her left, Grandma Rose peered at J.C. over her glasses. "Did you get fired again?"

Jeez. You get fired a few times—okay, five times, but that third time was *not* her fault—and suddenly it's, what, a habit?

"No. I'm still employed." J.C. drank some water. "I..."

"Come on, sweetie," her dad said, giving her a wink as he scooped sweet potatoes onto his fork. "Whatever it is, it can't be as bad as when you stopped going to college but didn't officially drop out, leaving me to foot the bill for a year's worth of classes you didn't take."

"Daddy," Liz admonished while Carter ducked his head and coughed—the sound suspiciously close to a laugh. "We all promised not to talk about that again, remember?"

J.C. twisted the napkin around her fingers. "I told you I'd pay you back."

"We've been through this," Nancy said, shooting her husband a loaded look. "You can worry about paying us back once you're on your feet." She sipped her wine. "Now, what is it you want to tell us?"

"You...you and Daddy..." Her voice shook so she took another drink, and then, staring at the table, said, "You're going to be grandparents." When no one spoke, J.C. raised her head.

A huge, proud smile broke out across her dad's face. He pumped Carter's hand, not noticing his son-in-law was too flabbergasted to return his handshake. "Congratulations. When are you due?" Don asked Liz.

"Due?" Carter repeated, his gorgeous face devoid of

color, his green eyes panicked as he gaped at his wife. "What's due? Who's due?"

"I thought you wanted to wait a few years before having children," Nancy said to Liz.

"Yeah," Carter choked out, his hand still being pumped by his father-in-law, "me, too. Why didn't you tell me?"

"I didn't tell you," Liz said slowly, "because I'm not pregnant."

Frowning, Don let go of Carter's hand and sat back. "What? But Janie said..."

Staring at her plate again, J.C. felt five expectant gazes turn on her. "Jane," her mother said sharply, "are you pregnant?"

Biting down on her lower lip, she nodded.

"Oh, dear Lord," Grandma Rose murmured.

"But...but I didn't realize you were seeing someone," Don said, sounding lost and hurt. J.C. winced.

"I'm not." Raising her head, she sent Liz a beseeching look. "It was a...a mistake."

"Oh, Lord Almighty," her grandma cried, throwing her hands up as if she were at a tent revival meeting.

Her mom shook her head, her disappointment palpable. "Didn't we teach you to have more self-respect than that?"

J.C.'s throat constricted. "It wasn't like that," she whispered.

No, it was worse. Because even though she'd known Brady was using her as a substitute for Liz, J.C. had gone along with it.

Liz rushed around the table and, crouching next to J.C., put her arm around her sister and squeezed. "Now, let's all calm down. This can't be easy for J.C."

Don stood. "What's his name?" he asked in a low, deadly tone J.C. had never heard before. Not even when she'd sold the car they'd bought her as a high-school graduation present to pay for a trip to Europe.

"It doesn't matter. He doesn't want anything to do with me or the baby." He slammed his palm down on the table, and they all jumped.

"Don!" Nancy admonished, catching her wineglass before it fell. "Calm down."

"I want his name, Jane Cleo, and I want it now," her father said.

J.C. wound the napkin around her finger so tightly, her fingertip went numb. "I... It..." Her stomach burning, she forced herself to meet Liz's eyes. "It was Brady."

Liz jerked as if she'd been slapped. "Brady? You...you and..." She shook her head slowly. "You slept with Brady? With *my* Brady?"

"Your Brady?" Carter asked, his eyebrows shooting up.

And with that, all hell officially broke loose. Don wanted to force Brady to "do the right thing" while Nancy tried to calm him down. Grandma Rose was worried what her Bunco group was going to say when this got back to them, and Liz and Carter were having a heated argument off to the side over Liz's lingering feelings for her ex-fiancé.

J.C. slouched down in her chair so far, her chin was level with the tabletop. For half her life all she'd wanted was Brady Sheppard to notice her. To want her. And now that he'd slept with her—albeit he hadn't exactly wanted *her*—this was what she got.

Her mother had always warned her to be careful what she wished for. As usual, she'd been right.

TWO HOURS LATER, Liz was elbow-deep in a sink of soapy water and seriously regretting not taking her mother up on her offer to stay to help her clean. But after the dinner disaster, she'd needed some peace and quiet.

Though peace seemed to be out of the question, she had more than her share of quiet.

"I've already apologized," she said, proud of how composed she sounded when all she wanted to do was hit something. Or someone. Or burst into tears. "Several times. How long are you going to continue with the silent treatment?"

Setting leftovers in the refrigerator, Carter glanced coolly at her over his shoulder. "You're the one who said you didn't want to discuss it."

Since when did he use that biting, condescending tone? She couldn't say she cared for it much. She threw the tofurkey into the sink. Shoved it down the disposal with a wooden spoon. As the whirring sound filled the air, she tapped the spoon repeatedly against the sink. And to think, she'd been so excited about hosting her first holiday as a married woman. Thrilled to be able to spend one of her precious few days off from the E.R. with her family.

Now she didn't think she'd ever be able to look at J.C. the same way again.

Liz turned off the disposal. "There's nothing to discuss. I made a mistake. A slip of the tongue." She tossed silverware into the water. "I don't see where you have any right to hold it against me."

Shutting the fridge door, he faced her, his shoulders rigid, his pale hair sticking up from where he'd run his fingers through it. "Some would say that slip of the tongue indicates your true feelings. Such as you still considering your ex as belonging to you."

"You're a pediatrician, not a psychiatrist. Don't try to analyze me. And I didn't appreciate you humiliating me in front of my parents by accusing me of still having feelings for Brady."

His expression darkened. "You were humiliated? How did you think I felt when your ex-lover crashed our wedding?"

She blew the hair off her forehead. "What did you want me to do, Carter?

Let your idiot friends throw him out?"

"No, but you could've trusted me to handle it."

"I didn't want a scene."

"Right," he said, his sarcasm setting her teeth on edge. "But it didn't bother you that I was embarrassed in front of three hundred people."

Of course it'd bothered her, but how could she worry about something that happened three months ago when all she could think about was what had happened at dinner? She scrubbed the bottom of the roasting pan. No, she shouldn't have reacted that way but she'd been...shocked... hearing that J.C. and Brady had...been together...she hadn't been able to censor herself.

Still, it wasn't like Carter to get so angry. To treat her so coldly.

When they'd first met while doing their residency training at George Washington University Hospital, she'd immediately been attracted to him. And guilt-stricken over that attraction since, at the time, she'd been wearing Brady's ring. For months she'd deluded herself into believing the pull between her and Carter was just physical, a result of only seeing Brady a few times a year. She'd tried to ignore the attraction, tried to think of Carter as only a friend, but after working with him day in and day out, her feelings for him became too big. Too real. She found his intelligence, sense of humor and easygoing attitude impossible to resist.

Especially after years of Brady's quiet intensity.

She wished Carter would display some of that laid-back attitude now.

"I'd think you'd be happy Brady has moved on," Carter said as he began drying dishes. "Weren't you the one who was worried he wouldn't be able to let you go?"

"I want him to move on. Just not with J.C."

"Why not?"

She gaped at him. How could he be so intelligent and still be so clueless?

"Because it's not right. She's my sister."

Drying a handful of spoons, he glanced at her. "Because it would be uncomfortable—for all involved."

"Exactly," she said with a sigh. Now this was more like it, and more like the man she'd fallen for so hard for. The man she'd chosen.

Carter nodded. "I get that. But from what J.C. said, he's not going to be involved with her or the baby."

The baby. Brady's baby. With her sister.

God, why did it hurt so much?

She swallowed past the lump lodged in her throat. "Brady would never abandon his own child."

"You sound pretty convinced of that."

"I am. I know him."

Carter tossed the towel over his shoulder and stood eyes downcast, feet apart, hands braced against the edge of the sink. "Do you still love him?"

She blinked. He'd never asked her that before. Not on their wedding night when they'd argued over her not wanting him to confront Brady. Not almost two years ago when she'd gone to him in tears because she'd ended her relationship with Brady. Ended it so she could be with Carter.

"Wha-what?"

He faced her. "Do you still love him?"

"I love *you*," she said, taking his hand in her wet one.

He shook his head and stepped away from her. "That's not what I asked."

Suddenly chilled, she crossed her arms. "I...I don't understand."

"I need to know if you still have feelings for Brady."

"Of course I do," she said carefully. "I'll always...care... about him. I was with him half my life."

"But you're not with him now," Carter said quietly. "You're with me. And I can't help but wonder if with me is where you really want to be."

HEADLIGHTS CUT THROUGH the darkness as the car pulled into the short driveway. A motion-detection light above the garage came on, illuminating the bottom half of the stairway on the side of the building. Where Brady sat at the bottom of those steps. He didn't move. Wasn't sure he could so much as stand since his leg had stiffened up during the two hours he'd been waiting in the cold for J.C. to come home.

She opened her car door, grabbed something from the seat next to her and then got out of the car. She took two steps before she noticed him and stopped, a huge purse clutched to her chest. Her gaze flicked from him to her apartment above the garage, then behind her to her car.

"If you take off," he said, figuring she was thinking of doing just that, "I'll still be here waiting when you get back."

She turned back to her car anyway but didn't get in. After a moment, she mumbled to herself and started walking toward him again. "What do you want?"

Gripping the wooden railing, he put all of his weight on his right leg and stood. "Things got out of hand this morning and I wanted to make sure we're on the same page."

"As much as it may shock you, I'm not a complete idiot. You don't want anything to do with me or with this baby. See? Same page. Now, I've had a really craptastic day and all I want is for it to be over. Goodbye."

Then she brushed past him and climbed the stairs, another motion-detecting light coming on when she reached the top. As he watched, she went inside and shut the door. No slamming this time, but somehow the quiet click was just as final.

That hadn't gone quite as planned. He shoved his frozen fingers into the pockets of his jacket. After J.C. left his house earlier, he'd tried to forget she'd been there in the first place. Forget what she'd told him...and how shitty he'd treated her.

While he'd sat in his living room staring into a glass of whiskey, she'd more than likely been telling her family— telling Liz—he'd gotten her pregnant.

And that he didn't want anything to do with his own child.

Oh, yeah, he'd wanted to forget all of it.

Unfortunately, his usual method of temporary amnesia hadn't worked.

He scanned the long, steep staircase. At least thirty steps. Shit.

The railing was on the wrong side to be of any help to him but he'd have to make the best of it. Have to take it one step at a time. Literally. He debated getting his cane from his truck, but when he faced J.C. he wanted to do it on his own two feet.

Clutching the rail, he leaned on his arm to take some of the weight off his left leg while he lifted his right onto the first step. He gritted his teeth against the pain and stepped up with his left leg.

He repeated the process. Then again. And again. Halfway up, he stopped to catch his breath. To think, less than a year ago he was running top speed up mountainsides in full combat gear. With that cheery thought still in his head, he glanced toward the dark house to find J.C.'s grandmother glaring at him from a bedroom window. From what he could remember, J.C. had moved into the apartment above her grandma's garage a few years ago after her latest attempt at college had failed.

He was just thankful Mrs. Montgomery hadn't come home with J.C. It was going to be hard enough to fix things with J.C., he didn't think he could handle facing anyone else in the Montgomery family.

By the time he reached the top, his shirt clung to his sweat-soaked skin and he had an inch-long sliver imbedded in his palm from his death grip on the wooden railing. But hey, at least he'd made it. Bracing his shoulder against the door, he wiped the sweat from his face with the bottom of his T-shirt before knocking. After a minute, he knocked again. Another minute, another knock.

He'd forgotten how, underneath that sunny personality, J.C. was as stubborn as they came.

"Last winter I waited in a cave in southern Afghanistan for over fourteen hours," he said, pitching his voice so she'd be sure to hear him through the door. "Sitting out here until you go to work tomorrow won't be a problem."

A moment later, the door opened to reveal a pinched-face J.C. holding the fattest white cat he'd ever seen. She stepped aside to let him in. "Like I said,

I'm tired so wh—"

"I thought you were allergic to cats."

"What?"

"I remember you wanting a cat when—" When he and Liz were together.

Seemed as if his life could be defined in two ways: when he and Liz were a couple, and now. "In high school. But you couldn't get one because you were allergic."

"I couldn't get one," she said with enough frost to cause the temperature in the apartment to drop at least ten degrees, "because Liz is allergic to them." The cat gave Brady a sneering, you-are-a-dumb-ass look, then leaped to the ground and waddled off. "I didn't get a chance to finish my dinner, so I'm going to make a sandwich. Do you want one?" she asked so grudgingly that even if all he'd had to eat for the past week were MREs—meals ready to eat, the packaged, precooked meals given to military personnel out in the field—he would've said no.

"I'm good."

"I guess you might as well sit down, then. I'll be back out in a minute." But when she would've walked away, he grabbed her by the wrist. Ignoring how she went as stiff as a new recruit at attention, he lightly tugged her forward, hooked his finger under the edge of the neck of her sweater and pulled it down. She swallowed and tried to step back but he didn't loosen his hold. All day long he'd tried to convince himself that he hadn't hurt her, that his hangover had dulled his recollection of what had happened. Of how bad it'd been.

The cat was right. He was a dumb-ass.

He brushed his thumb over the light bruises on her pale, delicate skin, his stomach turning. "I didn't mean to hurt you."

Apprehension flashed in her eyes. "I'm fine."

This time when she pulled away, he let her go. She disappeared through a doorway, and he crossed over to the white couch. He sat on the edge—the only spot available among six pillows of varying shapes, sizes and colors.

Stretching his left leg out, he rubbed his knee and glanced around.

Her apartment was a good deal smaller than his house, so how did she get so much stuff in it? He remembered the squat, light blue chair he used to sit in in her parents' living room next to her sofa. But not the two red velvet ottomans on the other side of a chipped, painted coffee table. Or the two hardback chairs on either side of a round table underneath the window. A large, glass-fronted case took up an entire corner, its shelves filled with everything from ceramic animal figures and music boxes to tea cups, crystal bowls and books, both paperbacks and hardcover. As if a rummage sale had blown up.

The cat padded in and jumped onto a low stool and then up onto the blue chair. J.C. followed a minute later, one hand curled into a loose fist. In the other she carried a glass of water with a sandwich balanced on top. She set the water on the coffee table in front of him and picked up the sandwich.

"Here," she said, holding out her hand to show him the two small, white pills in her palm.

"What are those?"

"Acetaminophen. It's all I have." When he didn't move, she shrugged irritably and set them next to the water. "From the look on your face when I opened the door, I thought you could use them."

Tossing the yellow pillow from the chair to the floor, she nudged the cat onto the arm rest and then sat, curling her bare feet under her. She took a bite of her sandwich and stared straight ahead.

Brady scratched his cheek. Realized he forgot to shave again today. He supposed he appreciated her bringing him the pills—though he knew from experience a few over-the-counter pain relievers would barely take the edge off. But she was too generous. Too sweet. After everything he'd done, she shouldn't give a crap if he was in pain or not. Not to mention how humiliating it was that he'd been so easy to read.

"Thanks." He took the pills and washed them down with the water. "Did you... Have you told your parents?" She gave a terse nod. Leaning forward, he picked up an ugly ceramic duck, turned it in his hands. Cleared his throat. "And Liz?"

J.C.'s mouth flattened. "Is that why you're here? To see how Liz reacted to finding out that we slept together?"

"No." Maybe. He rubbed his thumbnail over a chip on the duck's beak.

"How did...your family...take the news?"

"About as well as you'd expect." She bit into her sandwich again. "And so you won't be wondering...Liz didn't take *the news* well."

Okay. And what the hell was that supposed to mean? Not that he dared ask.

"I didn't handle things as well as I could have this morning." "You don't say," she said dryly.

"I've done some thinking and...I'm not going to shirk my responsibility."

43

She set the remainder of her sandwich on her lap. "What do you mean?"

Talking about this made it hard for him to breathe. Hell, it was as if his lungs were being squeezed by a vise. "That I'm willing to support you and the baby."

Her eyebrows drew together. "Support?"

"I'll call my lawyer tomorrow. We'll figure out some sort of financial agreement." He rubbed his damp palms up and down the front of his jeans. This was for the best. For J.C. and the baby. And for him. "I'll make sure you and the child are provided for, but...I won't be in Jewell much longer."

"Where are you going?"

He had no idea. "I'd only planned on staying until I was back on my feet." Which would probably happen faster if he showed up at his physical therapy sessions. "I'll probably be doing some traveling, so it'd be best if we don't set up any type of...shared custody or visitation rights."

"This is perfect," J.C. muttered as she got to her feet, her sandwich falling to the floor. The cat pounced on it and began eating while J.C. paced on the other side of the coffee table, swerving to avoid the ottomans. "So what am I supposed to say in a few years if your child asks about its father?"

The idea of J.C. having to tell her kid—their kid—he'd essentially abandoned them... He set the duck down with a sharp crack. "You can tell it whatever you want."

She shook her head, her dark curls bouncing on her shoulders. "What happened to you?"

What happened to him? He went to hell and he didn't think he'd ever get out. His hands fisted, so he forced himself to relax. To stand with no sign of weakness—when all he felt was weak. And out of control.

She wanted him to be the man he used to be. Someone

honorable. The type of guy who did the right thing no matter what the cost.

"People change," he said flatly. "Look, I'm willing to take responsibility—"

"But not too much responsibility, right?" She rubbed her temple and exhaled heavily. "You know what?" she said, dropping her hand. "Forget it.

Let's just pretend I never came to you this morning."

"What the hell are you talking about?"

"Don't bother meeting with that lawyer tomorrow. I don't want your money."

He pinched the bridge of his nose as he focused on keeping his voice even. "Then why did you come to me this morning?"

"Because I...God...I'm such an idiot." Then she met his eyes and shocked him for the second time that day. "I wanted you to ask me to marry you."

4
—————

BRADY GRIMACED. THE MAN ACTUALLY GRIMACED, HIS face going so white, J.C.

thought for sure he was about to pass out. At the thought of marrying her. Jerk.

"I don't think marriage is the best thing," Brady said in a low rumble. "For either of us."

Yeah, no kidding. But he didn't have to act as if it were the worst thing, either.

"I wouldn't marry you even if you tied me up and threatened to force-feed me a hamburger," J.C. said. "I wouldn't marry you if we were the last two humans left and the only way to save mankind was—"

"I get it. Then why did you say you did?"

"I said I wanted you to ask me." Noticing Daisy devouring the remainder of her peanut butter and jelly sandwich, J.C. bent and picked it up, much to her cat's annoyance. She met Brady's eyes. "You should've at least asked."

She went into the kitchen, tossing the sandwich into the garbage before getting herself a glass of water from the sink.

Staring at her reflection in the small window, she held her glass with two hands to steady it as she drank when what she really wanted was to put her head on the counter and weep.

God, could this day get any worse? Her grandmother was ashamed of her, her parents disappointed. And while she'd certainly disappointed them in the past, her failings—while numerous—had never been anything of this magnitude. But the worst part had been Liz's reaction. Her sister was hurt. So hurt J.C. wondered if she'd ever forgive her.

Which was a crazy thought. No matter how badly J.C. screwed up, Liz was always there for her.

And Liz always forgave her.

Brady's reflection joined hers as he stepped into the doorway.

"Why did you sleep with me, J.C.?"

She choked and bent over the sink to spit out the water in her mouth.

Coughed to clear her airway. "What?"

"Did you..." Walking into the room, he shoved a hand through his hair, causing it to stand on end. "Did you do this...on purpose?"

Her eyes widened. The glass slipped out of her fingers, but Brady caught it. Not that it mattered. What was a broken glass when her life was falling apart?

"You think I wanted to get pregnant? I'm only twenty-six. That's way too young to become a mother. I hadn't planned on kids until I was older." Her voice rose and she waved her hand in the air. "Mid-thirties, maybe. *Married.* I have plans. Dreams I need to fulfill before I get tied down with motherhood."

She bit her tongue before she told him everything. How she was unprepared to become a mother. And worse, how

47

unhappy she was about this pregnancy. How guilty she felt over feeling the way she did.

She sure didn't need his crazy accusations adding to her stress. "Why on earth would you think I did this on purpose?"

He looked at the glass in his hands and, as if realizing he still held it, set it on the counter. "When you were a kid you seemed to have a...a crush on me—"

"You knew?" she asked weakly. "Did Liz know?" He nodded.

Buzzing filled her ears. "I can imagine how much fun you two had laughing about it, about me. Poor chubby, silly Jane and her unrequited love for one of the beautiful people. Doesn't she have delusions of grandeur?"

"Neither one of us laughed at you," Brady said. "I was flattered."

"Flattered?" she repeated tonelessly. Groaning, she bent at the waist and covered her face with her hands, her curls falling forward to hide her face. "Oh, my God. Just kill me now. You're a Marine, you must know a hundred different ways to do it quickly and painlessly."

She heard him step forward but before she could move, he wrapped his fingers around her wrists and gently pried her hands from her face. "Did you sleep with me so we could...because you hoped we'd get together?"

Straightening quickly, the blood rushed to her head and she swayed. "You got me," she said, tugging free of his hold. "What started out as a childhood crush developed into a mad infatuation that's lasted all these years. So when you showed up at my sister's wedding, uninvited, unwanted and drunk, how could I resist? And the rumors about you drinking every night, getting into fights and sleeping your way through the females of Jewell make you all the more

48

enticing. Now I not only get an unwanted pregnancy, but I'm also a notch on Brady Sheppard's bedpost. It's like a dream come true."

"I'm trying to understand how this happened. Didn't we use a condom?" "What do you remember of that night?" she asked, her stomach sinking.

"You came up to me at the bar at the country club and asked me to leave, so I did." He frowned and stared off in the distance. "Then, when you found out I planned on walking home, you offered to drive me..."

She waited. And waited. "You don't even remember."

"Bits and pieces," he admitted, having the decency to look abashed.

"Let me give you the CliffsNotes version. I took you home and made you some coffee. We started talking and then you kissed me. You. Kissed. Me." She pointed her finger at him with each word. "Not the other way around."

"Janie, I—"

"It was sort of...intense. One minute we were kissing, and the next..." She shrugged. "The next we were having sex."

And she'd been so wrapped up in the fact that Brady wanted to be with her —and then so devastated by how it'd ended—she didn't even realize they hadn't used protection until she got home.

"Did I hurt you?" he asked quietly, his expression giving none of his thoughts away. "I didn't...I didn't force you, did I?"

"No. Of course not."

He shut his eyes briefly. Had he seriously thought he'd forced her?

"I knew what I was doing," she continued. And now she had to take responsibility for that decision. "But I didn't get

49

pregnant on purpose and I have no desire to trap you into marriage. Right now I'm not even sure I want to see you again." She pushed herself upright, locked her knees so they wouldn't tremble but couldn't stop her voice from shaking. "So now would probably be a good time for you to leave." When he didn't so much as blink, she pointed to the door. "Get out."

"Not until we come up with the terms for a financial agreement."

"The terms are I'll take care of this baby and you can pretend we don't exist." Because the reality was, she didn't know if she wanted to keep this baby. The poor thing hadn't been born yet, and so far neither its mother nor father wanted anything to do with it. How messed up was that?

There was so much involved in having a baby. Diapers. Doctors' visits. Day care. And she'd never once considered being a single parent, of being solely responsible for another life. She had enough trouble taking care of herself.

"Having a child is expensive," he said as if she hadn't spoken. "How are

you going to manage?"

She swallowed. Worked to keep her expression disdainful so he couldn't see the terror she was trying to hide. "Unlike you, I have a job."

Nothing. No reaction to her dig. The man really was made of stone. "I'm guessing tellers aren't the highest paid employees at the bank."

True. Another point to consider if she decided to keep the baby. She had a hard enough time making ends meet now. The only reason she could even afford this apartment was because her grandmother was her landlord. How would she support not only herself but a baby?

She clutched his arm above his elbow and pulled him

toward the door. His muscles tensed under her fingers but he didn't resist.

She opened the door, and the cool rush of crisp autumn air helped settle her stomach. And her nerves. "Goodbye, Brady."

"I want to help."

"Why?"

He seemed taken aback. "Because it's my responsibility."

More exhausted than she'd ever been in her life, she shook her head. "I'm officially absolving you of any and all responsibility, then."

Yes, she usually accepted help getting herself out of the many jams she managed to get into, but she didn't want him trying to assuage his guilt by tossing money her way. Bad enough he'd only slept with her because he'd been drunk... and that she'd slept with him when he'd really wanted Liz. She'd be damned if she'd take his pity, too. And that was all this was. But it wasn't enough.

Seemed she had some pride, after all.

"Damn it, Jane, you're—"

"You've done your part. If anyone asks, I'll be sure to tell them how you tried to get me to see reason. Go back to feeling sorry for yourself in your dark, dirty house. Drown yourself in Jim Beam for all I care." She nudged him outside so she could shut the door and put an end to this horrible day. "This baby doesn't need anything from you. And neither do I."

———

BRADY PULLED UP to the cottage and shut off the ignition. Every light in the place was on, and seeing as how they'd all been off when he'd left, that—plus the black sports car parked out front—meant one thing. He had company.

Damn, he hated company.

As he got out of the truck, his leg buckled. He tried to catch himself on the door but wasn't fast enough. He fell on his bad knee, landing hard on the cold ground. Gulping down air so he wouldn't howl with the pain, he pulled himself back up and reached into the cab for his cane. Slowly he made his way across the gravel to the front door.

He heard them as soon as he stepped inside. Seemed both his brothers had come calling. He stood there for a moment, the front door still open in case he changed his mind and decided to make a run for it anyway.

A nice dream, considering he could barely stand.

One of them—Matt, from the sound of it—laughed, the sound easily carrying throughout the small house. Brady scowled. How many times over the past few years had he wished he could be home for the holidays? Times when he would've given anything to come back to Jewell, if even for a day, to see Liz and his brothers and mother. Now he'd do anything to avoid them.

Too bad a few of them couldn't take a freaking hint.

Leaving the cane by the door, he went into the kitchen. Aidan, his older brother, leaned against the sink, his legs crossed at the ankles, not a wrinkle on his khakis or dark blue dress shirt. He didn't say a word when he noticed Brady, just raised an eyebrow over eyes the same light blue as Brady's.

"Why are the windows open?" Brady asked.

Sitting on the counter, wearing dark jeans and a light-weight, V-neck sweater, his light brown hair pulled back into a stubby ponytail, the youngest Sheppard grinned. "Because it smells like you're hiding a dead body in here," Matt claimed.

"Not yet," Brady muttered. "But the night's young." He tossed his keys onto the cluttered table. "Why are you here?"

"Happy Thanksgiving to you, too." He slid off the counter, landing with an ease Brady hated him for. "Missed you at dinner."

Brady grabbed a bottle of pain relievers from the table. He couldn't take one of his prescriptions, not with Aidan watching, but maybe adding a few of these to the ones J.C. had given him would do the trick.

Opening an upper cupboard, he frowned. He could've sworn he had a bottle of Jack Daniel's in there. Shoving aside a box of cookies he didn't even remember buying, he shifted his weight onto his right leg. "You two ever hear of a little thing called trespassing?"

"Heard of it," Matt said with his usual freaking good cheer. "But it doesn't count when we're all equal owners in this place."

"Your leg bothering you?" Aidan asked.

"It's good."

"You sure? Because you seem—"

"I said it's good." And since he was being watched, being judged, he carefully shut the cupboard door before opening the next one to find a few mismatched plates and bowls. But no bottle. His hand shook as he moved on to cupboard number three. "I'm not in the mood for company."

"There's a news flash," Aidan murmured.

"Go away."

"Now is that any way to treat the people who brought you Thanksgiving dinner complete with half a pumpkin pie?" Matt asked.

"I don't like pumpkin pie," he said, searching the meager

contents of his fridge for the six-pack of beer he'd bought the other day. Damn but he needed a drink.

"I do." Matt reached over Brady's shoulder and took out the pie. "Don't worry, Mom sent over two big slices of pecan pie, too."

"Looking for something?" Aidan asked.

It was his tone that clued Brady in. He leaned his arm against the fridge.

Shit. They'd cleaned him out.

"This your idea of an intervention?"

"What do you mean?" Aidan asked, unbuttoning a sleeve and rolling it up.

Brady's eyes narrowed. The smug son of a bitch. "What's the matter?" he goaded. "You're not man enough to admit you snuck in here and hid all of my booze?"

Repeating the process with the other sleeve, Aidan stepped forward, his unhurried strides at odds with the cold, hard expression on his face. "I didn't hide it. I trashed it. Dumped it down the sink. When are you going to be man enough to admit you've got a problem?"

Hands fisted at his sides, Brady limped forward until he and Aidan were nose to nose. "Why don't you go—"

"Back it up," Matt said, stepping between them. A surreal experience considering Brady used to be the one breaking up fights between the other two. "Remember Mom and Dad always said you have to set a good example for me."

The urge to throw a punch still vibrating through him, Brady went back to the fridge. He took out several of the plastic containers his brothers had brought along with a half-empty jar of mayonnaise. "What do you want?"

"Why didn't you show up for dinner?" Aidan asked. He sounded so much like their deceased father.

Sounded like Tom Sheppard, but wasn't. No matter how hard he tried.

"I was busy."

Setting everything on the counter, he swallowed a couple of the pain relievers before shoving aside a dirty frying pan and a stack of plates. He pulled out a few slices of bread from the loaf behind the toaster, checked for mold then searched for a halfway clean knife.

"You're lucky Mom didn't come here instead of us," Matt said. "She'd kick your ass if she saw this kitchen."

Sweat broke out above his lip at the thought of his mother seeing firsthand how messed up he was. "I'm all sorts of lucky," he agreed, slathering mayo on the bread.

"Mom cried."

Brady froze, his grip tightening on the knife. "I told her I couldn't come."

"It's Thanksgiving," Aidan continued. "The first one in years where you've been on the same continent and you didn't show up."

Brady slowly, deliberately, set the knife down. Opening all the containers, he found turkey, stuffing and sweet potatoes. He piled turkey onto a slice of bread. "Don't push it," he said, his voice quiet. "I've had a really shitty day."

And he didn't need his sanctimonious brother heaping the guilt on, he thought as he topped the turkey with stuffing and another slice of bread. Hell, he felt so much guilt right now, any more and he'd explode.

"Worse than watching your mother leave Thanksgiving dinner in tears because your selfish, idiot brother didn't bother to show?" Aidan asked.

Brady sat at the table, took a bite and pretended to think that question over as he chewed. "Yeah. Worse than that. Besides, something came up that I had to take care of."

"What could be so important that you skipped out on a holiday family dinner?"

Taking his time, Brady had another bite of sandwich before he answered.

"I'd say the woman who's going to have my baby was more important." Blessed silence.

"You're kidding," Matt finally said.

"Serious as Aidan gets about...well...everything." "Who?" Aidan asked.

A piece of turkey seemed to be stuck in his throat. He cleared it. "Jane Montgomery."

Another beat of silence. Then Aidan shook his head. "You slept with J.C.? Are you insane?"

"I'd sleep with her," Matt interjected.

Both Brady and Aidan stared at him. "What?" he asked, offended. "I would. She's got a body like one of those old-time movie stars. And that mouth of hers? The combination of that sexy mouth with those big brown eyes?" He nodded, a half smile on his face. "Oh, yeah, I'd—"

Aidan gave him a hard smack upside the back of the head. "Shut up."

Matt rubbed the spot. "I'm just saying..."

Sexy mouth? Brady frowned, picturing the way J.C. had looked when she'd shoved him out of her apartment. There hadn't been anything sexy about her then. He could see where some guys might find her attractive and she did have a certain...warm appeal. But compared to Liz, she was ordinary.

Aidan crossed his arms and glared at Brady. "What are you going to do?"

"Nothing."

"What do you mean, nothing?"

"J.C. said she and the baby didn't need me."

Which should be a relief, right? And what he wanted. No obligations. No ties to either J.C. or the baby.

"Doesn't matter," Aidan insisted. "You have a legal right to your child.

And now is the perfect time to rethink that job offer we discussed." Right. The job offer.

A few weeks ago, Aidan had driven Brady to the V.A. hospital for a checkup. On the way home, he'd offered Brady a position at the Diamond Dust Vineyard, the winery their father had started more than thirty years ago. Aidan had pointed out that Brady had been away from the wine business a long time. And while he'd worked at the winery as a teenager—all three brothers had—a lot had changed in the past twelve years. Change that would take Brady time to catch up on. So he'd suggested Brady ease back into the swing of things by taking over the bookkeeping of the Diamond Dust.

His brother wanted him stuck in some office behind a desk taking care of invoices and orders and adding figures. Trying to keep him away from alcohol, most likely. Sounded like hell.

"I don't need to think about it," he said. "I'm still not interested."

"You have other prospects?"

Brady snorted. He used to have prospects. He'd always planned on joining the Virginia State Police after he got out of the service. But like all his goals and dreams, that idea went up in smoke, starting when Liz decided he wasn't enough and ending with his knee getting shot up.

"I think I'll take some time to work on finishing my great American novel."

"How are you going to support a kid—"

"I'm not." He shrugged as if it didn't matter, but deep

57

down, he knew it did. "J.C. doesn't want anything from me. Including child support payments."

Aidan's lips thinned. "So that's it? You're just going to abandon your own kid?"

"I'm thinking about leaving—"

"To go where?" Aidan asked.

Brady stretched out his leg. "North. New Hampshire, maybe. Or Maine."

Somewhere far from Jewell. Where there wouldn't be a chance of him running into Liz and her new husband. Or J.C. and the baby. So his kid wouldn't have to grow up in the same town as him, knowing his father didn't want anything to do with him. Or her.

Even he wasn't that big a prick.

He wasn't trying to hurt J.C. or the kid or make their lives more difficult. He just...couldn't be what they wanted. What they needed.

"You are some piece of work," Aidan said, staring at him as if he were a lowlife. "Why did you even come back?"

"Now that's an easy one," Brady said, working to keep his voice even. "I had nowhere else to go."

Instead of laying into him like Brady expected him to, Aidan snatched his jacket from the back of the chair so quickly, the chair toppled over.

"You need to get your head out of your ass," Matt said before following Aidan to the door.

Brady slouched in his chair. What he needed was for his family to leave him alone instead of trying to bring him back into the fold like a goddamn sheep. He had no interest in joining the winery. Having all three sons run it had been his father's dream.

But his father wasn't here anymore.

And just because Aidan had quit law school after their

dad died to run the Diamond Dust Vineyard didn't mean Brady had to follow his footsteps. Matt hadn't. He'd lit out of Jewell right after graduating high school and hadn't looked back. He now made bucketfuls of money advising top wineries around the world. Brady wasn't about to cave, either.

Even if he didn't have any other options.

And he didn't. Not in Jewell, anyway.

Standing, he picked up a dirty coffee mug, rinsed it out and hobbled to his room. He grimaced as he stepped inside. His brothers hadn't bothered opening the windows in here...but he wished they had. The room smelled like his high school gym locker. Maybe he'd do a load of laundry, he thought as he sat on the bed and picked up the almost full bottle of whiskey on the floor between the nightstand and bed.

He filled the mug halfway and drank deeply, ignoring the tremor in his hand. He concentrated on how the alcohol seemed to wash away his anxiety.

Leaning back against the headboard, he took another, slower sip.

Tomorrow he'd worry about dirty laundry. About what he was going to do with his life now that his knee was useless and the woman he loved had exchanged him for some overeducated brainiac doctor. Tomorrow he'd think about what to do about J.C., with her warm brown eyes and huge expectations of him.

He finished the drink. Debated all of two seconds before pouring more into the mug. Yeah, he'd figure it all out.

Just not tonight.

5

SHE DIDN'T USUALLY MAKE MISTAKES. MORE LIKE... missteps. Paired the wrong shoes with an outfit. Picked up a real soda instead of sugar-free after a bad day. And when she was fourteen, there had been an unfortunate decision to perm her hair. But overall, Dr. Elizabeth Montgomery-Messler made the right choices.

Screwing up was J.C.'s department.

But as soon as the door opened, Liz knew she'd made a mistake, a huge one, in coming here.

"Good morning," she croaked, her face heating.

Linking her hands together in front of her, she tried to give Brady her professional smile—cool, calm and detached —but couldn't manage it. Not when he glowered at her, his hair tousled, his eyes red-rimmed.

Not when he stood in the doorway wearing a pair of low-slung, faded jeans. And nothing else.

"Liz," he said in his low voice.

"How...how are you?"

Widening his stance, he crossed his arms, the muscles in

his arms bulging, the eagle tattoo on his left bicep shifting. "Cold."

If the goosebumps covering his arms were anything to go by, he was freezing. But he didn't shiver. Didn't give any indication he was uncomfortable at all. At least not enough to invite her inside.

"Yes...it's quite...chilly this morning," she said lamely. Though it was almost 9:00 a.m., frost still covered the ground, the sun unable to penetrate the cloudy, gray sky. "We're due for some rain..."

He raked his gaze over her. "Why are you here, Liz?"

"I...I'm running errands... I don't have to work until this afternoon and I...I came here to..."

He raised one eyebrow. She'd forgotten how much that annoyed her.

"To...? To discuss the weather?"

She stuck her hand into the pocket of her brown leather jacket, her fingers closing around the velvet jeweler's box. "I wanted to see you. To see how you're doing," she amended quickly.

"Never better."

"Good. That's...good." The breeze picked up, blowing her hair into her face. She tucked the errant strands behind her ear.

"How's your knee?" she asked.

He seemed upset by the question. "It's fine."

"Are you taking physical therapy here in town or at the V.A. hosp—"

"Don't," he warned quietly.

"Don't what?"

"Don't pretend you give a damn."

Her throat constricted. "I...I wanted to visit you," she confessed, "when you were in the hospital."

"But you didn't." He leaned against the doorjamb, studying her in that way that used to make her feel like he could read her thoughts—when all she'd wanted was to keep a few of her thoughts to herself. "I guess your husband wouldn't have been too happy with you sitting by your ex's bedside."

No, Carter probably wouldn't have been happy, but he wouldn't have stopped her, either. When she'd discovered Brady had been injured, that he'd almost died, Carter had told her he understood if she needed to go to him. But she'd been too afraid to face him again.

Afraid he'd ask her to take him back. Terrified she'd say yes.

"After the way things...ended...between us," she said, staring at a point over his shoulder, "I thought a clean break would be best."

"And yet here you are."

She squeezed the box. Then pulled it out. "I wanted to give you this."

He went very still. "You've got to be kidding."

"I can't keep this, Brady. I...I want you to have it back."

"And you always get what you want, don't you? Sorry to disappoint you, but not this time." He pushed himself upright. "Toss it in the garbage. Hell, flush it down the toilet for all I care. But I'm not taking it back."

Her hand trembled. She should've returned his ring long ago but she hadn't wanted to send it overseas and risk it being lost or stolen. And she hadn't been brave enough to drop it off at his mother's house, knowing how angry his family must be with her.

But now she needed him to take it back. Things were still...tense... between her and Carter and if he discovered she still had it, he'd see it as a sign she hadn't let go of Brady.

Not completely. She had to show her husband she'd moved on. That she didn't regret the choice she'd made.

"I'm not taking it back," Brady repeated. "So, if that's all..." He started to close the door.

"Did you sleep with my sister to hurt me?" she blurted, then bit the inside of her lower lip. Hard. "Never mind. Let's forget I was even here."

Shoving the ring back into her pocket, she hurried down the steps, the high heels of her suede boots sliding on the wet wood. And wouldn't landing on her rear be the perfect ending to this misadventure?

She wrenched open her car door.

"No."

Her heart pounded against her ribs. "What?"

He looked down at the porch, his hands on his hips. "No," he repeated, lifting his head. "I didn't sleep with Jane to hurt you."

She nodded, got into her car, started it and drove down the gravel road. Well, that was a relief. Brady hadn't become the kind of man who'd deliberately set out to cause pain. Who'd use J.C. as a tool to get back at Liz.

He hadn't slept with her sister out of revenge.

He'd slept with her because he'd wanted to. Because he'd wanted J.C.

Her vision blurring, she wrung the steering wheel. Yes. That certainly was a relief.

BRADY'S TOES WERE NUMB. The tip of his nose tingling with cold. But he didn't move, couldn't force himself to turn from the sight of Liz driving away.

He did a few slow neck rolls. She thought he'd take it.

Well, why wouldn't she want to get rid of it? She couldn't still wear it, not when she had another man's ring on her finger. Yeah, he'd noticed. Hard not to notice a rock that size. One that made the diamond he'd spent three months' salary on look like a freaking speck.

Guess better jewelry was just one of the perks of trading up from a grunt Marine to a doctor.

A car came barreling toward the house and his heart beat faster but it wasn't Liz coming back. No, it was worse than seeing the woman who was everything he'd always wanted and couldn't have.

It was his mother.

Diane pulled to a stop and got out of her big boat of a luxury car. "You're up," she said, striding toward him. "Good."

"Mom."

By choice, he'd hardly seen her since he'd moved back to Jewell. Her mouth was set in a disapproving line, and her frame was a few pounds heavier than he remembered. But with her graying blond hair cut in a new style and the remnants of the tan she'd acquired on her trip to Florida a few weeks ago, she looked good.

Ready to tear him apart limb from limb, but good.

"Shall we stand out here staring at each other all day," she asked, "or are you going to invite me in?"

He shifted his weight. Let her inside? Now? Before he'd had a chance to rent a backhoe to clean the place out? "Do I really have a choice or is that one of those trick questions?"

She went in ahead of him—straight to the kitchen. "Oh, Brady," she called in disgust. "Look at this mess."

"I've seen it," he said as he entered the room.

Her eyes narrowed behind her glasses. "Are you sassing me?"

"No, ma'am," he responded automatically.

"Go put a shirt on while I make some coffee...you do have coffee, don't you?" He pointed toward the container next to the coffeepot on the counter.

"You and I," she continued, "are going to have a little chat."

Aw, hell. This couldn't end well for him.

By the time he came back, wearing a Carolina Panthers T-shirt, Diane had the coffeepot scrubbed, a fresh pot brewing and was at the sink tackling his mountain of dirty dishes.

"I was going to get to those," he said, brushing crumbs off a chair before sitting.

She didn't even glance at him. "I could see it was high on your to-do list."

He slouched down and stretched his leg out. "I've been busy."

"You obviously have some free time this morning," she said, not mentioning that without a job, he had free time every morning. "And I could use some help."

He wasn't stupid—or brave—enough to point out that they could air dry. He got up again and found a towel at the bottom of a drawer. They worked in silence while the coffee finished brewing.

"You haven't returned any of my calls," Diane said, rinsing a heavy white mug.

And here they went. "I meant to—"

"No. You didn't. You're avoiding me." She scrubbed at a spot of dried ketchup on a plate. "When you first came back to Jewell and insisted on living here instead of at the house with me, I thought you just needed time and space to accept all the changes you've gone through."

"I appreciate it," he said, guessing that her giving him space was about to come to an abrupt end.

"But," she continued, stressing the word, "when you didn't show up at Thanksgiving, I realized I was wrong."

Noticing he'd twisted the towel in his hands, he smoothed it out before drying a glass. "I didn't want to do the whole celebratory dinner, that's all.

Don't make more of it."

"The problem is, I haven't made enough of it. That needs to change." Her voice softened. "Let me help you."

"I'm fine."

"If you're so *fine,* then tell me why you've been avoiding your family." She tossed the dishcloth into the sink with enough force that water splashed them both. "And while you're at it, you can also explain why I had to hear from someone else that you're going to be a father."

Wincing, Brady scratched the back of his neck. This had to be some sort of gossip speed record.

"I was going to tell you..." In a few weeks. As soon as he'd figured out a few things. Like how to get J.C. to accept child support without wanting more from him. And what he was going to do with the rest of his life.

"Now you don't have to. Shirley Hanold down at the coffee shop told me, in front of my entire walking group, no less."

And so his day continued to get worse. He poured himself a cup of coffee so he wouldn't have to look at her. "Things are...complicated right now."

"Getting the sister of the woman you'd once planned to marry pregnant certainly is complicated. What are you going to do now?"

"About?"

"Don't play dense with me, Brady," she snapped. "Are

you, or are you not, going to take responsibility for this baby?"

"I've offered J.C. child support."

His mother waved that away with one hard stroke of her hand through the air. "Raising a child is about more than money. It's about being there, day in and day out. Nurturing your son or daughter. Loving them...no matter what mistakes they may make."

"Subtle," he muttered.

"You're too stubborn for subtlety." She poured herself a cup of coffee. "Your father and I raised you to be the type of man who steps up and takes responsibility for his actions."

He was willing to support the child for the next eighteen years. To make sure he...or she...was provided for. Wasn't that enough? He chugged a quick gulp of coffee and succeeded in burning his tongue.

"Does this have anything to do with Liz?" Diane asked.

And that was the last place he was going. Bad enough he still loved the woman. He wasn't about to admit it to his mother.

Besides, Liz was married now.

"Liz and I are over."

"Then why did I pass her car on my way here?"

His answer was a hard stare.

"That's it. I've had enough." Setting her cup down, Diane braced her arms against the table, getting right in her son's face. "You live like an animal. You refuse to go to physical therapy. When you're not ignoring your family, you're arguing with us. And your drinking is out of control."

He kept his expression blank. As if it didn't bother him that his mother knew how low he'd sunk. At least she didn't know about his nightmares. That he woke up in a cold sweat. He sipped his coffee.

"I'd think a winery owner would be all for drinking," he said.

"I'm disappointed in you, Brady." She cleared her throat and when she spoke again, her words were louder. Stronger. "I've never said that to any of my sons, never thought I would have reason to, but it's the truth."

What she'd said ripped him through him like a razor. He stood. "If that's all, I think I'm going to go back to bed."

"I'm not finished. You've done nothing to help yourself heal."

"The doctors at the V.A. hospital said my knee will never be a hundred percent."

"I'm not talking about your physical wounds." Hands trembling, she took her coat from the back of the chair and put it on, her movements jerky. "Every day I thank God your life was spared. That I'm not one of those mothers who's had to bury a child. You were given a gift, but instead of embracing your second chance, you'd rather dwell on the past. On what you lost. As much as I love you—and I do love you—I can no longer sit back and watch you self-destruct."

Damn it, that was not what he was doing. He may not be dealing with things how his family thought he should, but he was doing the best he could.

"Get yourself the help you need," his mother continued. "If you don't..." She swallowed.

"Don't stop there," he said softly.

The woman who raised three boys with equal doses of love and discipline stared him down. The woman who was as formidable and implacable as a drill sergeant. Who didn't make idle threats.

"If you don't, you'll have to find somewhere else to waste your life. Because you'll no longer be welcome here."

THE THIRD STREET DINER was packed with a boisterous lunch crowd, but J.C. spotted Liz seated in a small, two-person booth in the back. Hard to miss her, what with that halo highlighting her perfectly straight hair.

Okay, the halo was just the sun shining through a skylight. Still.

J.C. patted her hair. Yes, it was as big and frizzy as she feared. She made her way through the restaurant. She smiled and said hello to a few people but she didn't stop. She had to get her sister back.

"Hi," J.C. said when she got to the booth.

Even though she was sitting—and J.C. was a good three inches taller than her—Liz managed look down her nose at J.C. "You're late."

She checked her watch, then shrugged out of her coat. Bit her tongue instead of pointing out that anything under five minutes shouldn't be considered late. "Sorry. My last customer had a couple savings bonds and..."

And her sister didn't give a rat's behind about her job.

J.C. hung her coat on the metal pole next to the bench seat before sitting down. "I'm glad you came."

Liz folded her hands on the table. "I'm only here because Mom asked me to hear you out."

"Oh. Right. Well..." So she'd had to get her mother to talk to Liz for her.

She didn't have a choice. Liz had ignored all of her attempts to explain. J.C. couldn't remember a time when they'd gone five days without speaking.

Couldn't remember there ever being a time when Liz was so angry with her that she didn't want to talk to her.

Their waiter, a short, stocky college kid, took their

orders. Once they were alone again, J.C. cracked her thumb knuckle. "So...how are you?" she asked awkwardly.

"Fine."

J.C. drummed her fingers on the table. This was going to be harder than she'd thought. While she had plenty of experience apologizing for her blunders, she didn't know how to be the one who smoothed things over. She'd always relied on Liz for that.

The waiter delivered their drinks and J.C. unwrapped a straw and stuck it in her ginger ale. Took a sip to calm her churning stomach. She'd had her first prenatal visit yesterday and Dr. Owens had assured her the morning sickness would end soon, it being the second trimester.

And then, after receiving that hopeful news, J.C. had been informed by the doctor's office manager that her medical insurance would barely cover sixty percent of the expenses she'd incur during this pregnancy. No wonder she still felt sick.

"How's Carter?" J.C. asked. She'd been worried about the two of them ever since that awful Thanksgiving scene. When she'd left their house, she'd overheard them arguing in the hallway about Liz's reaction to the news of J.C.'s pregnancy. And who the father was. "Is...are you two okay?"

Liz, her mouth set in a thin line, squeezed a lemon slice into her water. "Of course," she said, but wouldn't meet J.C.'s eyes.

J.C. leaned across the table and covered Liz's hand with her own. "Lizzie, I...God...I'm so sorry."

Liz eased her hand away. "I knew you had a crush on him when you were a kid." She shook her head. "What did you do? Wait all these years for your opportunity? For us to break up?"

"It wasn't like that. And it's not as if he ever would've

looked at me twice —at any other woman—if you two were still together." She lined the salt and pepper shakers up with the front corners of the napkin dispenser. "It just sort of...happened."

Liz pursed her mouth. "How exactly does that work? You and my ex-fiancé were both naked and one of you tripped and fell on the other?"

"It was a mistake." She took another drink but it did little to ease the dryness of her throat. "One I'd give anything to go back and undo. It was wrong. *I* was wrong. I...I convinced myself it wouldn't matter to you because you'd broken up with him. That you didn't want him anymore."

"I don't." Her cheeks colored. "That's not what this is about."

"No. Of course not." Liz couldn't still want Brady. Not when she had Carter. Could she? "I didn't mean to hurt you."

"You never mean to do the things you do. You don't think about the consequences of your actions. You just charge forward, not caring about anything except what you want. Then, when it blows up in your face, you expect someone else to pick up the pieces."

Stunned, J.C. sat back. That wasn't fair. She could fix her own messes. She just never had to before.

That part about her only thinking about what she wanted? Total crap. Of course she'd thought of Liz, of her reaction, that night she'd slept with Brady. Had thought of her sister but hadn't let anything stop her, she realized, her queasiness now having nothing to do with being pregnant. She'd betrayed Liz because Brady had wanted her.

Because she'd wanted him.

"I thought I could do this, but I can't," Liz said, sliding

out of the booth as she dug into her purse. She tossed some cash onto the table but J.C. got out and stopped her.

"What about lunch?" she asked. What about their relationship?

"I'm not hungry."

"I'm sorry," J.C. rushed to say, her throat so tight it came out as a croak.

"Please...can you forgive me?"

Liz slowly looked at her. "Not today," she whispered.

Their waiter passed Liz as she walked out. "Everything all right here?" he asked, setting their food on the table.

Sitting back down, J.C. gave him a pathetic excuse for a smile. "Fine. Thanks."

He took the hint and didn't press. "Let me know if you need anything else."

This was bad. Real bad. Liz hadn't forgiven her. What if she never did?

J.C. studied her cheese and mushroom quesadilla and then shoved it aside. Liz just needed more time. To...work through her hurt and anger. She'd forgive J.C.

Because J.C. couldn't get through this without her.

6

J.C. LEANED AGAINST THE STEERING WHEEL AND STARED up at the white Colonial house that had been in the Sheppard family for five generations. It was lovely with tall, narrow windows, black shutters and wide porches on both the ground and second floors. The front door was a deep, inky shade of blue and had leaded glass windows on both sides, another one shaped like a fan on top. Listed on the Historical Register as one of the oldest structures in the county, there was nothing even remotely intimidating about it.

Right. That was why she'd been sitting there for twenty minutes.

She unbuckled her seat belt. After the week she'd had, failure was not an option.

Too bad. Failure was the one thing she excelled at.

Taking a deep, fortifying breath, she stepped out into the bright midday sun before she could change her mind. She tucked a small, white bakery box under her arm and crossed the cement drive. Once on the porch, she lifted her hand to knock only to lower it again.

Why did last-ditch efforts have to be so difficult?

Shutting her eyes, she rapped on the door. Maybe no one was home. Maybe they were all out in the vineyards doing...whatever people who had vineyards did. Pruning. Or...or fertiliz—

Someone tapped her on the shoulder.

"God!" J.C. whirled around, her heart racing.

A sleek, long-legged brunette in tight jeans and T-shirt proclaiming Conserve Water, Drink Wine smiled. "Not even close. But it's better than a lot of other things I've been called. I'm Connie."

Still trying to catch her breath, J.C. shook the woman's hand. "J.C. Montgomery."

Connie tipped her head to the side, the sunlight picking up reddish highlights in her short, choppy dark hair. "Montgomery, huh? Liz's sister?"

If she had a dollar for every time someone asked her that, she wouldn't have to look for ways to supplement her income. "Yes."

"I was a few years ahead of Liz in school. Plus, she used to come out here before..."

Before she broke Brady's heart.

Connie tucked her fingers into her jeans pockets. "So, is it J-A-Y-C-E-E or just the letters?"

"Uh...the letters."

"Well, J.C. just the letters, is there something I can do for you?"

She glanced at the door. "I'm looking for Aidan Sheppard."

"I need to see him, too. So what do you say we go in and track him down?"

Connie let herself in and J.C. followed her into a two-story foyer with elegant wainscoting, rose-colored walls and a wooden staircase leading to the second floor.

"Shouldn't we wait for someone to let us in?" she whispered.

Humor lit Connie's blue eyes. "I run the vineyards for the Sheppards. They're used to me coming and going."

Oh. Well. That made sense, then. At least J.C. wasn't letting herself into another house belonging to the Sheppards. The one time she'd done that, things hadn't worked out so well for her.

Connie pulled out a cell phone and pressed a number. "Aidan's office is upstairs. I'll call him." She lowered her voice conspiratorially. "He gets grumpy when people barge in on him."

J.C. smiled weakly. Of course he did. "Yes. That's so rude." Maybe she shouldn't have come without an appointment.

"He's not answering, which means he's probably on the office line. Let me text him that we're here—" her fingers flew over the keys almost as quickly as the words coming out of her mouth "—and he can come down when he's finished."

Then, sticking the phone back into her pocket, she walked around a corner. J.C. switched the box to her other hand. Should she follow? Sit on the cute wooden bench against the wall and wait for Aidan to come downstairs? Take her impetuous self and this whole crazy idea and get out there?

Connie poked her head back around the corner. "You coming?"

She sighed. "Right behind you."

They went into a family room so big, J.C. could've fit her apartment in it. And still have space left over. A stone fireplace took up most of the wall to the left while sliding glass doors led to a bricked veranda at the back of the house. The room opened up into a large kitchen with ceramic tiles on the floor, oak cabinets and stainless-steel appliances—including a double wall oven and a six-burner range top like the ones J.C.'s mother had been bugging her father to get for their own kitchen. Passing a small breakfast nook with three sides of floor-to-ceiling windows, J.C. crossed to the granite-topped island in the middle of the room. After setting the box down, she lovingly ran her hands over the cool surface.

"You want me to give you two a few minutes alone?"

J.C. returned Connie's grin. And how sad was it that she couldn't remember the last time she'd smiled? "Do you have any idea how many truffles I could shape on this much counter space?"

Connie tapped a forefinger to her lips. "Quite a few?"

"Eight...maybe even ten dozen. And I wouldn't even have to set cookie sheets of them on the coffee table or washer and dryer. I can't even reach the edge," she said, stretching her arms across the width of the counter.

"It truly is an amazing structure." Connie carried a large, frosted glass jar with a silver lid over to the island. "Which is why Diane likes it so much. She doesn't make truffles, but she's big on baking."

J.C. blanched. She'd been so worried about meeting with Aidan she hadn't even considered running into Brady's mom. "She's not...she's not here, is she?"

Connie shook her head. "She and Al are spending the weekend up in D.C."

Al being Al Wallace, Mrs. Sheppard's boyfriend—if you could call a sixty-something retired senator someone's boyfriend—and God bless him for taking Mrs. Sheppard away for the weekend. J.C. would gladly avoid Brady's mom for...oh...forever would work.

Not that she was afraid of her or anything. Ha.

Diane Sheppard had a reputation for getting what she wanted and had no qualms about stomping on anyone who got in her way.

What if she wanted to be a part of the baby's life? What if...what if she wanted to have a say in any decision she made regarding the baby?

J.C. rubbed her temples. Mrs. Sheppard might not even know about the baby. And if she did, well, this was J.C.'s body. Her baby. And ultimately her decision whether she kept the baby or not.

"Here," Connie said, holding out a thick, pumpkin-shaped sugar cookie with orange frosting. "You look like you could use a sugar rush."

J.C. reached for the cookie only to remember how, when she'd stood on the stupid scale at Dr. Owens's Monday, the nurse had moved the little metal slide up. Then she'd moved it some more. And yet some more.

"I'm good, thanks," she managed to say, lowering her hand. She may be eating for two, but that didn't mean she had to eat everything. Besides, being this virtuous was almost as good as a giant sugar cookie.

And the day she believed that was the day she hoped she stopped breathing.

Connie shrugged, then polished off the cookie before reaching for another one.

J.C. hiked herself up onto one of the two high-backed, black stools. "Even though we just met, I already hate you. But it's nothing personal."

Connie's laugh was deep and husky—and the perfect fit for someone so sexy.

"I'm guessing you're one of those women who can eat

anything she wants without gaining weight," J.C. continued. Connie grinned and went for a third cookie. "See? I have to hate you. It's the principle of the thing."

"A girl's gotta have her principles." Connie put the lid back on the cookie jar when the sliding glass door opened.

Brady stepped inside and stopped abruptly when he saw J.C. "Everything okay?"

She twisted her fingers together in her lap. Crap. She'd gone seven days without any more fun-filled run-ins with him. And she'd like to keep that streak alive for the next eighteen years or so.

"Everything's fine," she said.

His hair was mussed, the black T-shirt he wore underneath an open gray and black checked flannel shirt was wrinkled and the stubble from the last time she'd seen him had grown into a full-fledged, if scruffy, beard.

Not even glancing at Connie—who watched them intently—he crossed to the end of the island. Close enough that J.C. could smell the fresh air on his skin.

He studied her as if he were a scientist and she were some perplexing, never-before-discovered insect. "Why is your hair like that?"

"You are such a moron," Connie murmured.

J.C. couldn't agree more. She lifted a hand to her hair. "I straightened it."

"I called you a few times," he said, obviously not having anything else to say about her hair. Like how nice it looked.

Not that she cared. She certainly hadn't spent a solid hour and a half ironing her hair into submission for him. "I got the messages."

All seven of them. He'd called once a day since leaving her apartment

78

Thanksgiving and each time he said the same thing. "It's Brady. Call me." "You two together?" Connie asked.

J.C. snorted. "No."

"Beat it, Connie," Brady said.

"But I don't want to leave. Not when this is so fascinating."

Brady glared at her. "Goodbye."

She held her hands up in surrender. "I can take a hint." She gave J.C.'s arm a quick, reassuring squeeze as she walked past. "I'll go up and see what's taking Aidan so long."

He frowned. "Aidan? You're not here because you've changed your mind?"

Please. Even if she wanted his money, she couldn't accept it now.

"I'm not here to see you," she said, glad to hear a touch of ice in her voice. "I'm here on business."

He raised his eyebrows. "Business?" She nodded. "With the Diamond Dust?" Another nod, this one jerky. "Is that why you're dressed like that?"

"What's wrong with how I'm dressed?"

She forced herself to remain still and not fidget or tug at her clothes while he slowly inspected her from the tips of her pointy-toed shoes, up the black, wide-legged pants and over her small baby bump currently covered by a loose white button-down shirt. When she thought he was done and she could breathe again, his gaze lingered at the black lace peeking out of the top of her shirt.

Her breasts had already gone up a cup size and since she liked being able to breathe, she'd left the top three buttons undone and worn a silk camisole underneath. Now, as her skin warmed under his scrutiny, she wished she had on a sweater. Preferably with a high neckline.

He jerked his eyes up, his jaw tight. "You don't look like yourself."

That'd been the point. The hair, the clothes, they were supposed to show Aidan she was a businesswoman. Professional. Capable. Confident. Someone he would want to do business with.

———

"YOU'RE NOT HERE to see me?" Brady asked, trying to wrap his head around what she was saying. Why was she dressed like some sort of naughty librarian? With her hair straightened, there was a noticeable resemblance between her and Liz. A resemblance that was eclipsed by the way J.C. filled out that damn shirt.

"I'm really not here to see you. I was hoping to talk to Aidan."

"About doing business with the Diamond Dust?"

"Yes," she muttered.

What sort of business could J.C. have with his family's winery?

"Why don't I wait in the foyer for Aidan?" she asked. "I'm sure you have...things...to do."

He shrugged and went to the refrigerator. Out of the corner of his eye, he noticed J.C. pick up the white box from the island.

"Do you have an appointment?" he asked.

"An appointment?"

Brady took a container of some sort of leftover pasta out before closing the fridge door. "An appointment with Aidan."

She didn't. For one thing, if she had an appointment, Aidan wouldn't have told her to come to the main house.

His brother used their father's home office upstairs, but he held all meetings down the road at the converted farmhouse where the Diamond Dust's main offices were located.

And he never would've let her wait this long. Aidan was nothing if not organized. He'd be willing to bet Aidan scheduled every minute of his day, including his trips to the bathroom.

J.C. fumbled the box in her hands before setting it back on the island. "No. Do I...do you think that'll be a problem?"

"Only if you're serious about doing business with him."

She blanched. No, Aidan wasn't that big prick, to hold something like an impromptu visit against her. But the truth was, Brady didn't want her to go to his brother.

Not when she wouldn't even take his calls.

"Maybe I should leave," she said, biting her lower lip, her brow furrowed.

"You're already here," he pointed out. His knee began to ache so he lifted himself up to sit on the counter. "You might as well do what you came here to do."

"But if it's going to make Aidan angry—"

"You don't need Aidan." Brady took the lid off the container. Lasagna. Great. Even better. He opened the drawer between his legs and grabbed a fork. "You've got me."

She wrinkled her nose. "I've got you for what?"

He waved the fork. "To discuss your business idea."

"Have you been drinking?"

She didn't add *again,* but sure as hell implied it. "Not yet."

He would've started already but he'd been starving and all he had at the cottage was cereal...but no milk. Guess he needed to make a trip to the grocery store. The grocery store where he could limp behind a cart while everyone stared. Or asked him how he was doing, what his plans were next.

Better yet, he could have a flashback, proving to everyone how little control he had over himself.

Was it any wonder he needed the oblivion alcohol provided?

The only reason he'd come to his mom's house was because he knew she wouldn't be there. Despite her being pissed at him, she still kept him informed of her comings and goings and two days ago, she'd left him a message saying she was spending a long weekend in D.C. with Al.

"Are you working for Aidan?" J.C. asked.

He could be. If he gave in to his mother's threats and Aidan's pressure.

Brady scooped up more cold lasagna. "Tell me."

She tucked her hair behind her ear—just like Liz always did. "I've had some unexpected expenses. And I need to supplement my income."

He narrowed his eyes at her hesitant tone. "What kind of unexpected expenses?"

"It doesn't matter. But I—"

"Jane. What expenses?"

She shrugged, the movement causing her full breasts to rise and lower. He averted his gaze. "Some...doctor bills."

For the baby. *His* baby. "I'll pay them."

"No. You won't."

"I want to," he said, realizing it was true. He wanted to help her, even if all he had to offer was a few bucks.

"I told you, I don't want your money." Her hands were clenched at her sides, her shoulders rigid. "I have to do this on my own."

And that was when he saw the real reason she wouldn't accept his help.

Pride.

Hell. He knew a thing or two about that. And he wasn't about to try to injure hers.

"Go on," he said quietly.

She looked at him with such gratitude, he felt like a complete ass. Damn it, she shouldn't be willing to accept so little from him.

"When I saw that first bill," she said, "I was a bit stressed so I did what most women do when they're stressed."

"Found some poor bastard to castrate?"

"Ha-ha. No, but only because I didn't think you'd let me within ten feet of you if I happened to be carrying a machete."

He grimaced. "Ouch."

"I searched for some chocolate. But I didn't have any so I decided to make some." She took the lid off the box and carried it over to him.

He set the lasagna aside. "I didn't know you made chocolates." He inspected the candies set on waxed paper.

Then again, there was plenty he didn't know about her. Like why she'd slept with him. Or what her plans for the future were. How she would raise their baby on her own.

But being this close to her he did find out a couple of things about her. She smelled sweet, like vanilla. Her eyes weren't plain brown as he'd always thought, but a deep, rich caramel.

"I usually make them as gifts," she said, "for holidays and birthdays or if a friend needs a pick-me-up. And I made them for—" she dropped her eyes "— for Liz's wedding and they went over pretty well and I...I started to think maybe I could sell them. So, I took some down to Horizons—"

"Is that the gift shop Sandy O'Donnell owns?" he asked, remembering the one time he'd gone into the small store on

Main Street. He'd been on leave from basic training and had stopped in to buy a Mother's Day gift. But being surrounded by all those chick gifts—crystal glasses, tableware, picture frames and ceramic figurines—had given him the hives.

"Yes. She carries chocolates from a candy maker in Danville during the holidays and Easter, so I thought she might be interested in selling mine, as well. But she has an exclusive contract with the other guy." J.C. rolled her eyes as if her encounter with Sandy hadn't been all that pleasant. "I tried Kent Goodwin at the Main Street Mercantile and he said he would've been interested...if I'd contacted him back in August when he was accepting inventory for the holiday season. Then he gave me the old 'if I make an exception for you, I have to make an exception for everyone' speech and—"

"The point of all this?" he asked, pinching the bridge of his nose.

"I'm getting there. Rhonda, the manager at Country Crafts, declined because she'd tried gourmet food at her store before and it hadn't sold well. Of course, she didn't tell me that until *after* she ate half a pound worth of samples. I went to Delgato's but he wouldn't even hear me out. You'd think, seeing as how I was the one he fired, *I'd* be holding the grudge and not the other way around."

Couldn't she have just said all three gift shops in town and the only gourmet grocery store within an eighty-mile radius had turned her down? "And now you're here...?"

"I'm here because when I left Delgato's, I saw the flyer for the holiday open houses the Diamond Dust is hosting and I had an epiphany."

"An epiphany on Mechanic Street. That's not something you hear every day."

"That's what makes it special," she assured him

solemnly, but her eyes were lit with humor. "I think my chocolates and the Diamond Dust would be a perfect match. Sell the chocolates in the gift shop."

He carefully slid off the counter landing with his weight on his right leg, the box still in his hands. "You want to start making chocolates—"

"Gourmet chocolates." She closed the distance between them and picked out a candy. "Here. Try one." She popped it into his mouth.

The outer shell was dark chocolate, the inside a creamy milk chocolate that melted on his tongue. Damn, that was good. He looked into her eyes and found it difficult to take a full breath.

He pushed away from the counter, set the box down and took a glass from an upper cabinet. "Let me see if I've got this straight," he said as he filled it with water from the sink and took a long drink. "You couldn't find anyone in town willing to sell your chocolates so you decided the best place for them would be at the Diamond Dust?"

She crossed her arms, which drew his attention again to that damn lace covering her breasts. "You make it sound like this is my last resort."

"Is it?"

"So what if it is?" she asked irritably. "It's not like it's the end of my world if this doesn't pan out. I'm sure I can get a part-time job somewhere."

"You don't sound very convincing."

"It's just...I've had some trouble finding a job that suits me. And when some employers see my employment history they're not real anxious to give me a chance."

"How many jobs have you had?"

"Total?"

Sleeping with her was the biggest mistake of his life and

she was a pain in the ass for wanting more from him than financial support with this pregnancy. For expecting more from him than he could give. So why did he find her amusing as hell? "How about you give me a rough estimate?"

She pursed her lips. "Around a dozen. Give or take one or two."

Twelve jobs in less than what...ten years? There was no way Aidan would go for any sort of deal with her no matter how good her candy tasted.

Luckily, Aidan wasn't here.

"You've got a deal," he said. "You can sell your candy at the Diamond Dust gift shop."

For a moment, she seemed confused, but then she broke into a grin.

"Really?" she asked breathlessly.

"The details will still have to be ironed out." Which would be the perfect job for Aidan. His older brother loved nothing more than ironing out details.

"But, yeah, really."

Her cheeks flushed with pleasure. "This is so great. You won't regret it, I promise." He ground his back teeth together when she did a little hip-shaking, shoulder-wiggling dance that brought her closer to him. "Thank you, thank you, thank you!"

Then she grabbed his face with both hands, pulled his head down and kissed him.

7

J.C. STOPPED DOING HER VICTORY DANCE WHEN BRADY'S hands tightened on her hips as she pressed her mouth against his. There she went again, throwing caution aside and letting her spontaneity get the better of her. She'd meant for it to be nothing more than a celebratory kiss. Light and fun. To express her gratitude—and relief.

But as soon as her mouth touched Brady's, she knew it could never be any of those things. Not when her heart stuttered at the feel of his lips against hers.

Not when warning bells were clanging in her head.

Not when fixing things with Liz meant she had to stay away from him.

She fell back on her heels.

You just charge forward, not caring about anything except what you want.

No. Not anymore.

"Don't take that the wrong way," she warned him in a raspy whisper.

His eyes hooded, he studied her. "How should I take it?"

She shivered. And realized she was touching him, still cupping his face.

She dropped her hands and stepped back. But she could still feel the scratchiness of his beard on her palms. "It's been a tough week and I'm... grateful...and..." And she was babbling like an idiot. She held her breath for the count of five. "I'm happy. That's all."

"Do you kiss a man every time you're happy?"

"Every chance I get," she assured him soberly. "You should've seen the lip-lock I laid on Marty Boyd last month when he told me my car passed its inspection."

"That impressive, huh?"

"Well, I hate to brag, but it was enough of a kiss that I'm pretty sure he thinks we're engaged now."

And then, to her amazement, Brady smiled. Disheveled, miserable and, if she wasn't mistaken, broken Brady Sheppard smiled. At her. It didn't last long and for a moment, it seemed as if even that small bit of happiness pained him, but what else could she do but smile back?

Someone behind her cleared their throat. "I hope I'm not interrupting anything."

J.C. whirled around. Aidan stood at the other end of the kitchen, gazing shrewdly from her to Brady and back again. Her face flamed.

"Nothing that meant anything," Brady said. "Isn't that what you said, J.C.?"

"Uh...right."

"Connie said you wanted to speak with me?" Aidan asked J.C.

Like Brady, Aidan was tall with broad shoulders and blond hair, but that was where the differences ended. His eyebrows were heavier, his lips fuller, his eyes more green than blue. And though it was the end of the day, his button-down shirt and khakis were still neatly pressed, as if wrinkles dared not mess with this cool-eyed man.

Thank God she and Brady had made the deal and she didn't have to try to convince Aidan to do with business with her. Though Aidan was polite, the way he scowled at his brother made him seem about as approachable as a wolverine. And not the Hugh Jackman kind.

"No." She cleared her throat. "I mean, yes, I did want to speak with you but now I guess I don't have to..." The tension between the brothers was palpable. And nothing she wanted to get in the middle of. "I'd better get going." She smiled at Aidan as she sidestepped him toward the family room. "I have...things. To do."

"I'll walk you out," Brady said.

"Oh. That's not necessary."

But the expressions on the brothers' faces told her it was. And far be it for her to argue.

"Bye, Aidan," she said.

He nodded. "Nice to see you, Jane."

As they walked back toward the foyer, she snuck a glance at Brady. He reached past her and opened the front door. "I'll have Aidan call you with the details."

"Thank you," she said, careful not to touch him as she passed. She stepped off the porch and into the sunshine.

"I opened a savings account. For the baby."

Shading her eyes with her hand, she looked up at him. He didn't know how important it was for her to prove she could take care of herself. And the first step was to be able to pay her own way. When the office manager at Dr. Owens's office had told her that her insurance wouldn't cover all her expenses, she hadn't been too worried. No, she'd done what Liz accused her of doing. She'd gone to her parents to take care of her.

While her parents were far from thrilled with the situation, they'd told her they'd support whatever decision she made regarding the baby. And that they'd be more than willing to cover her medical expenses.

But she wasn't going to be that person anymore, the one who let everyone else take care of her. "We've been through—"

"My attorney will send you the account information. I'll deposit money into it each month." He stood gripping the porch rail, the muscles of his arms knotted. "You can do what you want with it. Use it or not. Either way, it'll be there. And whatever's left when the kid is eighteen will be turned over to him."

"I don't want to go over—"

"Do you really hate me so much that you'd deny your baby financial security?"

She made a soft sound of surprise. Was that what he thought? That she was doing this as some way to get back at him? That couldn't be further from the truth. But really, what was it hurting if he put money into a bank? She was still trying to figure out how she was going to pay her doctor bills. Knowing she had a cushion for the future would be a huge relief. And as he pointed out, she didn't have to use it.

She could still keep her pride.

She nodded. "Okay."

"Thank you," he said, as if she were the one doing something for him.

"Listen, you said you weren't staying in Jewell and, well, in case I don't... see you again...I want to wish you good luck. With whatever you do. And I...I want you to know...I don't hate you," she blurted. "I could never hate you."

He regarded her intently, his eyes a brilliant blue. Her

cheeks warmed. Her breath clogged in her lungs as the silence stretched on.

"Not that it matters," she added feebly.

Okay, then. She gave him a half-hearted wave and walked away, hoping he couldn't tell how unsteady her legs were.

As she opened her car door, his voice carried to her, soft as the cool breeze.

"It matters."

***

"YOU MUST BE MAKING PROGRESS," Aidan said when Brady came back into the kitchen. Aidan popped the top of a can of cola and took a drink. "I'm glad you're stepping up and doing the right thing."

Brady grunted and rolled his head side to side so that his neck cracked. Progress? He'd agreed to a business deal he wasn't entitled to make and had told J.C. about the account he'd set up for the baby.

But he was ditching her, leaving her to raise their kid on her own. He wouldn't blame her if she did come after him with that machete.

And what had been up with that kiss? It'd taken every ounce of control he still had left not to pull her closer.

"When's everything going to happen?" Aidan asked.

Brady picked out a dark chocolate from the box next to him and tossed it in his mouth, hoping to replace the lingering taste of J.C.'s kiss. "Everything?"

"You need to tell Mom." Aidan waved his can. "It shouldn't take too long to plan the wedding—"

"Wedding?" Brady choked out.

"Stop repeating everything I say. It's pissing me off."

Aidan's lips thinned and he straightened. "Aren't you and Jane getting married?"

"No."

"No? That's it?"

Brady pretended to consider that. "How about, hell no."

Aidan tapped his fist against his thigh. "Then why did she seem so happy? Did you finalize a financial agreement about the baby?"

"We did." Brady put the lid back on the half-eaten lasagna. Since there was no food at the cottage, he might as well take it back with him. If he took enough of his mom's leftovers home, he could put off the inevitable trip to the store for another day or two. "I'm going to pay child support." Whether she ever used his money, he had no way of saying.

"We'll name you Father of the Year," Aidan said.

And Brady wasn't about to get into it again with his sanctimonious brother.

"As to the reason she seemed happy, that's probably because I told her the Diamond Dust would purchase some of her homemade candy to sell."

The silence was broken only by the soft ticking of the antique wall clock that'd belonged to their mother's great-grandmother.

"You did what?" Aidan finally asked softly, a muscle jumping in his jaw.

"I told her we'd buy her chocolates. We can sell them in the gift store, offer them at the open houses."

"We? I hadn't realized you were on the payroll."

Brady went back to the fridge to see what else he could take home to stock his own fridge. "I'm going to need you to draw up a contract—"

"No way."

"What's the problem? You wanted me to step up and do the right thing with J.C. and I am. Besides, you've been bugging me to get more involved in the Diamond Dust for months. So, I got involved."

"I wanted you to work for the company. Maybe pitch in with some paperwork. Handle some shipping issues we've been having. Not offer someone a deal behind my back."

"It wasn't behind your back," Brady muttered, irritated. "I just told you, didn't I?"

"You made a deal on behalf of the Diamond Dust without discussing it with me or Mom."

Brady grabbed a container of cheese spread, some lunch meat and a half-empty carton of eggs, shutting the door with enough force to shake the condiments. "Isn't that what you've been doing all these years? You've never once asked for my opinion on anything you wanted to do with the Diamond Dust."

"I'm the president. Mom's the owner. You don't even work for the winery. The way I remember it, both you and Matt couldn't wait to get away from Jewell and the Diamond Dust fast enough."

"Dad didn't have a problem with my decision to join the Corps," Brady said, carefully setting the egg carton on the counter instead of hurling it at his brother's head like he wanted. "Just buy the candy from J.C. It's good. Which means we're sure to make a profit. It's a win-win situation."

"Doesn't matter how good it is. Our budget for holiday spending is already set. Tell her you can't keep your end of the bargain."

"No."

Aidan shifted into what Brady recognized as his fighting stance—legs wide, hands loose at his sides, weight on the balls of his feet. "That wasn't a request. That was me not giving you a choice."

Aidan picked up his soda dismissively. As if whatever he said was the last word on the subject. Brady wanted to go after his brother and knock his fat head in. Too bad that, with his bum knee, he didn't have a chance of beating up his brother.

Aidan did whatever it took to win. Even if it meant fighting dirty.

Maybe Brady should consider going to his physical therapy sessions once in a while. The pain would be worth it if he could kick Aidan's ass.

"Just try one." He shoved the box at Aidan.

Even as Aidan chewed, his expression remained sour. Which was nuts considering how good those chocolates were. Then again, ever since their dad died and Aidan's wife left him a month later, he always looked as if someone had switched his favorite Petit Verdot with grape-flavored children's cough medicine.

"Well?" Brady asked when he couldn't stand it any longer.

"You're right. It's good. But that doesn't change anything."

"I already told J.C. we'd do this."

"And your word is your bond?" Aidan asked dryly.

"When I say I'll do something, I do it," Brady managed through gritted teeth. He may not be living up to his family's high ideals but he kept his word.

He just didn't give it very often.

"Sorry," Aidan said, not sounding sorry at all, damn him. "But it's not going to happen. You'll have to assuage your guilt some other way."

"DO YOU HAVE any chocolates?"

J.C. blinked at Brady. Why was he at her apartment... carrying a large pizza box, no less? When she'd left his mother's house earlier today, she'd figured, other than occasionally running into him while he was still in town, she'd never see him again.

She nudged Daisy back into the apartment with her foot before the cat could slip out into the dark. "Halloween was last month. And you're about twenty years past the normal trick-or-treating age."

"I'm not out begging for treats," he said in his rough voice. "Aidan didn't go for it."

So much for being able to pay her doctor bills with the money she'd get selling her chocolates. So much for trusting Brady Sheppard. "But you said..."

Wait a minute. What exactly had he said? She'd asked if he worked for Aidan and he'd said...She searched her memory. Nothing. He'd said nothing.

"You have no authority to decide anything about the winery, do you?" she asked.

"No."

Guess she should've asked him that question earlier. "Then why did you act as if you did? Why did you say it was a deal?"

He glared, as if he had a right to stand on her doorstep all big and imposing and fierce. "Do you have any chocolates made or not?"

The strap of her tank top slid down her arm and she pulled it back up. "A few, but—"

"If you still want to sell your chocolates at the Diamond Dust, we need to do a pairing."

"I thought Aidan wasn't—"

"We're going to change his mind."

She crossed her arms. As if she'd accept his help after he lied to her about the deal in the first place. "How?"

"I thought we could discuss the particulars over dinner." He held up the pizza box, his expression unreadable. "What do you say? Can I come in, Jane Cleo?"

She felt warm, tingly. She'd never heard her name sound so...so sexy...before. Was that how Liz felt when he said her name, too?

How would Liz react if she knew Brady had come to J.C.'s apartment on a Friday night, even for reasons that were decidedly nonpersonal? Then again, Liz didn't have to find out. Not if J.C. didn't tell her. She stood on her tiptoes and peered at her grandma's house. Except for the porch light, it was dark. Grandma Rose must still be at dinner. And J.C. really had pinned her hopes on selling her chocolates.

She stepped aside.

"Bring them up," Brady called down the stairs.

Peeking around the corner, she saw a kid taking the steps two at a time, a large wooden crate in his skinny arms, a dark blue ball cap on his head.

"Where do you want it?" he asked Brady when he reached them.

Brady gestured with his chin. "On the table is fine."

The kid glanced up at J.C., then did a double take. "Hey," he squeaked, blushing. He cleared his throat. "How's it going?"

She smiled at him and his eyes seemed to cloud over. "Uh...I'm fine. Thanks." Had his voice gotten deeper from when he'd spoken to Brady?

"Eyes straight ahead," Brady said, then nudged the kid's shoulder.

As Brady and the boy walked over to the table, J.C. bent and scooped Daisy into her arms. The sound of someone choking made her spin around and she saw the boy staring at her, his mouth hanging open.

She took a hesitant step toward him. "Are you all right?"

"Don't make eye contact. He'll see it as encouragement," Brady said under his breath as he took a hold of the kid's arm and steered him past her. At the door, he shoved some money at the boy and practically pushed him outside. "Thanks. I appreciate it."

Now standing at the top of the stairs, the teen tore his eyes away from J.C. long enough to check out the amount of cash in his hands. "Hey. Thanks a lot. If you need anything else, call me." Then he grinned sweetly at J.C. "Or I could hang around. In case you—"

Brady shut the door in his face.

"Well, that was rude." J.C. stroked Daisy's soft fur. "What was that all about anyway?"

"You really don't know?"

"Know what?"

Brady set his hands on his hips, his jaw tight. "You made his night. And gave him enough material to stoke his sexual fantasies for the next year or so."

She almost dropped her cat. She set Daisy down on all fours but the feline didn't take well to nearly landing on her head. Sticking her chin in the air, she meowed and then took off like a shot.

"First of all," J.C. said, her nose wrinkling, "ewww. Second of all, I'm at least ten years older than he is. Why on earth would he..." She gestured vaguely with her hands. "About me?"

Brady's mouth quirked. So glad to see her confusion amused him. "Maybe he'd want to..." He repeated her hand

97

gesture. "Because you smiled at him. Or maybe it's because when you bent over in those shorts you're barely wearing, that kid thought he'd just seen heaven."

Her face flamed. "They're pajamas," she said in a strangled voice, tugging on the hem of her purple cotton shorts.

And she had on the loose—albeit tiny—shorts and matching tank top with eyelet trim because it felt as if her internal body temperature had gone up twenty degrees since she got pregnant.

Brady shrugged, his intense gaze never veering from her face. "Doesn't matter what you call them. They don't leave much to the imagination. And believe me, teenage boys have vivid imaginations, especially when it comes to barely dressed women."

Great.

She hoped the kid wasn't scarred for life.

J.C. crossed her arms and frowned at Brady's back as he went into the kitchen. She wasn't going to apologize for putting on her pajamas after she'd taken an early shower. She was in her own apartment, after all. And she'd seen no reason not to answer the door when she was just as covered as she'd be if she had on any other pair of shorts and tank top.

She went in after him. "What are you doing?"

He opened the top cupboard to the right of her stove and took down two of her mismatched plates. Held them up to her. "Plates." Taking the roll of paper towels off the counter, he brushed past her, his movements slow, his limp slight but still noticeable. He set the items on the table, came back into the kitchen and took milk out of the fridge.

"I never said I'd eat with you," J.C. pointed out.

In the act of pouring milk into a tall glass, he glanced at her. "Not hungry?"

Hungry? She shouldn't be. She'd had dinner a few hours ago. But the rich scent of tomato sauce and melted cheese made her mouth water. "I don't want to have dinner with you, that's all."

"You're willing to lose out on a chance to make that deal with the Diamond Dust?"

Possibly. Because at the moment, it felt as if she had to decide between making the deal that would enable her to prove to her family she could take care of herself, and loyalty to her sister.

"Will any of this even make a difference?" she asked. "And can I trust what you say?"

He flinched. Well, well. What a shock. Maybe he wasn't completely dead inside after all.

"I messed up," he said, putting the milk back in the fridge. "I never should've let you believe I had the authority to make a deal on behalf of the winery."

"Why did you?"

He tugged on his ear. "I wanted to help you."

He seemed sincere. As sincere as a hard-eyed, hard-drinking man could get.

"Fine. You can tell me about this idea you have while we eat. But," she stressed, "then you have to go."

Before Grandma Rose came home. If she found out he was here, it was sure to get back to Liz.

He didn't look relieved or particularly happy about her acquiescence. "I appreciate you hearing me out." Then his hooded gaze raked over her, from the tips of her brightly polished toes to the top of her still-damp hair. "Before we eat," he said gruffly, "could you put something...else...on? Teenage boys aren't the only ones with vivid imaginations."

99

8

BRADY WATCHED J.C. WALK AWAY, HIS GAZE LOCKED ON the sway of her hips, the curve of her ass in those damn shorts.

Pregnant women weren't supposed to be so...sexy...were they? He even found the slight roundness of her belly alluring.

He scrubbed a hand over his face. Alluring. J.C. Montgomery. Sweet God, but he needed a drink.

He set the milk on the table when she came back out. She'd put her damp, curly hair up into a knot on top of her head but a few spirals had already come loose. She wore a boxy sweatshirt and loose black sweatpants.

Too bad he was still imagining her in those pajamas.

He cleared his throat and handed her the glass of milk. "Here."

She looked at it suspiciously. "What's this for?"

"I thought maybe you'd want some." He felt like an idiot. Weren't pregnant women supposed to drink a lot of milk?

"Oh. Sure. Thanks."

His neck warm with embarrassment, he put a slice of cheese pizza onto a plate before handing it to her. "I got half plain cheese in case you were still doing the vegetarian thing."

"I can't believe you remembered that."

He sat and helped himself to two pepperoni slices. "Hard to forget you with that duct tape over your mouth at Easter dinner."

"I'd forgotten about that. As a protest against my mom's baked ham." She tore off a piece of crust. "It took two weeks for the skin around my lips to grow back."

He and Liz had been seniors that year, J.C. a freshman. "Liz did your makeup every morning so no one could tell what happened."

"Right." J.C. tossed the crust back onto her plate then brushed her hands off. "Look, you don't have to worry about getting Aidan to change his mind. It's not like I've always dreamed of being a candy maker. It was a spur-of-the-moment idea. Believe me, another one will come along. They always do."

He scowled at his half-eaten slice of pizza. She'd always been that way.

Brimming with plans, abandoning one grandiose scheme for the next.

Perfect. He had an out. She didn't want his help. Now maybe his guilt over making her a promise he couldn't keep would ease. Maybe now he could go back to not giving a damn about anything or anyone. It sure made it easier to get through the day.

"Do you always roll over when you don't automatically get what you want?" he asked more harshly than he'd intended.

Her nostrils flared and two spots of color stained her

cheeks. "No. But that doesn't mean I go around knocking my head against walls, either."

"When those other stores turned you down, did you even try to convince them to change their mind?"

J.C. shifted her chair to the side, and the cat leaped onto her lap. "What's the point? They already said they weren't interested."

"The point is to stop taking the easy way out and fight for what you want."

"Wow," she said through tight lips. "That's great advice coming from the man who either ignores his problems or drowns them."

Other than his fingers flexing on his thigh, he showed no sign she'd just made a direct hit. "When I want something badly enough, nothing stops me from getting it."

He just no longer let himself want.

She licked her lips nervously. "Aidan's already made up his mind—"

"So we get him to change it."

"How?"

"By proving your chocolates will sell."

The cat nosed J.C.'s plate, and J.C. moved her barely touched pizza out of reach. "Except I can't give him a guarantee people will buy them."

He finished off his first slice and dug into his second. "But we can market them so they tie in with the wines. Aidan will see an opportunity to increase sales. And believe me, nothing makes him happier than increased sales."

"But I thought wine went with real food. Not candy."

"It can go with sweet or savory. We figure out which of the Diamond Dust's wines go best with each flavor." He nodded toward the crate. "I brought the wine so we can do pairings."

"We?" she asked as if he'd suggested they take jobs as targets at the rifle range. "As in, you and me, we?"

He scratched his cheek. "I was thinking me and the cat. But you'll do in a pinch."

Her lips twitched. "You might be better off with Daisy, seeing as how I don't know anything about pairing wine with...well...anything. Besides, last I heard, pregnancy and alcohol don't mix."

"You're not going to drink. You tell me about the chocolates, what's in them and we'll go from there."

"But...are you sure you can do this? I mean...you don't work at the winery..."

"I grew up working there. Dad taught us every aspect of running the business."

"Right. Of course, but it's...you've been away from it—"

"It's not brain surgery, Jane," he said, keeping his frustration out of his voice. "What's the problem?"

She methodically stroked the cat's back, one hand over the other. "I don't want to be part of anything that encourages you to drink." She cleared her throat. "No offense."

He leaned back, stretching his leg out. "I won't get drunk."

As if he had such little control he'd get wasted sipping what would probably amount to a couple glasses of wine. When he wanted to get drunk, he went straight for whiskey.

Like the bottle he'd picked up at the liquor store earlier today.

"If it'll make you feel better," he said, "I'll use a spit bucket."

"That's disgusting."

"You don't taste with your stomach," he pointed out. "So there's no reason to swallow."

"I guess not," she said, sounding unconvinced. "But there's no way I'm dumping spit."

He closed the pizza box lid and set his empty plate on top of it. "When Dad held private tastings, that was our job, mine and Matt's."

And as usual, no matter what the job, Matt had complained the entire time.

"I haven't seen Matt in years," J.C. said, her elbow on the table, her chin resting on her hand. "How is he?"

He ducked his head so she wouldn't see his frown. He hadn't realized she had any interest in his long-haired, love-'em-and-leave-'em, too-pretty-for-his-or-anyone-else's-good brother. The brother who thought J.C. had a sexy mouth.

"He's fine," Brady said. "He was home Thanksgiving."

And gone the next day. Matt came back to Jewell for the holidays and their mother's birthday, but he never stayed more than a few days.

"Not long ago, the paper ran an article about him," she said. "About his job and all the awards he's won and how one of his wines made it onto some sort of top one hundred list—"

"*Wine Spectator*'s annual Top 100," Brady said, unable to stop staring at her mouth now. "He's doing well for himself."

Giving him a half smile, as if unsure if he deserved a full one, she used the back of her hand to brush her hair back. "I'll say. Funny that he works for wineries all over the world when his family owns one right here."

No, what was funny was how at ease she was now that they were talking about his brother. How, sitting this close to her, he could smell the soap she'd used in the shower. See the tiny freckles dotting her nose. And that with her eyes bright and those few loose curls framing her face, J.C. looked fresh and soft and...pretty.

"If you want," he said mildly, "I can tell Matt to call you next time he's in town. I'm sure he'd be more than happy to get together with you."

J.C. blanched. "Thanks, but I'll pass. So far my experience with the Sheppard men has sucked." Though her words were cold, he detected a slight tremor in her voice. "I'll get the chocolates. I wouldn't want to keep you any longer than necessary."

This time when she walked away, he studied the wall in front of him. Once she disappeared into the kitchen, he tipped his head back, hitting the chair. Then he did it again.

And because his hands were twitching, because he felt unsettled and edgy, because panic was there, right there at the back of his mind, he pulled a bottle out of the case. Merlot. Not his favorite—and a far cry from the whiskey he preferred—but it would do. He just needed it to get him back on an even keel. With that promise, he took the wine and the corkscrew he'd brought and headed to the bathroom.

Where he could have one drink without worrying about J.C. and her disappointment in him.

LIZ COULD THINK OF NOTHING better than coming home after a grueling twelve-hour night shift to the smell of bacon and Carter's special buttermilk pancakes. Unless it was the sight of him standing at the stove wearing nothing but a pair of red and green checked pajama pants.

"Hi," she said cautiously. He may be making her breakfast and, she glanced at the set table, bought her a dozen red roses, but that didn't mean either of them had forgotten the tension between them was still as strong as it'd been on Thanksgiving. "What's all this?"

A cup of coffee in one hand, a spatula in the other, he said, "It's breakfast."

Liz's heart did one slow roll.

"I can see that," she said, tracing her fingertip over a silky rose petal.

"But...why?"

On the Saturday mornings when Carter didn't have to make rounds at the hospital, he was usually still in bed when she got home from work. She'd slide under the covers and, more often than not, they'd make love before she drifted off to sleep.

After shutting off the stove, he transferred the pancakes to a tray and carried them to the table. "Because I wanted to do something for you." He took both of her hands in his, brought them up to his mouth and kissed her knuckles. "And because I hate this distance between us."

She squeezed his fingers. "Me, too."

"I've missed you."

She nodded. Though they'd been together the past week, they'd barely spoken. And when they did, their conversations were stilted. Overly polite. The only time they touched was when they slept. They'd wake up wrapped in each other, but it never went any further.

It'd been torture.

He sat and pulled her onto his lap. "I blew it all out of proportion, what happened on Thanksgiving. I was..." He exhaled and shook his head, his hair tickling her cheek. "I was jealous."

She couldn't catch her breath. That wasn't what she

wanted. She didn't want Carter to be jealous. Didn't want him to doubt her love, not even for a second.

But she couldn't tell him the truth, either. How betrayed she felt. The thought of Brady and J.C. together infuriated her. She couldn't even face her own sister. Couldn't forgive her.

Worse was that she'd dreamt of Brady, of the way they used to be together.

The way he'd kissed her. Touched her. Made love to her.

"You have nothing to be jealous of," she promised. "Brady and I are over. We've been over a long time."

He slid one hand up to her rib cage, his thumb brushing the side of her breast through her long-sleeved T-shirt. "I'm afraid I'm going to lose you," Carter said, his eyes searching hers.

"Never." She pressed her lips to the side of his neck, inhaled his familiar scent. Caressed the warm skin of his shoulders.

And thought of how Brady had looked the other day when she'd gone to return his ring. Angry. Lonely.

Tears stung the backs of her eyes. No. She wouldn't think of him. Not when she was in her husband's arms. Not ever again. She needed to get Brady out of her system. Before she lost everything. Her sister. Her husband. Herself.

"You'll never lose me," she repeated firmly.

Shifting so that she straddled him, she trailed biting kisses up his neck. He moaned, his hands going under her shirt to smooth her back, down her stomach. She trembled and pressed against him. Kissed him hungrily, loving how solid he was beneath her. How hard. How he was all hers.

"Liz," he said, cupping her breasts. "I love you, baby."

She arched into his touch, her hands gripping his shoulders. "I want you, Carter," she told him, gasping when he grazed her nipple with his thumbnail.

"Only you."

His eyes flashed and then he kissed her again. Grasping her under her rear, he stood and swept one arm over the table. Plates and food crashed to the floor, the vase of roses shattered. And as her husband laid her among the ruins of their breakfast, Liz had one man in her thoughts. In her heart. Him.

"HAS HELL FROZEN OVER?"

Brady glanced at Aidan sitting behind their dad's large mahogany desk, his cell phone up to his ear, one hand covering the mouthpiece.

"Why?" he asked as he entered his dad's—now his brother's—office. "Did you get laid?"

Aidan grinned as he leaned back in his leather, ergonomic chair. "It's not even eight—"

"Don't remind me." Brady slouched in one of the matching checked armchairs facing the desk.

"It's just...unusual...for you to be lurking outside your hovel before—Zachary," he said, turning back to his phone conversation. "It's Aidan Sheppard. Sorry to call you so early on a Saturday but..."

Zoning his brother out, Brady tipped his head back. Aidan's Irish setter, Lily, padded over and nudged his hand until he scratched behind her ears.

Aidan needed to redecorate. The room was the same as when his father had been alive. Sunlight shone in the large window to his right, splashing light on the cream area rug and the wide board oak floor. The built-in bookcases on either side of the window still held his father's books—everything from his favorite author's political thrillers to biographies to books on horticulture and winemaking techniques. Interspersed among them were framed family photos, a few knickknacks and Tom's prized baseball trophy.

Even the bronze statue of a frog, standing on two legs, dressed in knee-high boots and tunic playing a guitar—the statue their mother had claimed too ugly to be seen in any other room—stood in the spot Tom had proudly picked out for it.

And people accused Brady of not being able to let go of the past.

With Aidan's voice no more than a soft murmur in the background, Brady let his eyes drift shut. When he'd come out of the bathroom last night, he'd been steadier. Ready to deal with J.C. and, more importantly, ready to ignore the feelings she evoked.

He wasn't sure if she realized what he'd been doing in the bathroom, how he'd gulped down one glass worth from the bottle of merlot as some sort of anesthetic. But she didn't kick his ass to the curb.

By the time he got home, he was trembling with the need for a drink. After his first shot, he poured himself another and...hadn't been able to drink it.

Because he'd had too much to do to get ready for this impromptu meeting with Aidan, he reminded himself. Not because he kept seeing J.C.'s face. Not because every time he lifted his glass he felt as if he was failing himself.

His body relaxed, the constant tension that tightened his shoulders finally eased. Until the first memory hit him, hard and fast like a bullet. Thad's laughter as they drove down the dirt road. The cloud of dust kicked up from the tires.

The old man who'd stood on the side of the road, his face lined and weary.

The images came faster, flashing through his mind. The explosion. The sharp pain in his knee, his head smashing against the pavement. Coming to, his leg mangled. Through the thick echoing in his ears, women and children were screaming and comrades shouting, crying out for help. Smoke. Burning bodies.

His buddy lying in the street, his eyes sightless.

Lily whimpered. Brady was clutching the dog's fur. Breathing hard, he forced his fingers open and the dog slunk over to Aidan. He gulped in air, his shirt clinging to his sweat-soaked skin.

"You okay?" Aidan asked quietly.

Damn. How long had his brother been off the phone? Resting his elbows on his knees, his head lowered, Brady nodded.

"Here."

"Thanks," he said, taking the coffee Aidan offered and downing half of it.

Lukewarm.

"Want to talk about it?"

Talk? Hell, all he wanted was to forget it. "I'm good."

Aidan studied him, his hands clasped together on top of his desk. "All right," he said slowly. "But if you ever do—"

"Yeah. Thanks," he forced himself to add before finishing off the coffee.

He set the cup down and tossed the folder in front of Aidan.

"What's this?"

"It's all the reasons you should reconsider J.C.'s chocolates."

Aidan took off his reading glasses. "As much as I'd like to

help J.C. out, I already told you we don't have the money in this year's budget. Besides, I'm not so sure chocolates would sell well, especially with the economy being the way it is."

"Sales of gourmet chocolates have been rising steadily for the past few years," he said. "Plus, twenty-five percent of annual candy sales are made between Thanksgiving and Christmas."

Aidan raised his eyebrows. "You learn about candy in the Marines?"

"In boot camp, right after I learned how to take apart and reassemble my M16." He shifted. "I did some research." God bless the internet.

"That what this is?" Aidan gestured to the folder. "Your research on chocolate sales?"

"Among other things," he mumbled. He loosened his neck muscles, moving his head from side to side. "Just read it."

Aidan put his glasses back on, opened the folder and began to read the top sheet. It was a far cry from a real business proposal but it was the best he could do without experience.

Brady stretched his leg out and whistled softly for Lily. She hesitated, but when he held out his hand and snapped his fingers, she walked over, her ears back, her head down.

"Sorry, girl," he murmured, rubbing her head. She wagged her tail and dropped beside him. And as easy as that, she forgave him.

If only humans were that easy to placate.

After what seemed like an eternity, Aidan set the papers down and studied Brady over his glasses. "You did all of this?"

"J.C. came up with her projected costs. My pairings."

Aidan tapped a mechanical pencil against his desk blotter. "Expensive candy. I can go to the convenience store and pick up a candy bar for under a buck."

"She's making a quality product with high-end ingredients." According to J.C., anyway. Brady had been impressed with her refusal to use cheaper ingredients. "Don't you appreciate her high standards?"

"I do. I even agree with them. But that doesn't mean I want to do business with her. What if we agree to a deal and she can't hold up her end of the bargain? Or decides she's bored and would rather move on to something else?"

"She won't." Although for all he knew, those were very real possibilities. And if Aidan didn't stop tapping that damn pencil, Brady was going to shove it up his—

"You haven't been back long," Aidan said, dropping the pencil, "so you may not realize that as sweet as J.C. is, she also has a reputation for being unreliable."

"Is that where you get all your information? Local gossip?"

"Does it matter if it's gossip if it's the truth? I don't want to take a chance on conducting business with a vendor who may or may not provide her product."

"She'll provide it," Brady said, pushing himself to his feet. He'd make sure of it. "Make one of those consignment deals. That way you're not out cash and she still gets to sell her candy in the gift shop."

Aidan closed the folder. "Not interested."

Brady linked his hands together on top of his head. Blew out a breath.

"What do I have to do?"

"For what?"

He dropped his arms. "To make this happen."

Aidan smiled—never a good sign. "Work for the Diamond Dust."

"That's it?" He'd figured it'd be something...bigger. Stop drinking. Or go back to physical therapy.

Bare his soul to some shrink.

He almost wished it had been one of those stipulations. Then he could've walked away.

"There are a few provisions—"

"Of course there are."

"—such as you, and you alone, are in charge of getting J.C.'s chocolates in the gift shop. I don't care what type of agreement you make with her as long as we don't lose any money."

Brady pinched the bridge of his nose. "No pressure there."

But Aidan wasn't done. "You have to put in eight solid hours of work a day, five days a week. And the first time you show up for work drunk, the deal is off."

"You realize this is blackmail."

"Funny. In business, we call this negotiating. Take it or leave it."

Brady ground his teeth. He couldn't imagine working for his father's company after all these years. Or worse, having Aidan as a boss. And what if he had another panic attack or whatever that had been? He couldn't control when the flashbacks came. Couldn't control how he'd react.

Besides, J.C. told him she didn't need this. And he'd set up that savings account for the baby. She could dip into that anytime she needed. Except she wouldn't.

He shoved his hands into his pockets.

"When do you want me to start?"

9

"JANE MONTGOMERY? Is that you?"

J.C.—along with the rest of the people attending the Diamond Dust's Holiday Open House that Saturday—looked toward the sound of the high-pitched voice. A short, busty brunette in dark skinny jeans and killer red leather boots elbowed her way through the crowd.

"If she's not careful," Brady murmured from behind J.C., causing her to jump, "she's going to jiggle right out of that shirt."

"I can see where that would bother a guy," she said, her heart thumping against her ribs.

What was he doing here? She hadn't spoken to him since a week ago when he'd called and told her she could sell chocolates at the Diamond Dust's open houses on consignment.

"I didn't say it would bother me."

She looked up at him so quickly she almost wrenched her neck. "Holy cow. Did you make a joke?"

"I never joke about women and jiggling."

Before she could decide that yes, Brady Sheppard had

indeed shown some humor, the brunette reached them. With a squeal guaranteed to ring every eardrum within a five-mile radius, she threw her arms around J.C.

"I can't believe it's really you," the brunette said, rocking her side to side.

"You look fabulous! I hardly recognized you."

Rounding her shoulders and sticking her hips back in an attempt to keep her baby bump from touching the other woman, J.C. met Brady's eyes over the other woman's head. But he held up his hands. The universal signal for, "You're on your own."

"Uh...thank you," J.C. told her new hug-buddy. "Who are you?"

The woman pulled back, squeezing J.C.'s hands. "It's me! Tina Harris."

J.C. blinked. "Tina?"

Last she'd heard, Tina worked in real estate up in Richmond, having lived there since high school. J.C. scanned the other woman head to toe. No wonder she hadn't recognized her. While she could now see Tina in the pert nose and dimpled smile, her hair was shorter and a far cry from the brassy blond she'd dyed it to in high school.

And those boobs? Totally new.

"Wow. It's nice to see you," J.C. said. "You look terrific."

"Forget about me." Tina held their hands out to the sides as if to better showcase J.C. "You look amazing."

"Thank you. Do you remember Brady Sheppard?" She stepped back to include him.

"Of course. You went out with J.C.'s sister, didn't you? You two were such a dream couple. I imagine you're married with a few kids by now, am I right?"

Though nothing in Brady's expression changed, J.C. could feel his tension.

"Brady and Liz broke up over a year ago," she mumbled.

Tina's dimples disappeared. "That's such a shame. The same thing happened to me and Mike...you remember Mike Nivens, don't you?" she asked J.C. before turning to Brady. "Mike and I were high-school sweethearts like you and Liz except we dated a few months, not years and years like you two. But after graduation, we went our separate ways. Which worked out for the best," she said with a giggle, holding her left hand out.

Good God, how did she even lift her hand with that rock on her finger?

"Congratulations," J.C. said.

"I'm so lucky. Shawn...that's my fiancé...is the best. Guy. Ever. He's an orthodontist in Richmond...there he is now." Tina waved. "Honey? Honey, we're over here!"

J.C. winced and lifted her shoulder to her ear. For such a small person, her voice carried.

"There you are." Tina's great guy came up to J.C.'s chin, had a pot belly and a comb-over that started at his left ear. He smiled and wrapped his arm around Tina's waist. "I thought I'd lost you."

"Honey, I'd like you to meet Brady Sheppard—his family owns this winery. Isn't that cool? Brady," Tina continued, cuddling against comb-over's side, "this is my fiancé, *Doctor* Shawn Connolly. Shawn is the number one orthodontist in Richmond. If you're ever in the market for braces, be sure to look him up."

Brady shook Shawn's hand. "Nothing I'd like better than driving three hours to get metal bands slapped on my teeth."

J.C. reprimanded him with a slight shake of her head.

Shawn shared a look with Tina. "I'm sure you can find

quality dental care right here in Jewell. It seems like a beautiful little town."

"It is," Tina said, ignoring Brady's slight. "It was the best
place to grow up, so safe...why...everyone was like family.
And this is Jane Montgomery, an old friend of mine from
high school. But I tell you, I couldn't believe it when I first
saw her! She's lost a ton of weight."

J.C. gritted her teeth. "Actually, I didn't lose quite
that much."

And she and Tina sure hadn't been more than acquain-
tances. Cute cheerleaders didn't hang out with chubby girls
who'd rather volunteer at the local ASPCA than work on
homecoming floats.

Tina hugged Shawn around his middle. "Well, however
much you lost doesn't matter. You look so much better."

She didn't need to be reminded that she'd spent most of
her life overweight. Especially in front of Brady.

Brady laid his hand on the small of her back and she
almost jumped out of her skin. "What brings you to Jewell?"
he asked the couple in front of them.

Tears stung her eyes. She blamed it on hormones. She
couldn't even listen to love songs on the radio without
getting all blubbery. Not because the warmth of Brady's
hand seeping through the silky fabric of her dress made it
easier to pull her shoulders back and pretend Tina's
comments didn't bother her.

"We're going on a cruise for Christmas so we're doing
the holiday thing early with my family," Tina said. "But I
still need to get my sister-in-law's gift and was hoping to find
it here. She's such a snob. She returns everything."

"Chocolates," Brady said.

Tina looked at him as if he'd lost his mind. "Excuse me?"

"We now carry a line of locally produced gourmet

chocolates," he clarified, sounding as if he'd memorized a brochure. Reaching behind J.C., he picked up the tray of samples she'd set out and held them out to Shawn and Tina.

"None for me, thanks," Shawn said. "My teeth are like a walking billboard for my business."

"I don't have his willpower," Tina confessed, scanning the tray. "I can't pass up chocolate. Ooh...what's this one?" She pointed to a glossy dark chocolate truffle with a drizzle of white chocolate.

Brady nudged J.C. "That's cappuccino," she said. "The... uh...ganache is milk chocolate, coffee and cinnamon."

"Sounds yummy." Tina picked it up and bit into it, her hand underneath the candy to catch any loose bits. The expression on her face was practically orgasmic.

"The cappuccino flavor is one of the top sellers in J.C.'s line," Brady said.

"You made these?" Tina asked. As if J.C.'s candy-making ability ranked up there with walking on water and being able to yodel.

"It's just a—"

"Yes," Brady said, not even glancing her way. "She makes them all."

Ten minutes later, Dr. Shawn walked over to the gift wrap table with three boxes of mixed truffles. Tina waited in line at the checkout counter with a bottle each of the three wines Brady suggested made the best pairings.

And Brady was still by J.C.'s side, all silent and grim-faced in his worn jeans, faded Marine Corps T-shirt and work boots. His hair was beyond shaggy and getting close to unmanageable. She'd say he hadn't shaved in a week.

"I appreciate the sales job you did with Tina," she said.

He leaned back against the thick, wooden beam next to

her table and inclined his head. The Brady Sheppard way of saying *you're welcome.*

Well, if he couldn't take the hint that she wanted him gone, she thought irritably, she'd just ignore him. Humming "It Came Upon A Midnight Clear" with the two violinists playing softly in the corner, J.C. pulled on clean gloves and arranged a trio of her extra dark truffles on the silver tray then checked her watch. With less than thirty minutes left until closing time, she wasn't sure how many more she'd need to set out, but there were still at least twenty customers milling around the gift shop and tasting room in the large farmhouse.

Two walls were all windows, with silver pendant and gooseneck lights hanging from the exposed ceiling beams. Wide, wooden beams showed where original walls stood and ancient-looking narrow boards made up the floor. Finger foods, catered from The Old Library, the fanciest restaurant in Jewell, were presented on a covered board over three large wooden wine barrels.

"Why'd you let Tanya upset you?"

She dropped a chocolate on the floor. Picking it up, she tossed it into the garbage can under the table. "Her name's Tina. And I wasn't up—"

"Bullshit."

Sighing, she turned, only to find him standing too close to her. "I... It's hard for me to...to know what to say when someone comments on my weight. It's...awkward," she finished, her gaze on the table.

And she hated that there were days she still felt like that overweight girl.

Self-conscious. Second-best to Liz.

"Seems to me," Brady said after what had to be the

longest moment of her life, "you've done something to be proud of."

"All I did was lose weight." It wasn't as if she'd graduated from college. Or gone to medical school. She didn't help save people's lives every day she went to work.

"Was it easy?"

"What?"

"Was it easy to deprive yourself?"

"It's not about deprivation. It's about making better choices." She took the gloves off and crumpled them in her hand. "Everything in moderation. Fruit instead of junk food. Exercise more."

"You still needed willpower. Dedication. Determination. And these?" he asked, gesturing at the candy before settling his right hand on the table.

"They're good. Tanya—"

"Tina."

He shrugged. "She bought three boxes because they're good. Not because of anything I did."

"Well," she said, warmth spreading throughout her chest, "you sure told me."

"You don't give yourself as much credit as you deserve."

"That has to be one of the nicest things anyone's ever said to me. Except for when I was in third grade and Davey Rodgers told me my hair made me look like a little lion."

"Not a lion," he said, studying her intently. She would've stepped back except he lifted his free hand to her hair and wrapped a curl around his finger. "More like a sunburst around your face."

J.C. JERKED HER HEAD BACK, her hair tightening around

Brady's finger before sliding away. She tucked it behind her ear. "So, is this how you usually spend your Saturdays?"

He fisted his hand. "I'm working."

She tipped her head and studied him. "You get paid to stand around and look…"

He raised an eyebrow. "Intimidating?"

She opened a bottle of water and gestured at him with it. "I was going to say grumpy but intimidating works, too."

"I didn't say I was happy about working. And I sold three bottles of wine, didn't I?"

"That you did." She crouched to pull a box out from underneath the green cloth covering her table. "Do you get a commission?"

"Just a regular paycheck," he said absently, his attention caught by the way her bright pink dress swirled around her knees when she straightened.

"You're working here for real? That's great. You must not be—" She blushed and concentrated on setting out more of her candy. "Your knee. It…uh…must not be bothering you as much."

And if that was what she'd meant to say, he'd eat a cork stopper. "I don't drink on the job."

As per his brother's instructions, he'd been sober every day. Hungover, but sober.

"I never realized you were interested in working here," she said, choosing to ignore him.

"I'm not." He helped himself to a white chocolate truffle. "It's temporary."

"Do you still want to go into law enforcement?" At his sharp look, she shrugged. "Liz mentioned you wanted to attend the police academy when you got out of the service."

"I'd never pass the physical."

Not to mention the psych evaluation.

"Maybe if you find a good physical therapist—"

"My knee will never be a hundred percent," he said, tossing a second half-eaten chocolate in the garbage.

"I'm sorry," she said, laying her hand on his forearm. His muscles tensed under her warm fingers. "Now stop wasting my inventory."

He stepped back and her hand fell to her side. He nodded to the middle-aged couple approaching them. "Customers."

As J.C. went into her sales pitch—offering them a sample, explaining the different flavors and wine pairings—Brady edged away.

He didn't need her pity. He'd known the risks going in. Those risks were part of the reason Liz hadn't wanted him to join up. For as long as he could remember, he'd wanted to be a Marine. To be in the middle of the action.

Right. *Action.* He saw a snow-covered road carved from the side of a mountain. Heard the echoing, rat-a-tat of machine gun fire. His commander's shouts. His buddies' curses. Felt the surge of adrenaline as he dove for cover.

Returned fire.

His mouth dried and his heart began to race. Taking J.C.'s water, he drained it, his fingers denting the plastic.

"I could've gotten you your own water."

He lowered the bottle. "Sorry."

J.C. regarded him seriously. "Hey, are you—"

"Another sale?" he asked, motioning to the couple walking off.

"No," she said, drawing the word out. "But they seemed to like the Turtles."

He twisted the cap back on the bottle. "Can't win them all."

"That's so inspiring," she said. "I think I'll put it on one of those needlework samplers and hang it in my living room." She moved an oblong red ceramic tray of white chocolate dipped pretzels an eighth of an inch to the left. "Is there a reason you're standing watch back here instead of... whatever else you're supposed to be doing? That can't really be your job."

"As far as Aidan's concerned, anything and everything he doesn't want to handle—and thinks I can—is my job."

Pam, the gift shop's superefficient manager, needed him here as much as Aidan needed help being uptight. Pam had no sooner given Brady his first assignment—making sure all the chardonnay bottles were label side out—than he'd realized that Aidan had asked him to work an extra day to keep Brady busy.

As if he were a kid who needed to be entertained or else he'd get into trouble.

He'd been about to walk out, he should've walked out. But then he'd spotted J.C. at the back of the store setting up her table.

"I like it back here."

She smacked his arm. "Yeah. For the free chocolate."

"Among other things."

She caught her breath.

And someone cleared a throat. "Are we interrupting?"

J.C. GROANED AND QUICKLY stepped away from Brady. What had so far been a pretty decent day was about to go downhill. Fast.

"Liz. Hi," she said, her voice strangled. "Wha-what are you doing here?"

Crossing her arms, Liz glanced at Brady and then back

at J.C. "We ran into Lori Crandall at the grocery store and she mentioned you were selling chocolates here. I can't imagine why you didn't tell us yourself."

"Right. I saw Lori in here earlier." J.C. wiped her palms down the side of her dress. "I would've told you..." she lied, "but I figured you'd be too busy to come."

"Hey," Carter said as he joined them, a grin on his movie-star-handsome face, "we're never too busy for you."

Then he pulled her into a warm hug. Out of the corner of her eye, J.C. saw Brady roll his shoulders back as if preparing to go a few rounds.

Winner got Liz.

Luckily, if Carter had any violent thoughts about Brady, he hid them well. "How are you feeling?" he asked as he released her.

"Fine. Good. It's okay if you have to go," she told Brady in a rush. "I'm sure you have a lot to do."

"Nothing that can't wait. Aren't you going to introduce us?" he asked in a deadly soft tone as he inclined his head toward her brother-in-law.

"Not on your life." Taking him by the arm, she pulled him to the other end of the table. "Stay here. Please," she said, when he looked ready to argue. "Please, Brady."

He looked over her head at Liz and Carter. His mouth flattened. "Where are your boxes?"

"What?"

"The store closes soon. If you get the boxes, I can start packing up your stuff."

"You don't have to."

He sent another fleeting look at Liz. "All part of the job description, Jane."

J.C. felt numb. Still thinking of her sister but willing to

124

settle for her. Well, at least he got her name right this time. "Sure. Whatever. They're under the table."

"I can't...I don't think I can get them," he said tightly, stopping her before she could walk away.

She shut her eyes for a moment. She could do this. She could act as if him sending longing looks her sister's way—after he'd touched her hair so sweetly —didn't bother her. Grabbing the boxes, she set them on the table and then deliberately turned away.

Liz, in her black skinny jeans, white top and red jacket, and Carter, with the barest hint of stubble and his striped scarf tucked under the collar of a caramel-colored suede coat, could've been in the picture accompanying one of those fashion magazine's articles: How The Perfect Couple Dresses, Weekend-Style.

But on closer inspection, J.C. could see perfection was an illusion. There were tension lines around Carter's mouth. Liz held herself stiffly. And while Carter kept his gaze on the candy display, Liz kept looking at Brady only to drop her gaze when she thought someone noticed.

"It was really great of you both to take the time to support me like this," J.C. said when she reached them.

"I have to admit," Carter said, "once I found out what you were doing, I had an ulterior motive for wanting to come out here."

She swallowed and peeked at Liz, but her sister wouldn't look her way.

"I was hoping you'd have some of that chocolate bark with the cashews available," Carter continued. "The last time you gave me some to take to the office, I was a real hero."

She exhaled shakily. "Sure. I think I still have a few

boxes left..." Before she could look over her products, Brady slid two, one-pound boxes down the table.

Wonderful. He could not only hear every word they said, but he wanted them to be aware he was listening.

She tried to return Carter's smile but failed miserably. "Here you go. There's one milk chocolate and one white chocolate."

"Perfect," he said, the unusual edge to his voice the only indication Brady's presence still bothered him. "Do I pay here or up front?"

"Oh, no. They're my treat."

"You can't be giving away all of your profits," Carter said.

"We'll pay for them," Liz said firmly, finally meeting J.C.'s eyes. "We insist."

"Okay, then. Thanks." J.C. swallowed but it felt as if she had one of her truffles stuck in her throat. "You can...uh... pay at the cashier."

Carter pulled out his wallet. "Looks like they're getting ready to close." He shot a glance over J.C.'s head—presumably to where Brady still lurked. "Will you be all right here by yourself, J.C.?"

She could've sworn she heard Brady growl.

"Sure. I get to keep most of my stuff here—they're going to set up a small display of the chocolate I have left to sell during the week," she said, purposely misinterpreting his question. Would she be all right alone with Brady Sheppard? "I'll be fine."

Though he didn't seem convinced, he didn't push it. "I'd better get in line, then." He kissed her cheek. "And in case we don't see you before then, good luck Tuesday."

"Thanks."

"You ready, honey?" he asked Liz.

"I'd like to speak with J.C.," she said. "I'll catch up with you in a minute."

"I hate this," J.C. blurted as soon as Carter walked away. She lowered her voice so Brady couldn't hear. "Can't we please discuss this?"

Liz frowned at J.C. "What's Tuesday?"

And that had been the last question she'd expected. "Nothing. Just...I have an appointment with Dr. Owens..."

"And you told *my* husband about it?"

"*Your* husband," J.C. whispered, her movements jerky as she swept pieces of the curly gold ribbon she'd scattered across the table into a pile, "is the only person at your house who'll talk to me when I call."

Liz drummed her fingers on the table, next to the base of a glass pedestal holding the remaining bite-size samples of J.C.'s Turtles. "What's this really about? You selling chocolate here?"

"I need extra cash. For the holidays."

"Do you really think orchestrating it so that you're around him more is going to change anything?"

C.'s head snapped back. "I...I didn't orchestrate anything." But...but hadn't she let him talk her out of speaking with Aidan? And then she'd jumped at the chance he'd offered to sell her chocolates at the Diamond Dust. She'd even spent the evening with him pairing the wine and chocolates after he'd been so ugly to her. "He just happened to be working—"

"Isn't that how it always is with you? Things *just happen.*"

J.C. winced as she remembered how she'd tried to explain why she and Brady had gotten together.

It just sort of...happened.

"I didn't even know he was going to be here," J.C. insisted.

"You've always wanted whatever I had," Liz said, her hushed voice sounding thick. "And Brady is no different."

J.C.'s scalp tingled and she snuck a look over her shoulder. She edged closer to her sister. "I don't want Brady."

"Even if you did, he's not the right guy for you. You deserve someone who'll put you first."

She knew that. She didn't need Liz and her condescending attitude to remind her.

"Because no way a man could possibly want me after they were with you," she said, her hands fisted. "Mediocrity just doesn't cut it after you've had perfection, right?"

Liz blushed. "I didn't say that."

And then, Brady was there, his hands on her shoulders. "Your husband's waiting for you," he told Liz. "You'd better go."

Liz blinked several times, but J.C. caught the sheen of tears in her eyes before her sister walked off.

For several heartbeats, J.C. didn't move.

Brady squeezed her shoulders. "You okay?" he asked, his mouth close to her ear.

She cringed. As if he gave a damn. As if his whole show of support hadn't been for her sister's benefit. It was as fake as Liz's so-called concern.

Trembling with anger, with humiliation, she jerked away from him. "Do me a favor. The next time you want to try to make my sister jealous, leave me out of it."

10

WELL AWARE OF THE INTEREST THEY WERE GETTING from the people left in the store, Brady wrapped an arm around J.C.'s waist. Though she stiffened, she didn't fight him as he led her down a short hallway and into the stockroom.

They'd no sooner stepped inside when she twisted away from him.

"Is there a problem?" he asked.

She stared at him incredulously. "You used me as some sort of...of..." She glanced around, as if she'd pick the right word out of the air. "Tool...to get back at Liz. Did you think she'd toss Carter aside and jump into your arms because of me? I hate to break it to you, but I'm the last person Liz would ever be jealous of."

How he'd stepped on this landmine, he had no clue. He hadn't been playing games and he sure as hell hadn't been trying to make Liz jealous.

He scratched the underside of his jaw. Playing hero brought a man nothing but grief.

Sure, he may have felt a slight surge of satisfaction at

Liz's reaction to him coming to J.C.'s aid. But that only proved he was human.

And not as dead inside as he'd like.

"I don't want to get back at Liz," he said.

"Then what was with all that touchy-feely stuff? You deliberately made it seem as if there was something going on between us."

"By telling her she should leave?"

"You touched my shoulders," she said with as much indignation as if he had pinched her butt.

Behind him, someone rapped lightly on the still-open door.

"Sorry to interrupt," Pam said curiously, glancing between them, "but I need to get—"

"Later," Brady said before shutting the door and leaning against it.

No doubt when Aidan heard about it, he'd rip Brady for being so rude to a valued employee.

"Your fight was starting to draw a lot of attention," he said with what he considered remarkable calm in the face of her irrationality. "I thought it best to intervene before it came to blows."

"We weren't fighting. We were having a discussion. A private discussion that you were eavesdropping on."

"Seeing how I was the main topic, I'd say I had a right to overhear."

You've always wanted whatever I had.

I don't want Brady.

J.C. rubbed her temples. "She hates me."

Impossible. Liz had always doted on her little sister. She'd been J.C.'s biggest champion.

He shrugged. "She's pissed. She'll get over it."

"That's a big help," J.C. said acidly. "Thanks so much."

"You want a shoulder to cry on," he said before he could stop himself, "try your brother-in-law."

She looked at him as if he was a few rounds short of a full clip. "What?"

"Nothing."

Damn it. Maybe his paranoia was getting worse. How else to explain him taking issue with J.C. cozying up to Liz's husband? Just because she'd been thrilled to see him and had asked Brady to back off when he'd been itching to take the guy down a peg didn't mean anything. It certainly couldn't mean that Liz had been right about J.C. wanting whatever her sister had.

Even if she had told that bastard about her doctor's appointment Tuesday.

An appointment Brady had no idea about.

"You're tired..." Didn't pregnant women get tired easily? And cranky? And blow things out of proportion? "Why don't we finish packing up your stuff then I'll drive you home."

"I don't need your help getting my stuff together and I sure don't want you taking me home."

Damn but she was stubborn. And starting to seriously tick him off. "You shouldn't drive when you're so upset."

"I've been upset before," she said as she stalked toward him, "and unfortunately, I'll be upset again. But I'm still capable of taking care of myself."

In other words, he could take his help and shove it.

He opened the door and stepped aside so she could pass. He watched her walk away, her hair bouncing to her long strides, her arms swinging.

I don't want Brady.

Looked like the Montgomery sisters had more in common than anyone realized.

"I WAS THINKING we'd try that new salmon recipe tonight," Liz told Carter as she set the last of the bulging cloth grocery bags on the kitchen table. "Unless you think it's too cold for grilling."

"That's fine," he said, not even pausing as he carried the dry cleaning into the living room.

She squeezed the package of salmon fillets. If he'd at least try to keep up his end of the conversation, maybe she wouldn't have to continue with her inane chatter. The sound of her own voice was grating on her last nerve. But she couldn't shut up, either. Not when the silence was so tense. So... uncomfortable.

Not when she was afraid of what Carter would say if she'd stop talking long enough for him to get a word in edgewise.

Laying a loaf of French bread aside, she unpacked the baked chips and organic eggs. He'd been fine all day. They'd slept in, enjoyed a leisurely brunch at their favorite restaurant and then ran their errands. Up until they'd gone to the Diamond Dust, Carter had been himself.

Lips pursed, she shook her head as she stacked yogurt containers in the fridge. Naturally he'd been upset about seeing Brady. She never would've guessed he'd be at the gift shop, let alone hovering over J.C. If she had, she would've put up a bigger fight about going there. But Carter had insisted she at least take a hold of the olive branch J.C. had extended with her daily phone calls. Though Liz wasn't ready to make peace yet, she hadn't wanted Carter to think her resistance had anything to do with Brady.

Rinsing the salmon at the sink, she heard Carter's footsteps as he came back into the kitchen.

"I'll make the marinade," she said, laying the fillets on a clean towel, "and you can put together a salad. And do you want rice or potatoes?"

He came up behind her and shut the water off.

She laughed nervously. "What are you—"

"We need to talk."

Her stomach dropped at his serious tone, his carefully schooled expression. She kept smiling. "If we want to make it to that movie…" But he just continued to watch her. She couldn't escape what was going to happen next. "All right."

Taking her time, she patted the salmon dry and set it in a plate. After washing her hands, she put the fish in the fridge.

Carter sat at the table, his hands in his lap as he stared out the window above the sink. The evening was darkening.

What had she done? She'd been careful, so very careful, not to show any reaction to finding Brady and J.C. together.

She pulled out the chair opposite him.

"Honey, what is it?" she asked, certain she'd be better off not knowing. "What's wrong?"

He dug something out of his pocket then laid it in the center of the table between them.

A small velvet blue box.

Brady's ring.

Her lungs squeezed painfully and she couldn't draw a full breath.

"Where… How…"

"Mr. Sandburg found it in your coat," Carter said quietly.

She shut her eyes. While she'd run into the pharmacy for a few items, Carter had gone next door to pick up their dry cleaning. Including her brown leather jacket, the one she'd been wearing when she'd gone to see Brady.

Sitting on the edge of her seat, she leaned forward. "It's not what you think."

"What is it I think?"

"I...I'm not sure. Maybe you see my having that ring as a way of holding on to...to him."

He linked his hands together on top of the table. "Is it?"

"No. No of course not. I...I was giving it back—"

"You were carrying it around with you in case you bumped into him?"

Her vision blurred and she blinked furiously. "I saw him last week," she whispered.

His body twitched. "When?"

"Monday."

"You weren't going to tell me."

"I didn't want to upset you." She reached out but he slid his hands back to his lap. "I tried to give him the ring but he wouldn't take it so I...I stuck it in my pocket. That's all. Look, it's so insignificant, I forgot it was even there."

She held her breath. He remained motionless, his face drawn. Had she thought his anger at Thanksgiving was bad? She'd take it any day over this.

"I saw how you looked at him."

Her blood chilled. "What?"

"Today. You kept watching him."

"I didn't—"

"And at the end, when he came up behind J.C., when he stood so close to her, you were upset."

"I was...I hadn't realized they were there..." And that shock, along with her hurt and anger, had almost brought her to her knees. "That they were... together."

That it seemed as if they were together. Or could be.

Carter wiped a hand over his mouth. "It might not seem like it, but I'm trying to understand why you can't let this thing between Brady and your sister go. Why it upsets you so much."

Tears ran down her cheeks. She knuckled them away. "I don't know."

"If I thought it was just the fact that she was with your ex, it'd be different but..." He shook his head. "There's more to it than that."

"No. I—"

"You kept his ring. You went to see him without telling me." Carter's voice turned gravelly. "You look at him the same way you look at me. The way you're only supposed to look at me."

Stunned, tears running unheeded down her cheeks, she watched as he walked out the door. She wished she could call him back. Tell him that she needed some more time to adjust to...everything. But she'd be lying. She wasn't sure she'd ever be able to accept J.C. having Brady's baby. Or Brady being a part of her sister's life.

And because of that, she couldn't even tell her husband what he needed to hear most. That he was the only man she loved.

———

J.C. ARRIVED FIVE MINUTES LATE for her appointment with Dr. Owens on Tuesday to find the waiting room filled with women of all ages. Several were way more pregnant than her, and two had recently given birth—as evidenced by the newborns in their arms and their post-baby bodies. To her left, a middle-aged woman read a pamphlet on improving your sex life after menopause. And all of them were shooting glances at the corner.

She followed their gazes...and tripped over her own feet.

Brady Sheppard, his left leg out straight, his hands linked on his flat stomach, watched her steadily.

Unreal.

"What are you doing here?" she asked.

"Waiting for you."

"Why?"

"I didn't want you to have to do this alone."

Her jaw dropped. *This* as in her doctor's appointment? Or could he possibly mean...? No. He'd made his stance about the baby very clear. And seeing as how he hadn't so much as mentioned her pregnancy recently, she doubted he'd changed his mind. That he'd ever change his mind.

"How did you even know I have an appointment today?" she asked.

He tipped his head to the side. "I heard you and your brother-in-law talking about it at the gift shop."

She switched her purse strap to her other shoulder. "It's...nice...of you to...think of me but I won't be alone. My mom is supposed to meet me."

He sat up. "I'll wait until she gets here."

"Oh, but—"

"Jane?" Rhonda Darcy, her round body stuffed into an impossibly cheerful set of Snoopy scrubs, stood in the doorway leading to the examination rooms. "Come on back, hon, and we'll get your vitals."

"You don't have to stay," J.C. told Brady.

She didn't want him to stay, she told herself as she followed Rhonda down the hallway to a small, windowless room. Not after how he'd acted at the gift shop. Not when he'd heard what Liz had said to her. How her sister had practically accused her of throwing herself at Brady.

As if she'd throw away her relationship with her sister for a man. A man who didn't even want her.

"Weight first," Rhonda said.

J.C. toed off her shoes and stepped onto the scale. Staring straight ahead, she could see Rhonda's hand moving the lever to the right but couldn't make out the numbers.

And if Rhonda so much as breathed what those numbers were, J.C. might resort to violence.

Rhonda noted J.C.'s weight in a small laptop. "Hop on down." She gestured for J.C. to sit in the chair next to a metal table where she sat to put her shoes back on. "I'm sure glad we didn't call the police on your young man out there."

J.C. about fell right off the chair. "Did...did he do something wrong?"

He hadn't seemed drunk but their conversation had been brief. And as she'd learned, he didn't need alcohol to say incredibly stupid things.

"All that boy did was wait." She moved J.C.'s hair aside and checked her temperature with an ear thermometer. "Even when Missy told him she couldn't give out your appointment time, he just thanked her and took a seat. Didn't kick up a fuss like some folks would. But after two hours, Dr. Owens started getting nervous about him being here so long."

"Wait," J.C. said, her head coming up in surprise. Two hours? "How long has he been waiting?"

Rhonda wrapped the blood pressure cuff around J.C.'s arm. "He showed up right when we opened at nine."

While Rhonda took her blood pressure, J.C.'s head spun. Nine. It was now after four. Brady Sheppard had spent the entire day sitting in her obstetrician's waiting room.

For her.

"Anyway," Rhonda continued, hooking her stethoscope around her neck, "The doctor pointed out how you might not want him here and maybe we should call the police to escort him home. Which we can certainly do if that's what you'd prefer."

"No." She cleared her throat. "No, he's...fine. He's..."

Rhonda took a hold of J.C.'s wrist. "With both Missy and I knowing him— Missy went to school with one of his brothers, and Diane Sheppard and I go way back—so we convinced Dr. Owens he wasn't hurting anyone."

Hurting anyone, no. Confusing the hell out of her? Definitely.

Rhonda finished checking her pulse and sent her back out to wait for the doctor. J.C. walked down the hall. Just because Brady showed up here didn't mean anything. She wouldn't let herself read more into it than a sign he was curious about the baby. Or that he was crushed over her being upset with him, and he'd wanted to make amends.

She snorted softly. That would be the day.

And since she'd told him to leave, she doubted she'd ever find out.

She opened the door and sure enough, his seat was empty. But, as she stepped out of the exam room, she saw that it was only because Brady was on his feet, his expression pained as he faced her parents.

J.C. hurried over and stepped between them. "Mom. You made it." She winced at her own false cheeriness. "Hi, Dad. I hope Mom didn't drag you away from the office early."

"Your father insisted he wanted to be here," her mom said, equally chipper. Equally false. "Isn't that nice, dear?"

"Great," she croaked.

"It's not every day a man's baby girl gets to see the ultrasound of her own baby," Don said gruffly, glancing at her.

"Daddy..." She stood on tiptoe and kissed his cheek.

But when she fell back to her heels, his expression hardened. "Move aside, Jane. Brady was about to explain what he's doing here."

As much as she'd love to hear that as well, she didn't want to hold this particular discussion in the middle of one of Jewell's busiest doctor's office.

"Now, Don," Nancy said. "I'm sure Jane asked him to be here."

They both looked at her. She felt Brady's gaze, too, burning a hole in the back of her head. All of their expectations weighing down on her.

"Yes," she said. "I did. Ask him, that is." And while that might not be true, her next words were. "I want Brady to go in with me for the ultrasound."

BAM...BAM...BAM...

Twenty-five minutes later, Brady stood next to an examination table in the cold, sterile ultrasound room.

Bam...bam...bam...

If she didn't stop making that racket, he was going to lose his mind.

His head pounded. Memories circled the edge of his mind, waiting to overwhelm him. Because J.C., sitting at the edge of an exam table, kept swinging her feet, her heels hitting the metal with a resounding bam. Like bombs going off.

Brady shot his hand out and grabbed her knee. "Do you mind?"

She stilled. "Sorry."

He released her. Her skin had been warm through the soft fabric of her black pants.

"I'm nervous," she blurted. "About..." She gestured to the

ultrasound machine next to the bed. "Seeing the baby."

"You worried something will be wrong?"

"No," she said so quietly, he had to lean forward to catch the rest of what she said. "That it'll make it real." She stared down at her clasped hands. "I...I don't know if I want this."

He straightened. "The ultrasound? If you're not feeling up to it—"

"The baby."

His head snapped back. He stepped around in front of her. She stared at the floor. He gently took a hold of her chin and raised her face. "Talk to me."

She pulled away from his touch. "How can I raise a child? I've never seen anything through in my life." She rubbed her palms up and down her thighs. "God, this is so selfish but...I'm not sure if I'm ready, or even capable, of committing the next eighteen years of my life to someone else."

"What are you thinking? Adoption?"

The thought of it left him cold. Of having a child out there, not knowing where he or she was, if the kid was safe. He shoved a hand through his hair. As if he had a right to be upset. As if he had the right to tell her what she should or shouldn't do with their child.

A child he'd already walked away from.

"No. Maybe. It kills me to think about giving this baby away," she said. "But I have thought about it. I'm afraid if I keep it, I'll mess up both our lives."

Damn. He should've seen this coming. All this time when she spoke about the pregnancy it was *this* baby. Or *the* baby.

Never her baby. Never their baby.

She was being torn up by the distance between her and Liz and her fears of raising a baby alone. And he'd been so focused on himself, on his own problems, he hadn't even noticed.

"Whatever you decide," he said, forcing out the words she needed to hear, "you have my support."

Words that gave her permission to put their child up for adoption. Words that were unbelievably hard to say.

"But...what about our families?" she asked in a rush.

"This isn't about them. It's about what's best for you and the baby."

She brushed her hair back and gave him a shaky smile. "Thanks."

"Could you...When you make the decision, could you let me know?"

She frowned. "If you want me to. But...aren't you leaving town? How will I get a hold of you?"

"I'll be here until after the first of the year." And when he'd made that decision, he had no idea. "But when I do leave, I'll make sure you have a way of reaching me. In case you need anything." In case she needed him.

Before they could respond to a knock at the door, a short blonde in black heels and a red and black dress covered by a lab coat came in.

"Hello, Jane," she said warmly. "How are you feeling?"

"Fine. You were right, the morning sickness went away."

"Wonderful." She offered her hand to him. "I'm Nanette Owens."

"Brady Sheppard."

Dr. Owens opened a small laptop, scanned the screen and shut it again. "Your blood pressure's normal. Pulse was a bit elevated but that's not unusual." After using some hand sanitizer she clapped her hands. "Now let's check out your baby."

Brady eased back a step as the doctor had J.C. undo the

bottom buttons of her white blouse and fold her shirt back.

"Okay," Dr. Owens said, "go ahead and pull your pants down to your hips."

He jerked his eyes up, stared sightlessly at the plain gray wall. But he could hear J.C. rustling around.

Sweat beaded on his forehead.

The doctor tucked a disposable sheet around J.C.'s pants and Brady glanced down. J.C.'s stomach protruded slightly, as if she'd swallowed a water balloon. The doctor squirted gel a few inches below J.C.'s belly button, then flipped a few switches on the ultrasound machine. After typing for a minute, she picked up a wand and placed it over the gel.

"Showtime." Dr. Owens moved the wand. Blurry black and gray images filled the screen and Brady looked away. "And there's baby."

Brady went numb. He couldn't look. He needed to keep some distance. It was his only protection.

"I don't see it," J.C. said.

"Here's the head." The doctor pressed something on the machine that made a clicking sound. "And here are the arms." More clicking. "From what I'm seeing here, I'd say you were right on about the date of conception. Baby's at seventeen weeks."

J.C.'s arms were straight by her sides, her hands clenching the sheet under her. He lightly traced a finger over her knuckle. Bent close to her head.

"Breathe," he said into her ear.

She exhaled, her fingers relaxing.

And he couldn't resist any longer. He had to see. It wasn't the clearest image but he could make out a head. Moving arms and legs.

Damn. J.C. had been right. This made it much too real.

Dr. Owens worked the machine for another five

minutes. When he looked over at J.C., he could've sworn she wiped the side of her face...as if she was crying. But with her head turned away from him, he couldn't be sure.

"Everything's fine," the doctor said, using paper towels to wipe the gel off J.C.'s stomach. "Heartbeat is strong, growth right on track. Do either of you have any questions?"

"When's it coming out?" Brady heard himself ask. His neck warmed. "I mean, when's J.C.'s...what do you call it?"

Dr. Owens smiled. If she found it odd he had no clue when the baby was supposed to be born, she didn't show it. "Her due date?"

"May fourth," J.C. said tonelessly as she buttoned her shirt.

May. Where would he be then? What would he be doing? Used to be he knew exactly what his life would be like. Who he'd be with. What kind of man he'd be.

"Would you like to know the sex?" Dr. Owens asked.

J.C. stood and pulled her pants up and though he tried not to look, he caught a glimpse of the curve of her hip. "Isn't it too soon to tell?" she asked.

Brady didn't blame her for sounding incredulous. He could barely make out the baby's head, let alone anything else.

"It's early, but the baby was positioned right for me to tell..."

Brady bit the inside of his cheek to keep from saying anything. Bad enough he'd seen the ultrasound. He didn't want to know any more about their baby.

Not if he wanted to walk away.

But he'd lost the right to offer an opinion.

Nibbling her lip, J.C. nodded.

The doctor grinned. "Congratulations. You're having a son."

11

FRIDAY EVENING, Brady sat at his kitchen table, a bottle of whiskey at his elbow, a spotty water glass in front of him, his cell phone in his hand. He'd left the window above the sink open, hoping some fresh air would help ease the tightness in his chest. The feeling that he was suffocating.

Pressing Redial on his phone, he held it to his ear, ground his back teeth together as it rang. And rang. When J.C.'s recorded voice came on and told him to leave a message, he hung up. Turned the phone end to end a few times and then tossed it aside.

The wind picked up, blew the take-out menu from his favorite Chinese place onto the floor. The evening air was thick with the threat of rain. A storm was coming. Several, if the local weather forecaster was to be trusted.

Southern Virginia was in for a long night of violent weather.

His hand shook as he poured whiskey into the glass. As a kid, he'd loved a raging thunderstorm, especially the raw power of it. If the electricity went off, all the better. He'd stare out his bedroom window, watch the sky light up. Press his cheek against the glass to feel the vibrations shake the house from a strong rumble of thunder.

He heard thunder in the distance.

His breathing felt ripped from his lungs. The nape of his neck tingled. The edge of his vision grew dark. He inhaled for the count of five. Exhaled for the same amount. And told himself that no matter how much it sounded like an IED—improvised explosive device—it wasn't.

Goddamn, he hated storms now.

He lifted the glass to his lips. Set it down again and ran a hand back and forth, back and forth through his hair.

He wanted a drink. Hell, he needed ten of them. The oblivion they promised. The relief. He needed something to get him through the next few hours while the storms raged. More to get him through the night.

Congratulations. You're having a son.

He shoved away from the table and stood. The bottle tipped. Instead of catching it, he watched dispassionately as it fell, whiskey pouring onto the table. At the last second he remembered to grab his phone. Shook off a few drops of alcohol, then tried J.C.'s number again. Still no answer.

He gripped the sink and stared out at the rain. It blew through the screen and he lifted his face, letting it dot his skin. Then another muted boom of thunder. He slammed the window shut and pressed the heels of his hands against his eyes as he bent at the waist, rocking slightly. His head pounded. His stomach roiled. Sweat soaked through his shirt as terror beat down on him.

It was bad. Real bad.

He glanced over at the glass on the table. If he drank it, he'd stop shaking. The gnawing, endless craving would end. And maybe he'd even have a dreamless night. Instead of tossing and turning. Sleeping only in the few reprieves when his brain shut down enough to pause the nightmares. He went back to the table. Sat down. Jumped back up and paced the length of the kitchen.

Last night had been the worst. He'd spent a fitful night, not falling asleep until a few hours before dawn. When he'd finally drifted off, he'd dreamt of Liz. Of the way they used to be. The way he'd always thought they would be forever.

It was their wedding night and Liz had her back to him, her dark hair over her shoulder so he could unfasten the buttons running down her gown. He'd kissed the nape of her neck, flicked his tongue out to taste her and she'd shivered. Taking his time, he'd pushed each tiny button free, trailing his lips over each inch of skin he exposed until finally the gown had slid down her naked body. She stepped free of the silk pooled around her feet and turned to him, but she wasn't Liz anymore.

She was J.C.

J.C. with her wild curls and sensuous curves and warm smile. And when she stepped up to him in his dream and kissed him, he didn't back away. He didn't wake up when, in the dream, his clothes somehow disappeared. No, he remained in that dream as J.C. pushed him back onto a large bed. As she straddled him, her breasts swaying, her eyes closed.

Then he'd woken up, hard and aching for her.

His body stirred at the memory of it.

And he looked at the spilled whiskey and realized exactly what he needed to help him get through the night.

———

"IN MY DAY," Grandma Rose said, "expectant mothers took

care of themselves. They rested. They certainly didn't work all day and then spend all night on their feet."

As the soapy water drained from the sink, J.C. rolled her eyes at the ceramic Victorian Santas lined up on her grandma's windowsill. Funny how Grandma Rose hadn't complained about J.C. staying on her feet when she'd offered to do the dinner dishes.

J.C. dried her hands and then folded the towel. "Didn't everyone smoke and drink while they were pregnant, too?"

Like the drum roll punctuating a joke, thunder rumbled in the distance.

Sitting at her kitchen table as regal as a queen, Grandma Rose sniffed delicately. "I don't understand why you'd choose to spend your Friday night making chocolates."

"I told you, I made a commitment to the Diamond Dust." And while the commitment part usually didn't mean all that much to her, she was determined to see this project through. To just once, complete a task she'd set for herself.

"But you could be out—"

"I thought you wanted me to rest?" she asked with an exasperated laugh.

"If you were out with some nice young man, you could rest. You could have dinner. Or see a movie."

"I just had dinner, I'm too busy for a movie and from my personal experience so far, nice young men don't ask out pregnant women."

"They might if you took some care with your hair," she said, eyeing J.C.'s frizzy ponytail, "and didn't wear such awful clothes. Why, that shirt needs to be thrown out. And it wouldn't hurt you to put on some makeup."

Used to her grandma's nit-picking about her appearance —at least this time she hadn't asked her why she couldn't be more like Liz—J.C. kissed Rose's soft, wrinkled cheek. "I'd better get going. Thanks for dinner."

"Wait." Rose stood and hurried to the refrigerator, where she pulled out a plastic container. "Take some pasta home. You can have it for lunch tomorrow."

"Great." Smiling, she took the leftover fettuccine in alfredo sauce.

"Thanks."

They walked past the living room. Her grandma's artificial tree, complete with festively wrapped packages underneath, was done up in blues and silver. Green garlands, white lights and silver and blue candles decorated the mantel over the fireplace.

J.C. tightened her ponytail. She'd been too busy or too plain exhausted to think about putting up her own decorations but seeing as how Christmas would be here in just over two weeks, she should get a tree. And maybe start shopping for a few presents.

In the foyer, she slipped on her pink and white polka-dot flip-flops. "I'll see you Sunday at Mom and Dad's." Lightning flickered.

"Oh, dear. You'd better take an umbrella," Rose said, hurrying over to the umbrella stand in the corner.

"I don't need one." J.C. raised the hood of her light blue sweatshirt and, looking back at her grandmother, opened the door. "'Night," she called over the heavy rain and wind, then turned.

She squeaked at finding Brady standing on her grandmother's porch.

"Brady. God. Don't scare me like that."

"Brady?" Rose repeated sharply as she peered past J.C. "What's he doing here?"

She shrugged. Rain dripped off his hair. Ran in rivulets

down his cheek. The bottoms of his jeans were as soaked as his jacket. And as usual, he was scowling.

"My grandmother would like to know what you're doing here," J.C. said.

"Evening, Mrs. Montgomery."

Grandma Rose pulled her shoulders back. "Don't you 'evening' me, Brady Sheppard. I'm not some impressionable young girl. You can't charm me."

He shifted. "No, ma'am."

"And don't for one second think that I don't know what you're after." Rose shook her finger at him. "Well, you're not going to get it. Not again. You hear me?"

He glanced at J.C. "Yes, ma'am."

"And you," she said to Jane, "need to remember what my own grandmother told me—no man buys the cow when he gets the milk for free."

J.C. considered pointing out that she'd already given him the whole farm. Instead, she nodded somberly. "No free milk. Got it."

And before J.C. could be taken to task for being cheeky, she slipped outside and shut the door. The strands of white Christmas lights decorating the porch swayed in the breeze. Cold, needlelike rain hit J.C.'s face. She turned her head and hunched her shoulders.

"Did you need something, Brady?"

He wiped the rain off his face. Stared at a point above her head. "I wanted to make sure you were all right."

"Why wouldn't I be?"

"You seemed upset. At the doctor's office." He met her eyes. "You're disappointed the baby's a boy."

"Don't be ridiculous," she snapped, then pressed her lips together.

Lightning lit the sky. "Look, I appreciate you coming

over here to check on me —three days after the fact—but I'm fine. And I really have a lot—"

Thunder cracked sharply. Brady shivered. "Do you think I could come up...? For a towel," he added at her hesitation. "And maybe...a cup of coffee?"

Bad idea. Bad, *bad* idea. She'd bet a week's pay her grandmother was already on the phone with J.C.'s mom. And while she could easily excuse his presence at the doctor's office as her giving him his parental rights, and their pairing wines and being at the gift shop together as purely business, this was different.

She'd have no excuse for being with him tonight.

"It's getting pretty late—"

"Please," he said quietly. Gruffly. "Please invite me up, Jane."

Slowly she nodded. Then she raced down the porch steps and into the pouring rain. Water ran down the sleeve of the hand holding her hood in place. Cutting through the front yard, she rounded the corner to the garage and climbed the stairs as quickly as possible.

At the top, her flip-flop skidded on the wet wood, her foot shooting out from under her. Her arms flailed, and the plastic container flew out of her hand as she pitched backward. Her hand hit solid wood and she latched on to the railing, the sudden change in momentum causing her to lurch forward. Her legs buckled and she twisted so she wouldn't land on her stomach. Instead, her shin hit the sharp edge of the stair. Pain shot through her. Left her gasping.

Getting unsteadily to her feet, she picked up the plastic container and glanced behind her. Brady was halfway up the stairs, his face in shadow. She limped inside and left the door open for him—Daisy wouldn't go outside, not if it meant getting wet. As she went into the kitchen, she unzipped her soaking sweatshirt and peeled it off, letting it drop onto the floor. The T-shirt she wore underneath it was wet, as well, but she wanted to check her leg before she changed into dry clothes.

After wiping her face on a hand towel, she sat at the table. "You okay in there?" she whispered, rubbing her stomach. She didn't feel any different.

Other than her leg, she had no pain. No cramping.

She shuddered out a breath. Thank God.

She gingerly pulled her pant leg up to her knee. A fist-size bruise was already forming. But there was no blood. Just some slight scraping of the skin.

"You all right?"

Brady stood in the doorway, his hair matted to his head. Water dripping off him, forming a small puddle at his feet.

"Yeah. It's not so bad," she said, twisting so he could see her shin. "It hurts but I don't think there's any major damage."

"The baby?"

"Fine. I didn't hit my stomach." She stood. "Before I make the coffee, I'll get you a towel and then change."

But when she went to move past him, he didn't budge. Lightning flashed, illuminating his harsh expression. He looked...dangerous. And pissed off.

"Give me your shoes," he ordered.

She glanced down. She hadn't even bothered to kick them off when she got inside. "What?"

Another rumble of thunder. "You almost fell because you're wearing those damn things. You could've broken your neck."

"But I didn't."

He stepped toward her, his movements menacing, his expression hard.

"The shoes."

"You're nuts," she said, edging away from him until her spine hit the edge of the counter. "Look. I'm cold. I'm wet. And I need to call the doctor to see what, if any, pain relievers I can safely take. So why don't you—"

"Hold on."

Hold on? To what...him? Not likely. Not when she just wanted him out of her way.

Wrapping his fingers around her uninjured leg, below the knee, he lifted her foot off the ground.

"Hey!" She clutched the counter for balance. "Watch it, grabby hands."

He plucked off her flip-flop and tucked it under his arm. He very carefully lifted her other leg and took off that shoe, as well. All she could do was stare as he searched through her kitchen drawers. When he finally found what he was looking for—a paring knife—she drew her shoulders back.

"You wouldn't dare," she breathed.

He raised one eyebrow. Then he held up a flip-flop, tilted his head and... with his eyes locked on hers...sliced through the strap. Tossing the flip-flop over his shoulder, he repeated the process with the second one then laid the knife on the counter and gave her a look that told her he'd not only enjoyed destroying her shoes, but he'd do it again in a heartbeat.

She shook her head. "There is something seriously wrong with you."

He closed the distance between them. Water dripped from his coat onto her bare feet. "You're the one stupid enough to wear those shoes."

She pressed back against the counter again. "At least I don't go around dismembering people's shoes."

"Damn it, you could've been hurt," he snapped, grasping her upper arms and lifting her on tiptoe.

A lump formed in her throat. He'd been scared for her. How awful it must've been for him in that split second when it'd seemed as if she was going to fall backward. How helpless he must've felt. How angry because he couldn't race up the stairs.

Thunder shook the apartment.

Brady shuddered, his fingers tightening on her arms. His breathing grew rapid.

She remembered his violent reaction that morning she'd first told him about the baby. How he'd seemed to space out at the gift shop last week.

All this time she'd thought the changes in him, his drinking, were because of Liz. Because he couldn't let her go. And maybe that was part of it. But it wasn't all of it.

"Hey, it's okay," she soothed him. She laid her hands on his chest. Under the soggy, cold shirt, his muscles tensed. His heart raced. "It's just a storm.

Everything's fine."

A muscle jumped in his jaw. He slid his hands up to her shoulders. Brushing his thumbs against the sides of her neck, he tipped her head back and met her eyes. She dug her nails into his skin. His narrowed gaze dropped to her mouth.

And any hope she'd had about truly being over her feelings for this man died when he swore under his breath and then kissed her.

HIS MOUTH AGAINST HERS, Brady swallowed J.C.'s gasp. He kept the kiss gentle. Almost reverent. He was afraid if he pushed for too much, too fast, she'd pull away. Tell him to go.

He couldn't let that happen. Not when the panic was already receding. He was able to blot everything else out because she was in his arms. Kissing him back.

He had no right to touch her, to discover that she tasted as sweet as he'd imagined. To sink into her kiss and forget how screwed up his life had become. But he couldn't stop. He needed to surround himself with her warmth. It was the only way to get rid of the fear that gripped him every day.

He slid his tongue along the seam of her lips and she pulled back slightly, but not far enough away to break contact. Forcing himself to slow down, he skimmed his lips across her jaw, over her chilled cheeks to her temple and down along her hairline.

Her skin was cold, so he rubbed her arms. Pressed closer to her as his own body heated despite his wet clothes. He wanted to tear her hair band out. Watch her shake her head so the curls framed her face. But he didn't have the patience for it.

He pressed an openmouthed kiss behind her ear. Her head fell back on a soft moan that seemed to wash over his body, caress his skin.

He kissed her mouth again. Her lips parted and the tip of her tongue touched his tentatively and about blew his mind.

He yanked her against him. Speared one hand into the damp hair at the nape of her neck to hold her still for his kiss. His other hand slid under her shirt to her waist, the curve of her belly pressing against his palm.

Deepening the kiss, he shifted his weight off his bad leg

by slipping it between her thighs. She wrapped her arms around his neck, her fingers combing through his wet hair. The movement brought their bodies center to center. He hissed out a breath. Her breasts rubbed against his chest, her beaded nipples burning through his shirt.

He shifted to the side and broke the kiss long enough to wrench his coat off. Letting it fall on the floor, he raked his gaze over her and his body tightened. She was...stunning. Her lips were red and swollen, her breasts, the roundness of her belly pressing against her shirt. Her cheeks flushed, her eyes dark with desire.

He took her mouth in another voracious kiss. Grabbing her ass, he pulled her even closer. She was all soft, lush curves. And the mewling sounds she made in the back of her throat were driving him crazy. Unable to resist, he rolled his hips and almost whimpered himself. He needed to be inside her.

Right now. Or else he'd lose his mind for good.

He would've dragged her down and made love to her there on her kitchen floor, was in the process of doing just that, when she stopped kissing him.

He lifted his head. "What's wrong?"

"I...I don't want this," she said, holding herself as stiffly as possible in his arms.

"Are you sure?" he murmured, unable to stop himself from trailing a finger down the smoothness of her cheek. "I want you."

She laughed harshly. "You don't want me. You want a warm body." When she pushed him, he dropped his arms and stepped back. "I'm convenient."

"What the hell is that supposed to mean?"

"It means you're looking for someone to help you through the night."

No. Not anyone. Her. But she'd never believe it.

"Is that so wrong?" he asked. "We're both adults. Both unattached."

"It wouldn't be wrong," she said with a sigh, "except you'll never be unattached. You're always going to be in love with Liz."

He wanted to deny it. Wanted his denial to be the truth, but he wasn't sure it would be. "She has nothing to do with this."

"How can she not have everything to do with this?" J.C. crossed her arms. "She's my sister and the woman you've loved half your life. What happens between us affects her, too."

"So I'm supposed to...what? Let Liz vet all the women I might sleep with? Because she sure as hell didn't ask my opinion when she decided to dump me for her husband."

"There's too much between us. Call it history or family ties or whatever. All I know is I've already let you use me once," she said wearily as she straightened from the counter. "I'm not about to make that mistake again. Especially not for a man who only wants me so he can pretend he's with my sister."

12

"YOU'RE EITHER THE WORLD'S MOST PATIENT MAN," J.C. said in exasperation, coming back to the kitchen when he'd refused to leave, "or the most stubborn."

"Both," he admitted.

She'd swept out of here twenty minutes ago, no doubt hoping that if she took long enough changing into dry clothes, he'd give up, maybe even get pissed and take off. But he wasn't going anywhere. Not when she had such a messed-up view of what'd happened between them. Of why he'd kissed her.

"Here," she said, tossing him a dark blue towel and a gray sweatshirt.

He caught one in each hand. "Thanks."

She shrugged and brushed past him, close enough he could smell a light vanilla scent as she went to a corner cupboard. She'd changed into a pair of striped pajama pants and an oversize, stained shirt with a scowling Garfield holding a coffee cup above the words *I Don't Do Mornings.* She must've redone her hair because the sides were smoothed back, the ponytail higher on her head. Several curls, having escaped confinement, trailed along the back of her neck.

The skin he now knew was soft and warm and sensitive to his touch.

Squeezing the towel in his hands, he stepped back so he wouldn't pull her against him.

She turned—spray cleaner in one hand, a dry cloth in the other—and, without so much as a glance his way, went back to the table. Rain pelted the roof, its intensity waning as the storm moved past. But another one would follow. And if he was alone, he didn't think he could make it through the night.

At least not sober.

By the time he'd peeled off his damp shirt, rubbed the towel over his chilled arms and chest, and dried his hair, she'd wheeled a small, three-tiered cart between the table and wall and taken a round, plastic container from the fridge.

"Thank you," she said, still not looking at him, "for cleaning up the floor."

"No problem." Since she'd left him to stew, he'd had plenty of time.

He tugged on the sweatshirt, shoving up the short sleeves. Sitting to her left, he clasped his hands between his knees. Inhaled deeply. "When I'm with you," he said slowly, his gaze fixed on her profile, "I don't pretend you're Liz. And I sure as hell wasn't thinking of her when I kissed you."

"You sure about that?" she asked, spraying cleaning solution over the table. "It wouldn't be the first time."

"Whatever I did the night of Liz's wedding, I didn't mean to hurt you."

"It wasn't all your fault." She wiped the table with brisk, rough strokes. "I convinced myself you wanted to be with me. And I kept on believing. Right until the end when…" Her voice broke, and she vigorously scrubbed the same spot. "When you called out Liz's name."

He linked his hands at the back of his neck and leaned back. Blew out a heavy breath. "Shit."

His memories of that night were blurry. Disjointed. He'd known he'd used J.C. to help him through his pain and anger. But he hadn't realized how low he'd sunk. Wincing, he shut his eyes. How low he was still sinking. Not thirty minutes ago he'd had her in his arms wanting only to shove aside his panic, to ignore the memories for a little while.

She unfolded a plastic tablecloth. When she spread the material over the table, he sat up and snagged her hand. She froze, her fingers curling. He traced his fingertip over the delicate skin of her inner wrist. Back and forth. Back and forth. Finally, she raised her head.

He wrapped his fingers around her wrist. Felt her pulse beat. "I'm sorry, Jane."

"Sometimes…" she said softly as she withdrew her hand. "Sometimes being sorry isn't enough."

J.C. DIDN'T SO MUCH as glance Brady's way as she set out what she needed— gloves, wax paper, tape, melon ball scoop, cookie sheets. After taping wax paper to the cookie sheets, she opened the container of ganache she'd made earlier. Wind rattled the windowpane.

"Won't be long before another storm comes," she said casually. As if having him sit there wearing her University of Virginia sweatshirt, all big and male and brooding, didn't bother her in the least. As if it hadn't taken all of her willpower to push him away. "If you don't want to get caught in another downpour, you'd better get going."

"Last time you wanted me out of your apartment, you told me outright."

"Fair enough," she said, pulling on a pair of gloves. "I'd like you to leave."

Scooping up a small amount of the dark ganache, she rolled it lightly between her palms, then set it on the wax paper. Repeated the process.

Brady stretched his leg out. Bent it again. Drummed his fingers on the table.

She sighed. "Brady—"

"I haven't had a drink in four days."

Her fingers tightened on the scoop and she glanced at him. Four days... She caught her breath. Four days ago he'd accompanied her to her doctor's appointment.

"Are you bragging?" she asked, keeping her tone neutral. "Or complaining?"

He slouched. "Just stating a fact."

"Oh. Well, that's—"

"I wanted to," he muttered. "Every damn day I've wanted a drink worse than the day before."

Using the scoop, she scraped a tic-tac-toe pattern into the ganache. "Maybe you need to decide what you want more. To have a drink. Or to stop drinking."

He stood. Put his hands into his pockets. Took them out again. The next storm rumbled in the distance and he hunched his shoulders.

"Don't like thunder?" she couldn't stop herself from asking.

"I've been jumpy since..." He shook his head.

"You were hurt?"

"Since I've been stateside." His expression was hard. "Sometimes...loud noises cause me to...zone out."

She frowned. "You mean you have flashbacks?"

He glared at her. "Sometimes I think about what happened back there." *There.* Afghanistan. Where his friends had been wounded. Killed.

And now a thunderstorm had the power to cause this strong man to tremble.

Her heart broke for him.

"Can I stay?" he asked, his tone belligerent. His feet wide, his arms loose at his sides as if ready for a fight.

"What do you mean?" If he said stay as in stay the night in her bed, she'd kick his butt to the curb—she didn't care how emotionally damaged he was.

He kept opening and closing his fist, like a gunfighter getting ready to draw his weapon. "If I go home now," he said, as if he were forcing the words out, "I'll drink. And I don't want to drink. Not tonight."

She squeezed the last of the ganache between her hands. He was using her. Again. She was his safety net. Except she couldn't save him. And even if she could, she wasn't sure she wanted to.

"Should I be your crutch?" she asked, unable to keep the bitterness out of her voice. "How about if I throw myself on any alcoholic beverages that get within a few feet of you?"

"I was thinking more along the lines of you just...talking to me," he said quietly. "Letting me keep you company while you work or do your laundry or...whatever you had planned."

She tore off her chocolate-coated gloves and dropped them into the empty bowl. She wanted to send him away. To protect herself from him. If she let him too close, he'd hurt her again. But then she met his eyes and, for the first time since he'd come home, glimpsed the man he used to be. She had to let him stay.

"BRADY," DIANE SAID TWO days later as she passed him the serving bowl of green beans, "there's something important Aidan and I would like to discuss with you."

They were seated at the small table in the breakfast nook rather than in the ornate dining room—the spot for Sunday dinners when he'd been a kid. His mother sat with her back to the dark window, Brady to her left. Aidan, as always, was her right-hand man.

Spooning beans onto his already full plate, Brady raised his eyebrows. "Don't keep me in suspense."

Diane smiled at him. "How would you like to take on a bigger role at the winery?"

His fingers tingled and he set the beans down. Every week since he'd been back in Jewell, his mother had invited him to Sunday dinner. And every week he'd declined. Until yesterday, when his mother had casually mentioned she was making all his favorites.

Damn. Lured into a trap by the promise of fried chicken, homemade buttermilk biscuits and her double fudge brownies.

He picked up his drumstick. "I wouldn't."

"Told you," Aidan murmured before sipping his chardonnay.

"But why not?" she asked. "Now that you're...getting better—"

"She means now that you're not stinking drunk or hungover all the time," Aidan offered.

Diane fixed Aidan with a look guaranteed to make most men feel as if they were ten years old again. "When I need you to help explain what I mean," she said, her slight Southern accent thickening, "I'll ask."

Aidan stabbed a bean. "Just trying to help."

Brady bit into his chicken, determined not to let the topic ruin his favorite meal.

"Your father always dreamt of having his sons work at the Diamond Dust with him," Diane said.

And his food now tasted like sawdust.

"Don't waste your time," Aidan told their mother. "The only reason he's working here in the first place is because I forced him into it."

"I never pretended otherwise," Brady said mildly.

"But it doesn't have to be that way," Diane said. "Won't you at least consider it?"

He couldn't. He'd already lost Liz and any chance he'd had of becoming a member of the Virginia State Police. If he stayed in Jewell, if he worked at the Diamond Dust, it'd be like admitting he accepted the way his life had turned out.

He wiped his fingers then his mouth on a cloth napkin. "I never planned on working here. Dad knew that."

"Yes, and we fully supported your decision to join the military, but things are different now. You need to start thinking of your future."

"I am," he said. Or he would. Soon.

"Well, then, how are you going to support yourself? And what about Jane and the baby?"

"What about them?"

She seemed taken aback. "I thought you and she were..."

on friendlier terms."

The memory of how J.C. had felt in his arms, of how she tasted, hit him with great force. "Nothing's changed."

Except that he continued to dream about her. Had kissed her.

Even after everything he'd done, she still let him sit at her kitchen table the other night while she worked on her chocolates. She'd kept up a steady stream of chatter and hadn't seemed to mind when he'd lapsed into silence.

"Everyone in town's talking about how you spent an entire day at the obstetrician's office so you could see her," Aidan said, laying his fork on his empty plate.

Brady rolled his shoulders. Damn small-town gossip, he thought for the nth time. "It wasn't like that."

His brother smirked. "What was it like, then?"

"I think it's wonderful that you and Jane are working out your differences," Diane said, pausing to eat a bite of mashed potatoes. "Especially as I'd like to have some sort of relationship with my first grandchild. You wouldn't believe the horror stories I've heard about grandparents being refused the right to even visit with their grandchildren after a nasty divorce. In some cases where the parents were never married, the mothers disappear with the child. Can you imagine?"

Imagine? He'd been trying not to think about it ever since J.C.'s admission that she wasn't sure she wanted to keep their son.

And he'd told her she had his full support because she'd been so upset, he'd wanted to let her know he didn't judge her. And because... He swallowed the nausea rising in his throat. Because if she did decide to give the baby up for adoption, it'd let him off the hook.

She'd brought up their families and wondered how her

decision would affect them. He hadn't wanted to think about it. Hadn't wanted to care.

"J.C. would never keep the baby away from you," he said.

Diane set her water down. "When relationships go bad, some people change."

"Not her."

"I'm sure you're right." Diane cut her chicken into tiny pieces before setting her knife down. "After all, it was your idea to have her sell those chocolates in the gift store. Pam said J.C.'s sales yesterday were up fifteen percent from last week."

Figuring they both needed some space after Friday night, he'd stayed far away from the gift shop yesterday. "Good." He looked over to find Aidan regarding him steadily. "What?" Brady growled.

"I find it interesting how well you seem to have gotten to know Jane."

"I was with her sister for twelve years," he pointed out. "I've always known J.C."

He tapped his fist against his thigh. Just because he'd dreamt of J.C., kissed her, and wanted to take her to bed, didn't change what'd been in his heart since he was sixteen years old. He would always love Liz.

———

J.C. WAS FINISHING UP with one of her favorite customers late Wednesday morning when Liz walked into the lobby of Hampton Bank and Trust Company.

"Going to do some Christmas shopping?" she asked Mr. Carns as Liz waited in line at the end of the roped-off area.

Mr. Carns, an elderly gentleman with thinning silver hair and an easy grin, slid his money into a bank envelope.

"My wife handles all the gift buying. She leaves me in charge of making sure her wallet's always full of money." He winked.

J.C. smiled. "She's a lucky woman."

"That's what I keep telling her." Hitting the counter with the flat of his hand, he straightened. "If I don't see you before, you have a merry Christmas."

"You, too, Mr. Carns."

As usual for the middle of the week, business was light. "Silver Bells" played in the background and in between each teller's window hung a swag of evergreen boughs tied with a red velvet ribbon. Behind her, Mary Jo Hanold spoke to a customer using the drive-up window. Two windows down in the lobby, Shirley Dodge counted out a deposit from one of the local grocery stores.

"Hello, J.C.," Liz said, stepping up to the window with obvious reluctance.

"It's so good to see you. I've tried calling but—"

"I'd like to cash this." She set down a personal check while seemingly engrossed in watching the hands of the large clock on the wall above the door turn. "Large bills are fine."

J.C. narrowed her eyes. "Yes, ma'am."

Other than the slight stiffening of her shoulders, Liz gave no indication she even heard J.C.

"What do you want from me?" J.C. asked as she processed the transaction on her computer. "Blood?"

"All I want is to cash a check."

"Fine," J.C. said. She was so very tired of being the only one trying to make things right between them.

She quickly counted out the cash, recounted it out loud for her sister's benefit and then tapped it into a neat pile.

"Next time," she said, sliding the money across the counter, "try one of our convenient ATM locations."

Liz put the money into her wallet. "Grandma Rose mentioned Brady spent quite a bit of time at your apartment Friday night."

"Grandma Rose," J.C. said vehemently, "has a big mouth."

"So it's true?"

J.C. straightened a stack of withdrawal slips. "He stopped by."

"Are you...are you two...together?"

Heat washed over her as she remembered how he'd kissed her, as if he could never get enough of her. Held her breast, his voice scraping along her nerve endings when he'd said he wanted her. How...relieved he'd been when she'd told him he could stay through the worst of the storms.

"No." She picked up the withdrawal slips and fanned herself. "Of course not."

When Liz didn't respond, J.C. glanced up, shocked to see her sister fighting tears. Liz must be close to her breaking point to show that much weakness in the middle of the bank lobby.

J.C. set up her Next Window Please sign.

"Don't move," she ordered and then told Mary Jo she was taking a five-minute break.

By the time J.C. had walked out from behind the teller station, Liz's eyes were dry. But she still let J.C. lead her through the lobby to the corner office they used to open new accounts.

J.C. flipped on the light and shut the door. "What is it?" she asked, taking Liz's hand. "What's wrong?"

Liz linked her fingers with J.C.'s. "Carter and I..." She

cleared her throat. "We're having some…problems."

"What do you mean by problems?"

"He thinks I have…feelings…repressed feelings…for Brady."

Her mouth went dry. "Do you?"

"If you mean do I still care about Brady, about what happens to him, then yes." She tugged her hand free and began to pace. "After all our time together, how could I not? But Carter refuses to believe it's not more than that. He wants us to go to marriage counseling," Liz said, as if her husband had suggested they join a wife-swapping club.

The idea of admitting her marriage was in trouble must be devastating.

"Maybe counseling's not such a bad idea," J.C. offered.

"It's a horrible idea. We don't need it. Where would we attend sessions anyway? I could never face our colleagues after discussing our most intimate issues with one of them." Crossing her arms, Liz shook her head. "No. We don't need therapy. We'll get through this on our own. But I need you to do something for me."

The hair at the back of her neck stood on end. "I'll do whatever I can—"

"Stay away from Brady."

She licked her lips. Clasped her hands in front of her. "I told you, we're not together."

"But you've been spending time with him and I…I miss you." Liz's expression softened. "So much. But things can't go back to the way they were between us if…if Brady's in your life. And you said yourself that he didn't want any part of the baby, right?"

She remembered Brady's expression when he'd seen the baby's ultrasound—small part wonder, huge part fear. "Right, but—"

"I'm not just asking this for me. I'm asking for Carter, so he doesn't have to risk coming face-to-face with my ex when we see you. And I'm asking for you, too."

"Me?"

"You may not believe this, but I don't want to see you get hurt."

Brady's not the right guy for you. You deserve someone who'll put you first.

Someone who hadn't loved her sister first.

"Okay," J.C. managed to say through the tightness of her throat. "I won't see him anymore."

Liz shut her eyes briefly. "Thank you."

And as her sister enveloped her in a warm hug, J.C. assured herself she'd made the right decision. She'd give Brady up.

As soon as she figured out how to give up a man who was never really hers in the first place.

13

"BRADY," J.C. SAID, WHEN SHE OPENED THE DOOR FRIDAY evening. "What do you want?"

He raised his eyebrows and she forced herself not to wince. Well, he couldn't show up at her doorstep out of the blue whenever he liked. It wasn't fair to her. And having him standing on her doorstep, clean shaven with his recently cut hair ruffling in the breeze, didn't make keeping her promise to her sister any easier.

"There's a ten-foot Scotch pine strapped to the roof of your car," he said.

She widened her eyes. "It must've fallen onto my car when I drove home from work. Funny how I never noticed."

His eyes narrowed to slits. "How did you think you were going to get it off the car, let alone up the stairs, by yourself?"

"I didn't plan that far ahead." Stopping by the Christmas tree lot on the way home had been an impulse. It had seemed like such a good idea, spending Friday night decorating her tree. With her luck, it'd still be on her car Monday morning. "Is that why you stopped by? To tell me about my own Christmas tree?"

He studied her in that intense way of his that made her blush. "Did I do something between last week and today to piss you off?"

"You haven't even spoken to me since then. What could you have done?"

She grimaced. That sounded as if she'd expected him to call.

"So there's no reason for you to not invite me in," he said.

She lightly hit the dangling silver earring in her left ear with her fingertip, set it swinging. "Actually, there is. A reason."

"Should I guess?" he asked when she remained silent.

"I..." She swallowed. "I just got home," she said on a rush. "I haven't even changed yet."

His gaze skimmed over her black pants. Lingered on her shiny burgundy top before meeting her eyes. "I don't mind."

Her mouth dried and she stepped behind the door, closing it slightly, showing only her face through the small opening.

"Since I'm not going to see the other side of your door any time soon, you might as well take this now," he said, holding out a plastic shopping bag.

She eyed it suspiciously. "What is it?"

He pulled a large, plain cardboard box out of the bag. "Do you want it or not?"

She took it, flipped it over then back again. Letting go of the door, she lifted the lid. And blinked down at a pair of purple and white polka-dot flipflops.

The tips of Brady's ears were red. "They were out of pink," he said almost defiantly.

"That's okay," she whispered. "I love purple."

He scowled. "I wasn't sure of your size."

"They're fine. They're perfect," she said. "Thank you."

He inclined his head, the barest of nods. "Good night."

"Wait." She stepped onto the landing, pulling the door closed in case Daisy made a run for it. "Don't you want to come in?"

"Do you want me to come in?" he asked cautiously.

She clutched the box, holding it over her racing heart. "Yeah, I do."

He gestured for her to go ahead of him and she hurried inside. Before she changed her mind.

She kicked off her shoes. "Do you want a soda?" she asked, setting the box on top of her coffee table before making her way toward the kitchen. "I think I have regular—"

"How are you going to get the tree up here?"

She placed a hand over the fluttering in her stomach. "I'll call my dad tomorrow."

He glared at the sheet and tree stand under the window. "I can't bring the tree up."

"I didn't ask you to." And then she realized what he meant. What bothered him. "Is this about your knee? Because even if I wasn't pregnant, I couldn't drag that tree up all those stairs, either."

He tossed his jacket onto the sofa. "That's different."

"If that isn't one of the finest examples of the male ego at work, I don't know what is."

"It's not ego. Not all ego. More like I hate not being able to do all the things I used to."

"So you can't haul a large evergreen up a flight of stairs. At least you can still climb them," she said, sick to death of him focusing on what he couldn't do. What he didn't have, such as Liz. "You're able to get out of bed by yourself. You can work at a job—even if it's not the one you'd always planned on. You're surrounded by people who care about you. Who are more than willing to give you a hand when you need one. And if all of those reasons weren't enough for you to thank God each and every day," she said, her face hot, her voice breaking, "I'd think the fact that you're alive would be."

The room seemed too quiet after her outburst. All she could hear was the sound of her own ragged breathing. Her pulse kicked up as Brady closed the distance between them, the surprise on his face giving way to admiration.

He stopped a few inches from her. Close enough she could feel his body heat, smell the fresh winter air clinging to his clothes. "You're right. Those things weren't enough for me. I'm not sure they'll ever be." He tucked one of her stray curls behind her ear, his fingertip grazing her neck. "But you're wrong, too. Because right now, I can honestly say I'm very grateful to be alive."

"DID YOU FIND SOMETHING to drink?" J.C. asked as she came back out into the living room ten minutes later. After her impassioned speech and his own admission, she'd bolted with the excuse of changing out of her work clothes.

Sitting on the sofa, her cat curled up next to him, Brady held up his can of soda. He watched as J.C. walked past him. She'd pulled her hair back and had on the same clinging black pants she'd worn last week when she fell on the steps and a loose T-shirt the color of peaches.

As she disappeared into the kitchen, his fingers tightened on the can. He took a long swallow. "You hungry?" he called.

She came back into the room eating from a bag of pretzels. "What'd you say?"

He grinned. "I asked if you were hungry."

She sat on the other end of the couch. "Nowadays that's pretty much a yes no matter when you ask me."

"We could order some dinner," he said casually. "Maybe get some Chinese?"

"Sure," she said after a long moment, as if having takeout with him was some sort of momentous decision. "That'd be nice." Handing him the bag of pretzels, she stood. "Let me grab the take-out menu for The Golden Dragon."

"I don't need it. I'll have a number three and a number fifteen."

"You have the menu for the Chinese restaurant memorized?"

The cat stood and stretched, stepped onto Brady's lap and lay down again. "Just the dishes I like."

She rubbed the side of her stomach. "I take it you don't cook."

"Not if I can help it."

"Me, either. Between my parents, Grandma Rose and Liz and Carter, I—" She blushed, acting as guilty as if she'd admitted to hiding terrorist operatives under her bed. "I'll go order dinner," she said before rushing out of the room. Again.

He didn't call her back. Not when he had no idea what to say to her. He knew what he should say—that J.C. could go ahead and talk about her sister all she wanted. That Liz was a part of her life and as such, she shouldn't worry about bringing her up in an innocent conversation.

Leaning his head back against the couch, he stared at the ceiling. Yeah, he should say all of that. But he'd be lying. He didn't want to hear anything about Liz. Didn't want to be reminded of her existence. Not when he'd gotten to the point where he could go all day without once thinking about her.

Someone knocked, and Brady set the cat aside and stood. He opened the door, nodded at Matt and then noticed J.C.'s tree on the stairs behind his brother.

"Thanks," he said, figuring he could manage to drag it up the last few feet. "I've got it from here."

Matt pushed the door back open when Brady tried to shut it in his face.

"Don't I even get invited in? After all, I dropped everything to do you favor."

Dropped everything, Brady's ass.

"Favor's appreciated," Brady said, refusing to fall for his brother's bait.

When he'd called Matt fifteen minutes ago, Matt had been at The County Line, one of the higher end bars in Jewell. And Brady sure as hell didn't feel guilty for tearing him away from a watered-down drink and whichever local girl he'd been trying to charm into sleeping with him.

"Well, appreciation's great and all," Matt said, leaning against the door. "But I'd rather have a beer."

"J.C. doesn't have—"

"Food should be here in twenty minutes," J.C. said, coming up behind Brady. "Oh. Hi, Matt." She glanced curiously between the brothers. "I didn't know you were home."

"Since I had to fly back to Australia the day after Thanksgiving, I thought I'd come in early for Christmas."

Funny how Matt's accent became thicker whenever a female was within hearing distance. His green eyes lit as he scanned J.C. head to toe and back up again. "Jane Cleo, you get prettier every time I see you."

Brady stopped himself from laying a proprietary hand on J.C.'s shoulder.

"Any women stupid enough to buy your tired lines?" he asked.

Matt grinned, his hair, too long, blowing around his face. "You'd be surprised."

"I wouldn't," J.C. said. Brady scowled while Matt laughed. "What?" she asked. "I'm just saying there are plenty of stupid women out there."

He laid a hand over his heart. "You wound me, sugar. And after I hauled your Christmas tree up all those stairs. Your very heavy Christmas tree."

At that moment, Brady would've given anything to have full use of his leg back so he could kick Matt down the steps.

"You brought my tree up?" J.C. asked, her brow knit in confusion.

"Sure did. Now, why don't you hold the door open and I'll bring it the rest of the way in."

Brady stepped out onto the landing. "Better let me help you," he said. "Seeing as how this is one of those extra-heavy Christmas trees."

He carefully took a hold of a thick bottom branch while Matt did the same. Walking backward, they pulled the tree up over the doorstep and into the apartment. The sharp needles pricked and scratched his skin. The pungent scent of pine filled the room.

"Want me to set it up for you, Jane?" Matt asked.

"No," Brady said before J.C. could so much as open her mouth.

"You sure?" Matt hooked his thumbs in his pockets and sent J.C. one of his patented grins guaranteed to charm the ladies. "I'd be more than happy to stick around."

"We've got it," Brady ground out. "Thanks for coming over."

"Yes," J.C. added, giving his brother a warm smile. "Thank you so much, Matt. This was really sweet of you."

"No problem." He walked to the door and stood on the landing. "Call me if you need anything else," he said to J.C. "Come to think of it, why don't I give you my num—"

Brady shut the door. "I don't suppose you have a hacksaw?" he asked, his hands on his hips as he studied the tree. The cat came over and delicately sniffed the trunk. "We're going to have to cut this down by—"

He broke off, went rigid when she pressed against his side. Stretching up, she kissed his cheek. "Thank you for getting my tree inside."

"I didn't do anything," he said, stepping back when what he really wanted was to pull her closer.

"You called your brother when it must've been hard for you to ask for help."

J.C. flinched, her hand going to her side.

"What is it?" he asked. "Are you sick?"

"No, I...I think I felt the baby move."

"You're not sure?"

"I'm new at this, remember? Dr. Owens said I'd know what it was like when I felt it, whatever that's supposed to —" She gasped, her face filled with wonder. "That had to be it."

Brady watched her stomach, as if he could somehow get a glimpse of movement through her clothes and skin. "Does it hurt?"

"No, it's...weird. Here." Shifting so they were toe to toe, she took his hand and slid it under her snug top.

His fingers grazed her warm skin and he clenched his fist. "J.C., I—"

"Don't you want to feel it, too?"

Forcing his fingers to uncurl, he let her guide his hand to her side. Her skin was incredibly soft and he couldn't stop himself from cupping the roundness of her stomach, his thumb by her belly button, his fingertips brushing her hip bone. They were so close, he breathed in the fresh scent of her hair. Had the torture of her breasts brushing against his chest with every small move she made.

He cleared his throat. "I don't feel anything."

"That's because he hasn't moved yet." Another second passed. And another. "There! Did you feel it?"

He shook his head. "What's it like?"

"The first few times, it felt as if there were butterflies in my stomach— literally." Making a sound somewhere between a laugh and a cry, she raised her head, bringing their faces to within inches of each other. Her smile faded.

"Butterflies, huh?"

"Uh...yes...It was this...sort of fluttering," she whispered, staring at his mouth. "But now it's more of a...rolling sensation. Sort of...how you feel when you're falling..."

She lifted her hand to his cheek. Her lush breasts pressed against him, her breath washed over his lips.

And then she kissed him.

She kept the kiss delicate. Light. But in that instant, with her mouth supple and warm against his, her lips tasting of salt and a sweetness that was uniquely her, his senses spun.

Yeah. He knew all about falling.

He also knew how much it hurt when you hit the ground.

She eased back. Her smile was so purely Jane—simple

and honest and bright enough to chase away nightmares—it took all his waning willpower not to yank her to him.

"In case you were wondering," she said as she adjusted her shirt to cover her stomach again, "that was one of those happy kisses."

He frowned. Happy what? And then he remembered. That day when she'd kissed him in his mom's kitchen, she'd claimed she'd only done it because she was happy.

"Good thing I was here," he said.

"It was awfully convenient. Although if I'd felt the baby move a few minutes earlier Matt would've still been here so..."

"You would've still kissed me."

She laughed. "Well, you would've had a fifty-fifty chance."

He set his hands on her waist and pulled her forward. Sliding his arms around her, he held her to him, pressing his palms against the flat of her back.

"You would've kissed me." His gaze followed the movement of her throat as she swallowed, then shifted back to her eyes. "Say it," he demanded in a soft undertone.

She gripped his forearms, her short nails digging into his skin. "I would've kissed you."

He dipped his head in acknowledgment and dropped his arms. "I'll check in the garage for that hacksaw," he said. And maybe, if he helped her put up her tree, she'd be so happy she'd kiss him again.

THIS IS MY FAVORITE PART," J.C. said late the next night as they watched the DVD of *It's A Wonderful Life.*

"You said that before."

Tossing popcorn into her mouth, she didn't even bother glancing at Brady.

Not when Mary and George were about to kiss for the first time. And, okay, she may have said her favorite part was the scene after the school dance when Mary and George walk home, but this was her absolute favorite scene.

"You're not going to cry again, are you?" Brady asked.

On the screen, George stormed out and Mary smashed the record of their song into pieces.

"I haven't cried yet," J.C. said. She may have welled up a few times, but what did he expect when she was watching the most fabulous movie ever? "But if tears bother you, I should warn you that I bawl at the end for a solid five minutes."

"Great," he muttered, slouching down even farther on the opposite end of her couch, staring at the brightly lit Christmas tree across the room.

Setting the popcorn bowl aside, she picked up her water glass and took a sip. "Are you all right?"

He sent her an unreadable look. "Fine."

"Are you sure? You seem...distracted." He lifted one shoulder in a shrug.

She huffed out a breath, trying to figure out why he was acting like his old brooding, angry self. It was as if he didn't want to be there—although when they'd talked at the Diamond Dust's gift shop earlier, he was the one who'd asked if he could stop by. She couldn't refuse him, not after last night when he'd helped put up her tree and then had kissed her so tenderly before he left.

And for once, she hadn't felt guilty for wanting to spend time with her sister's ex. Or worried about telling Liz she'd made a mistake when she'd promised to stay away from Brady.

She paused the movie. "We don't have to watch—"

"I said I'm fine."

She crossed her arms at his clipped tone. "Yes. That's obvious."

"I just..." He ran his palms up and down his jeans. "I really want a drink."

"Oh." She sipped more water, but it did little to ease the dryness in her throat. After pulling the hem of her shorts down, she tucked her legs underneath her. "Are you going to have one?"

"If I could stop at one drink, it wouldn't be a problem now, would it?"

"No, I suppose not."

When she remained silent, he sat up. "Aren't you going to tell me not to drink?"

"Is that why you're here?" she asked, proud of how calm she sounded, how rational. "So I can stop you from drinking?"

"You don't get it," he burst out. "I don't need you to babysit me so I won't drink. I want a drink because... because, maybe if I get drunk," he continued, the low rumble of his voice scraping along her nerve endings, "I can forget how much I want you. Even for a little while."

She caught her breath. "I...I don't..."

"It's killing me to sit here and not touch you," he admitted raggedly, his hands fisted on his thighs.

It all made sense now. How Brady had barely looked her way all evening.

Why he'd sat as far away on the small sofa as possible.

She knew what was at risk. Her family wouldn't understand. Wouldn't approve. And her sister? If J.C. followed her heart, if she chose Brady, she may never be able to salvage her relationship with Liz.

Her heart pounding, she unfolded her legs and knelt on the cushion, facing him. He watched her warily, his jaw taut. Swallowing back her trepidation, she said the words that had the power to change everything between them.

"Touch me, Brady."

For a moment, he didn't move. Other than the rapid rise and fall of his chest, it was as if he were made of stone. Then he groaned and pulled her forward for a voracious kiss. She tumbled, catching herself against his shoulders, and still he didn't release her mouth. His kiss was hard. Hungry.

Almost punishing.

When he lifted his head, they were both breathing hard. He kissed her jaw up her cheek to her temple and back down again. His fingers kneaded her neck, his other hand squeezing her outer thigh. He captured a fistful of her hair and tugged her head back. He pressed his lips against the hollow of her throat before scraping his teeth across her collarbone.

She whimpered and clutched his shoulders, her nails digging into his skin. He kissed his way back up her throat to her mouth again, his tongue sweeping inside to touch hers.

He straightened and combed both hands through her hair, his touch incredibly gentle. "Where's that purple top?" he asked.

"What?"

"The tank top you wore with these shorts before."

"I'm wearing it."

He stared at her black sweatshirt so intently she half expected it to burst into flames. "Under that shirt?"

She nodded and he lowered his hands to the hem of her shirt. She lifted her arms as he pulled the fleece up, his knuckles grazing the sensitive skin on the inside of her arms as he pulled it over her head and let it drop.

She glanced down. The ribbed tank top clung to each curve, hugging the mound of her belly and her breasts, her hard nipples jutting out. She held her breath as he edged closer, his leg bumping her knees. He brushed his fingertips over the fabric covering the upper slope of her breasts and she exhaled softly.

"I really like this shirt," he said solemnly, dragging his fingernail down between her breasts and back up. His cupped her breasts in his hands, his thumbs brushing back and forth over her nipples.

"I'll..." But the promise to wear it more often died on her lips when he bent his head and his open mouth was over her breast. The heat of his breath washed over her, causing her nipple to tighten even more, if that was possible. His tongue rasped against the cloth and she jerked, her hands clutching his thigh.

He raised his head, got to his feet and held his hand out.

Though her nerves battled with her anticipation, she didn't hesitate.

Linking her fingers through his, she stood and led him to her bedroom.

She let go of him to cross the room and turn on the lamp on her nightstand. Brady came up behind her. Wrapping an arm around her waist, he pulled her to him, his arousal pressing against her back. Reality about what they were about to do, how it was going to change everything—again —crashed over her and she stiffened.

"I won't hurt you, Jane," Brady said, brushing her hair aside and kissing her neck.

He would. Of course he would. Eventually. Because she

wasn't who he really wanted. But he did want her tonight, right now. And that would be enough.

She forced herself to relax against him and felt his own tension ease, as well. He turned her around and kissed her deeply as he backed her toward the bed, helping her onto the mattress. Straightening, he quickly toed off his shoes and stripped his shirt over his head.

Her blood quickened. He was all lean muscles and golden skin, his mouth unsmiling, his eyes glittering. He was gorgeous. And as always, she was plain Jane Cleo.

But he didn't look at her as if she were plain, but rather as if she were... special.

Beautiful.

He climbed onto the bed and lay down on his side next to her. He dipped his head for a kiss and she sighed. No more second-guessing. No more insecurities.

She ran her hands over him. Over his broad shoulders, down his arms and back up again, then trailed her fingertips down his back to the waistband of his jeans. He was so warm. His skin smooth, his muscles flexing under her hands.

Then his kiss became more urgent.

In one quick motion, he sat up, pulling her up with him. He grabbed the bottom of her tank top and peeled it off.

"You're beautiful," he said huskily. Reverently.

Warmth filled her, grew to searing heat when he eased her back again, bent his head and sucked one nipple into his mouth. She whimpered, then bit down hard on her lower lip. Her hands curled around her bedspread. With each tug and pull on her breast, desire built inside her. He moved to her other breast, giving it the same attention until she squirmed.

He kissed his way down to the slope of her stomach, his

hands on either side as if holding a precious—albeit large—egg.

"Hello, baby," he murmured.

J.C. felt the baby move as if he couldn't help but respond to Brady's deep voice.

Brady rubbed the sides of her stomach a moment longer, placed a kiss just under her belly button and then slid his hands to the waistband of her shorts.

J.C. lifted her hips and he tugged the material, along with her underwear, down her legs.

It hurt to breathe as he stared down at her. She squeezed her eyes shut. As much as she wanted to watch him undress, as much as she wanted to see him— every part of him—she couldn't. Her stomach turned with nerves as she waited for him to enter her. What if the unsatisfying sex last time hadn't been Brady's fault? What if she'd somehow messed up? Moved the wrong way or—

Her eyes snapped open as his hand smoothed up her inner thigh. He was lying on his side next to her, still wearing his jeans. "Wha-what are you doing?" she asked.

"Touching you."

"Why?"

"Because you're soft." He nudged her legs farther apart with his hand then pressed his nose to the side of her neck and inhaled deeply. "Because you smell good." His hand trailed along the crease of her thigh up to her hip bone, then back and forth over her lower stomach. Her pelvis contracted. "Because I want to make you wet for me."

Heat suffused her at his words, said in such a dark, seductive tone. "I..." Her breath whooshed out when he brushed his fingertips over the tight curls between her legs. Back and forth. Back and forth. She lifted her hips but he didn't deepen those featherlight touches like she wanted. "I think I'm already there so if you want to…"

"I do want to," he said with such a wicked smile, she couldn't help but smile in return.

Until he slid his hand down. It was like an electric shock, feeling his hard, work-roughened hand on her most intimate place. She gripped his wrist, tried to pull his hand away, but he didn't budge.

"What's wrong?" he asked, looking so confused and sexy, for a moment she couldn't remember why she'd stopped him.

"Nothing," she managed to squeak out, her voice about three octaves higher than usual. "I…You don't have to…I've never done this before," she said, forcing the words out. "This…part…I mean…"

"J.C.," he asked slowly, "were you a virgin the night we—"

"No! No, there were…two other guys—"

His head snapped back. "Two?"

"Three…since we should count you," she added faintly.

For several long moments, Brady just watched her. Her body started to cool and all the reasons why they shouldn't be doing this seeped back into her brain.

Until he sat up. Keeping his hand above her center, with his other hand he brushed her hair away from her face. Then he kissed her. Their lips clung for one heartbeat. Then two. When he lifted his head, he traced the arch of her eyebrow, the slope of her nose with one finger. Her resistance and her doubts melted away.

"I want to touch you," he said quietly, his hand now in her hair massaging her scalp. Before she could point out that he was touching her, he continued, "I want to touch you like no other man has touched you. Make you feel things no other man has made you feel."

He was. He did. But she couldn't say that out loud. He rubbed large circles over her stomach as he swirled his tongue around her nipple. When he bit her nipple lightly, her hips rose off the bed.

Then his hand on her stomach moved between her legs. At his slow, sure strokes, her pleasure built, almost impossible to bear. Sweat coated her skin which suddenly felt too tight. Sensitive to his touch. Her need to find relief from his talented hands and tongue grew until her hips pumped up and down. Brady once again sucked on her breast, his teeth scraping the sensitive bud the same time he slipped a finger inside her.

She teetered on the edge, but then she looked down at the sight of his head at her breast and she fell. Her back arched off the mattress and her vision blurred as her orgasm flowed through her, a rush of pleasure followed by smaller tingles of electricity. Tears stung her eyes.

And she knew that her worst fear had come true after all.

She was one hundred percent, totally and unequivocally in love with Brady Sheppard.

14

HIS BODY ACHING, SCREAMING FOR RELEASE, BRADY raised his head and watched J.C. come down from her orgasm. Her eyes were closed, her full lips parted, her heavy breasts rising and falling as she panted softly, a sheen of sweat coating her skin.

At that moment, she was the most beautiful thing he'd ever seen.

As if of its own accord, his hand moved back up to her belly. He couldn't seem to stop touching her there, where she carried their child. Couldn't get past how...hard...her stomach was. He could only imagine what she'd look like next month. Or four months from now. How much more would her body grow and change?

And did it even matter if he wasn't sure he'd be around to see it?

He rubbed her stomach, his body growing harder as she wiggled and sighed. Her eyes slowly opened. She skimmed her hand over his shoulder and down his bicep, her touch hesitant. Shy, almost.

Which made sense, considering her sexual history.

Obviously neither of the two guys she'd slept with had taken the time to give her pleasure. Idiots.

And he was idiot number three for not only neglecting J.C.'s satisfaction the first time they'd made love, but by not even remembering being with her and calling out her sister's name. Make that king of the idiots.

And yet, by some miracle, she hadn't turned him away tonight. Instead, she'd trusted him with her body.

I won't hurt you, Jane, he'd promised.

J.C. stared at him, or rather the bulge in his pants. She reached out, her hand a few inches above his arousal. Behind his zipper, his body twitched.

"Don't stop," he said in a husky whisper when she took her hand away without touching him.

"I'm not stopping," she said. "At least not until I've had my fill of you."

J.C. rose onto her elbow, the movement causing her breasts to sway. He lightly pinched one hard, dusky tip and she moaned. He lifted his head to take her into his mouth again but she moved back, out of reach.

"Let me," she said, nudging his shoulders until he reclined on the bed once again.

He held his breath as she laid her hand against his cheek. She stroked the side of his neck, then his shoulder and down his arm. Outlining the edges of his USMC eagle tattoo with her fingertip, her frown thoughtful. He expected her to ask him about it, why he got it, what it meant. Instead, she smoothed her hand back up to his shoulder and down his chest. Under her soft, seeking touch, his heart skipped a beat before finding a steady rhythm that quickened as her fingers traveled down to his belly button.

He inhaled sharply, his stomach muscles contracting. With as much concentration as an explosive ordnance disposal unit defusing a bomb, her other hand went to the waistband of his jeans. Both his lungs and his groin tightened almost to the point of pain. But he forced himself not to move. To wait and see what she'd do next.

"Could you take your pants off?" she asked in a rush.

He thought she'd never ask. He undid his jeans, shimmied them and his boxers down his legs and kicked them off before sitting back up.

She blinked. "Wow. That must be some sort of land speed record."

"I aim to please," he managed. Not an easy feat when J.C. stared at his body as if he were one of her candies.

"So do I," she murmured. His mouth went dry.

J.C. rose to her knees. Lying flat on his back, he couldn't watch her like he wanted so he grabbed a pillow, folded it in half and shoved it under his head, the scent of her shampoo surrounding him.

As she sat back on her heels beside him, she looked confused, as if she had no clue what to do. He almost took her hand and placed it on a part of him where he'd love for her to start. And finish. And spend any amount of time and attention on.

She leaned forward and softly kissed his scarred knee.

He jerked, his hands fisting into her bedcovers.

She lifted her head and turned to him, her hair falling to the side, the ends tickling his lower thigh. "Does it hurt?"

"No."

But he couldn't stop himself from tensing when she laid her right hand above his knee. Blindly staring up at the ceiling, a lump formed in his throat as she traced each and every one of his scars, her touch as gentle, as soothing as a summer breeze. No one had touched his knee in a nonprofessional way since the attack. He couldn't remember anyone ever touching it, touching any part of him with as much compassion and tenderness as J.C. did now.

When she was done with his scar, she caressed his thigh. Up and down, from his knee, along his outer thigh to his hip bone and back again. Each time she seemed to get more confident. And a lot bolder as she worked her way toward his inner thigh, stopping shy of his erection. Grinding his teeth, he raised his head to look down at her only to find her watching him.

As soon as his eyes met hers, she wrapped her hand around him. His vision blurred. Then she started stroking him leisurely. He about went over the edge. He hissed out a breath and fought for control. But he couldn't take his eyes off her, the sight of her pale, small hands on him and the way she watched him carefully, her eyes bright, as if there were nothing she'd rather do than touch him, explore his body.

She was...amazing. Her generosity and warmth. Her sensuality. Her beauty—both inside and out. And she wanted to be with him. Even after all of his mistakes, she still wanted him. She humbled him.

She scared the hell out of him.

He lost the ability to think at all when J.C. did some sort of gentle twisting motion that felt so damned good that he groaned.

And she smiled.

That did it.

He jackknifed up, had a glimpse of her startled expression right before he took her mouth in a hungry kiss. Clutching his biceps, she kissed him back as he lowered her to the mattress and followed her down, supporting his weight on his elbows.

Breaking the kiss, he shifted to the side, picked up his

jeans and shook them until his wallet fell out of the pocket. He flipped it open and took out a condom.

"I'd say it's a little late for that," J.C. said, the lightness of her tone unable to completely cover her underlying nerves.

He opened the packet and covered himself. "It's never too late to be safe."

Besides, though he'd gotten a clean bill of health when he'd had a physical before starting physical therapy, he didn't want to take any chances with J.C.

He settled himself between her thighs, his arms shaking with the effort to hold himself back.

"Are you sure this is okay?" he forced himself to ask. "For the baby, I mean."

"Dr. Owens said it's safe."

She no sooner got the last word out when Brady lifted her hips and slid inside her. Her body tensed, her expression unsure. He withdrew slightly and didn't move. It took every ounce of self-control not to take what he needed so badly from her.

But he couldn't find any of those things at J.C.'s expense. Not again. Not when he was finding his way to who he was. He kissed her, careful to keep his weight off both the baby and his bad knee.

He continued to kiss her until some of the stiffness left her. When she combed her fingers through his hair, he rolled his hips, filling her. She gasped into his mouth and he smiled against her lips before pulling back and repeating the motion. Again. And again until the tension built to a fever pitch. Her hands pulled at his hair, her body soft and pliant under his. But still, he could feel her holding back from him.

He lifted his head but her eyes remained closed, her hands now at his hips. "Jane." Her eyes popped open, her nails digging into his skin. "It's just you and me here," he continued hoarsely, increasing his tempo as he moved in and out of her body. "No one else I want here. Only you, Janie."

Reaching between them, with the pad of his thumb he rubbed the hard nub at her center. Her mouth opened and her eyes grew cloudy. Her body squeezed around him. She tipped her head back but kept her eyes on his as she came, her body pulsing around him. Pushing him to follow.

He gripped her under her thighs and plowed into her. Again. And again.

His concern for the baby, his vow not to hurt J.C. keeping his control in check.

Keeping him from taking her as hard, as fast, as he wanted.

His climax built.

"No," he ground out when J.C.'s eyes began to close. "Watch me, Jane. Watch what you do to me."

Her eyes, so dark they seemed bottomless, locked on his. With a guttural groan, he threw his head back and emptied himself.

J.C. ROLLED OVER and reached for Brady but found his side of the bed empty. The sheets cold. Shoving her hair out of her face, she glanced at the glowing numbers of the digital clock on her nightstand. Two thirty-two. Flopping onto her back again, she flung her arm across her eyes. After she and Brady had made love, he'd pulled the comforter over them both and she'd immediately fallen asleep in his arms.

Hoping he'd still be there in the morning.

She tossed off her covers. Since she was up, she may as well get a glass of water, maybe use the bathroom. Swinging her feet over the edge of the bed, she sat up and flipped on the light. "You okay?"

She yelped and almost fell off the bed. She spun around to find Brady, wearing only his jeans, sitting on the floor, his back against her closet, one leg bent, his injured leg out straight.

"Don't scare me like that!" Grabbing the comforter, she wrapped it around herself.

"Sorry."

She frowned. Something was wrong. And it wasn't just that he sat on her floor in the middle of the night. His expression was tight. His hands clenched.

Holding the end of the comforter so she didn't trip, she walked over and sat next to him. "What are you doing on the floor?"

"I couldn't stay." His head fell back against her closet door with a thump. "But I couldn't leave, either."

"I'm sorry, I don't understand."

"I should go," he said. "But I don't want to."

She wouldn't read more into any of this—what he said or how he acted or how he'd looked at her when they'd made love. She was going to take it one day, one minute at a time.

And she wouldn't get her hopes up or start wishing for things that weren't going to happen. Like him loving her back.

"I'm glad you stayed," she said. "But I think you'll be more comfortable in the bed."

"I can't."

"Sure you can. It's plenty big enough for two."

"No. I mean, I really can't. I have these...dreams." He

faced forward and wiped an unsteady hand down his face. "Nightmares. And sometimes I get...sometimes it's like I'm... back in Afghanistan and I...I'll throw a punch or..." He shook his head, and his voice dropped so low she had to strain to hear him. "I don't want to hurt you. Or the baby."

Oh, God. Unable to catch her breath, not strong enough to face the bleakness in his eyes, she curled her knees up to her chest and stared at the floor.

As much as it shamed her, as big as her feelings for Brady were, she wanted to run. She had no idea—absolutely no clue—how to help Brady, what to say or do.

"These dreams..." She cleared her throat. "Are your dreams like the flashbacks?" The flashbacks he never confirmed nor denied having.

Sometimes I think about what happened back there.

He remained silent. She didn't press. She waited, hoping he'd open up to her. Time passed and her toes got cold so she tucked the comforter around them.

"We were on patrol," Brady finally said, speaking in a slow monotone as if unaware she was even there. "Jonesy was driving, Thad was riding shotgun, and me and Van were in the back. One minute Van was telling us about when he'd accidentally hired a male stripper to show up at his brother's bachelor party, and the next...I was coming to on the side of the road. We'd all been laughing and then..." He swallowed. "The explosion was so loud, after it was as if I was listening to everything through a filter. But I could still hear Van yelling for help. Jonesy's cries of pain."

She shivered. God, she couldn't even imagine what he'd gone through. How close he'd come to dying. "What about your other friend?"

"Dead," he said flatly, his lips a thin line. "He had a wife and two little kids and now..." He blew out a heavy breath and lowered his head into his hands. "It should've been me."

"Don't say that." She scrambled onto her knees in front of him, cupping his face in her hands and raising it so he looked at her. "What happened was horrible for you all but—"

"He should've lived," he said, bracketing her wrists with his hands. "He had people to live for."

J.C.'s eyes stung but she wouldn't cry. Not when Brady sat there dry-eyed, thinking he had nothing to live for.

"Have you considered talking to someone about this?" she asked. "A psychologist or—"

"No."

Shaken and humbled he'd trusted her with this, she pressed her forehead against his. "I'm glad you told me. But I think," she said carefully, not wanting to say the wrong thing, "you should consider getting professional help."

He exhaled shakily, his breath washing over her face. "I know you're trying to help—"

"I am. And I won't push you, I swear, but could you at least think about it?"

"Yeah," he said gruffly. "Okay."

"Thank you," she said. Then she pressed a kiss against his mouth. As she stood, she let the comforter slide off her shoulders to pool at her feet. "Come on. Let's go back to bed."

After a moment's hesitation, he accepted the hand she held out and let her help him get to his feet.

As much as she wanted to, she couldn't heal him. But she could help him get through tonight.

BRADY CARRIED HIS SHOES as he soundlessly made his way to the bedroom door. He glanced back at J.C. She was still asleep, the covers pulled up to her chin, her lips were parted, her hair a mass of wild curls.

He wanted more than anything to slip back into bed with her. To be here when she woke up so they could make love again.

He snuck out of the room. Sitting on the sofa, he put his shoes on, grabbed his jacket from the chair where he'd tossed it last night and stepped out into the cold. His leg had stiffened during the night and descending the stairs became an awkward and painful process. But less awkward than it would've been if J.C. had woken up while he was still there.

He couldn't face her. Not now. He needed time to sort things out. Like why he'd told her about the nightmares when he'd never told anyone else. Why he'd enjoyed holding her so much as she slept.

A black Lexus pulled into the driveway as Brady reached the bottom step. Goosebumps appeared on his arms as the driver got out.

Stopping below him, Liz glanced from him to J.C.'s apartment and back at him again.

As if she had any right to try to make him feel guilty.

"You slept with her? Again?" Liz asked, crossing her arms over her red jacket.

He moved to the left but she blocked his way. Her breath turned to a cloud before disappearing. "What's between me and Jane is none of your concern," he said.

"That's where you're wrong. Anything having to do with my family is my concern. Especially when someone is using my sister to get to me."

"Get to you? Why the hell would I do that?"

"To hurt me for what I did to you or...or maybe you think if you make me jealous, I'll come back to you."

"I'm not into revenge," he snarled. "And what makes you think I'd ever want you back?"

Liz tucked her hair behind her ear, her hand trembling. "From what I understand, you've made it clear you want nothing to do with the baby. Why else are you with J.C. if not to hurt me?"

"You act as if she has no redeeming qualities other than having you as a sibling."

Liz blushed, rubbed her gloves hands together. "J.C. is plenty special on her own but I'm not blind to her faults. She's a dreamer, unreliable and can't stick with one project, job or college for more than three months at a time."

"She's also sweet and funny and sexy..." Brady shook his head to clear his thoughts.

Liz's took a step back as if she'd been slapped. "Oh, my God," she breathed. "You're in love with her."

The back of his neck tingled, like it used to in Afghanistan before a firefight broke out. As it did moments before the bomb exploded. "I'm not in love with Jane Cleo," he growled, noticing the relief in Liz's eyes.

Loving one Montgomery sister had almost killed him. And he never made the same mistake twice.

"All the more reason to stay away from her," Liz said emphatically, the breeze lifting her hair. "Before she gets hurt. I mean it, Brady. Leave her be."

Damn it, he knew that. "You gave up any say into how I live my life when you wrote me that Dear John letter."

"This isn't about you and me," she said unsteadily.

"It's only ever been about us," he said, his voice rising. "I loved you, I wanted to marry you. We'd planned our life together and then suddenly you met someone new and it's over?"

Her mouth trembled. "It wasn't like that. With Carter, I mean. I never...We didn't..."

"You didn't what?"

"I never cheated on you."

"Is that supposed to make it all right?" he asked, taking that last step, forcing her to back up. She bumped into J.C.'s car. He kept walking until he stood mere inches from her. "How long after you sent that letter did it take the two of you to get together?"

Her eyes welled with tears. "Brady, please don't..."

A car drove by but both Brady and Liz ignored it. "I deserve to know," he said, his stomach in knots. He needed to know. "How long? A week? A month?"

She wiped her fingers over her cheeks, brushing away the tears. "One."

"One week?"

She stared at the ground. "One day," she said faintly.

His blood drummed in his ears. "So while I was over seven thousand miles away, thinking you and I were still engaged, thinking you still loved me, you were back here screwing another guy?"

She blanched. "I never meant for it to happen. And I'm sorry I hurt you, Brady, but people change. Feelings change. You need to accept it and move on."

Accept it? She'd lied to him. Used him. And the best she could do was toss him an *I'm sorry?* And now she wanted him to move on—just not with her sister.

To hell with her.

"Just because it was that easy for you doesn't mean that's how it works for everyone." He started pacing, the breeze doing nothing to calm his anger. "You have everything you've always wanted." He spun to face her and she shrank back against the car. "Everything you were supposed to have with me. Instead, I'm five months away from becoming a father to a baby I don't want with a woman I'll never be able to love because she's not you!"

Behind him, he heard a sound—as if someone had just been punched in the stomach. Brady's scalp tingled, his skin grew clammy. He turned to find J.C. in the same pajamas she'd had on last night, standing on the next to last step, her feet bare, her eyes huge. With one hand she gripped the railing, with the other she held her stomach protectively.

His panic spiked. He sensed he was close to losing something important—something he might not be able to get back.

He didn't move.

Now, he wouldn't have to worry about facing her again. Trying to keep his distance. About the feelings he had for her he couldn't explain. Things between them could end here, now, before they became even more complicated.

Before he had to admit to himself that what he'd just said had been nothing but a lie.

15

TODAY WAS SUNDAY, J.C. THOUGHT STUPIDLY AS SHE stood there, the wind blowing her hair in her face, causing her eyes to tear. How could she forget it was Sunday. And that on Sunday mornings when Liz didn't work the night before, she took Grandma Rose to church.

"J.C., let's go inside where it's warm," Liz said as she walked toward her.

J.C. didn't so much as glance Brady's way. She couldn't. If she looked at him now, she'd never get through the next few minutes without breaking down.

Liz climbed up to stand next to her. "Oh, honey, you don't even have any shoes on."

"I didn't think I'd need them," she said absently.

Liz put her arm around J.C.'s shoulder, either ignoring or not noticing how J.C. stiffened. "Come on. We'll go in, ask Grandma to make some of her blueberry pancakes. You'll feel better after you have something to eat."

J.C. blinked. "Yes, I'm sure some pancakes will make this all better.

"At least you'll be out of the cold and away from..."

Away from Brady.

Brady, who hadn't moved since he noticed her.

Brady, who didn't want the baby. Who still loved Liz.

A sob rose in the back of her throat and she covered her mouth to hide the sound.

"None of that," Liz admonished gently. "You don't want him to see you cry, do you?"

Why not? He'd already seen her at her absolute worst and best. She was about to tell Liz exactly that when she saw the pity in her sister's eyes. Any small pieces of her pride that'd survived Brady's impassioned speech died.

She shrugged Liz's arm off. "You go ahead, I'd like a few minutes alone with Brady."

"I don't think that's a good idea," Liz said.

J.C. stared hard at her sister. "I didn't ask your opinion. Or your permission."

Liz was taken aback. "If that's what you want..."

"It is."

"All right. But remember, I'm right inside if you need me."

"I won't," J.C. said with such conviction, she almost believed it herself. "I can handle this on my own."

Looking far more hurt than J.C. thought she had a right to, Liz rounded

J.C.'s car and walked over to their grandmother's house. J.C. finally turned to Brady. As she'd suspected, his hooded gaze was on her, his hands in his front pockets, his hair still mussed from her bed. From her fingers.

Brady stepped toward her, stopping when she backed up a step.

"Jane..." he said in his deep voice.

"Is this where you tell me last night was a mistake?"

"It was."

202

"So it meant nothing to you? Or maybe you're too big of a coward to admit it did mean something."

"I'm sorry."

"Don't," she warned, unable to keep her voice from shaking. "Don't you dare patronize me by giving me some trite apology."

He glanced down at the ground. "It's the best I can do."

Her toes were numb, her legs shaking from the cold. "No. It's all you're willing to do." The baby moved, strengthening J.C.'s resolve not to let him see how much he'd hurt her. "I feel sorry for you."

His posture grew rigid. "Don't bother."

"Why not? Isn't that what you want, what this is all about? Poor Brady Sheppard lost his one true love and his plans for the future. Welcome to the real world, Brady, where people get their hearts broken every day. Where plans fall through, jobs are lost and loved ones pass away. The world where we don't always get what we want, but most people make the most of what they do have."

"I'm trying to," he said with a definite edge to his voice as he stepped onto the stair below her, bringing them eye-to-eye. "Once my knee heals more—"

"You'll what, be whole again? Be able to act like a human, like someone who stands up and brushes himself off when he falls? Your leg is an excuse, like your drinking."

His expression darkened and he walked away, his gait uneven.

"Oh, no, you don't," J.C. muttered. Careful of the damp stairs, she didn't start jogging until she stepped onto the cold, rough cement of the driveway. She rounded the garage and sped past him to stand in front of the driver's door of his truck.

His keys jingled in his hand. "Move," he ordered.

She swallowed. "Remember when I told you I've never seen anything through because it's easier to quit when things get tough?" He inclined his head. "Well, that's only part of it." She tried to slow her breathing, to get her heart rate back to where it belonged. "The truth is, if I quit, then I can't fail." And if she never failed, that was almost as good as always succeeding.

Like Liz did.

"But I've realized," she continued, pulling the sleeves of her sweatshirt down to cover her cold hands, "that by giving up so I don't fail, there's also no chance I'll ever succeed. And if succeeding means taking risks and putting myself out there, putting my pride on the line, then that's what I'll do."

She'd do it because, right now, success was more than getting what she wanted. It was proving to herself she had the courage to try.

"Brady, I..." She took a moment to regain her composure. "I'm in love with you."

He flinched. "No. You aren't."

"You don't have to love me back," she told him quietly. "You don't even have to like the fact that I'm in love with you. But don't you ever tell me what is or isn't in my heart."

He held his head with both hands, as if to stop it from exploding. "Damn it, Jane. Don't make this harder than it has to be."

"How could I? You're the one who made love to me last night then couldn't slip out of my bed fast enough this morning. You're choosing to hold on to Liz, to what you had. Wishing for things to be different, for a life you could've had if Liz hadn't fallen in love with Carter. If you hadn't been injured. If you hadn't slept with me and gotten me pregnant."

Brady stared straight ahead, not showing even the tiniest flicker of emotion, of reaction to her words.

Tears stung the backs of her eyes. "I can't tell you what your life would've been like. But I can tell you what you could've had. Me. And our son. You could've had a home filled with laughter and love and hope. But you'd rather wallow in self-pity."

He glanced at her, took in the tears running freely down her cheeks. "Is that all?" he asked tightly, a muscle jumping in his jaw.

She used her sleeve to dry her face. "One last thing. If you ever start thinking you'd like to be a part of our lives after all—don't bother. My son and I will be fine without you. We don't need you." She'd make sure her baby had all the love and support she could give him. Hopefully it would be enough to make up for his father's abandonment. "But I wonder, Brady," she asked softly, "how do you think you'll be without us?"

———

LIZ WAS ADDING FROZEN blueberries to her grandma's pancake batter when J.C. finally walked into the kitchen. Her relief at seeing her sister died quickly once she noticed J.C.'s tear-streaked face, red nose and chattering teeth.

"You poor dear," Grandma Rose said, wrapping her arm around J.C.'s middle and leading her to the table. "Sit down while I fetch a blanket."

"How about getting a pair of socks, too, Grandma?" Liz asked. Grandma Rose waved her hand to indicate she'd heard as she hurried out of the room.

"Here," Liz said, setting a tea cup in front of J.C. "Don't

worry," she added when J.C. just stared at it, "it's decaf. And I added extra honey."

J.C. picked up the cup, sloshing tea over the side. Liz was about to help her when J.C. raised the cup and took a sip.

Grandma Rose came back into the kitchen carrying two blankets and a pair of fuzzy slipper-socks. "We'll have you warm again in no time," Rose said, wrapping a fleece blanket around J.C.'s shoulders while Liz pulled the socks over her cold feet. The second blanket they laid across her lap.

And that whole time, J.C. didn't move. She didn't even blink. Liz and her grandmother exchanged worried glances.

"Hey," Liz said, covering J.C.'s cold hand where it rested on the table. "Are you all right?"

"Fine." She pulled her hand away and put it on her lap. "And you'll no doubt be happy to know that Brady's gone. Once again, you get exactly what you wanted."

Liz sat back. "Excuse me?"

"You didn't want him in my life and now he's not."

"He never should've been there in the first place," Liz pointed out. "And as I remember, you promised me you wouldn't see him anymore." She lowered her voice so Grandma Rose couldn't hear. "And yet, there he was, sneaking out of your apartment not twenty minutes ago."

And the sight of Brady leaving her sister's place after having obviously spent the night had been enough to knock the air out of her lungs.

J.C. pulled the blanket tighter around her shoulders. "The only reason I agreed to that promise was because I was willing to do anything to get you to forgive me. But you already knew that, didn't you?"

Liz flushed hot, then cold. "Don't be ridiculous."

"And then you added in that story about you and Carter—"

"What about Liz and Carter?" Rose asked, setting a plate of pancakes in the middle of the table.

"Nothing," Liz said, her cheeks burning. She sent J.C. a loaded look, one that clearly said, "Keep your mouth shut."

"Carter thinks Liz is still in love with Brady," J.C. said with more than a hint of venom in her voice. "Liz denies it, but either she's protesting too much or not enough, because Carter thinks they need to attend marriage counseling."

"Is that true, Elizabeth?" Rose asked.

"Carter and I are fine," she snapped, glaring at J.C. "And we'll be even better now that Brady Sheppard is out of the picture."

J.C. shook her head. "You'd like to believe that, wouldn't you? You'd like to pretend that Brady is at the root of all your problems."

Liz stabbed a pancake and set it on her plate. "Pretend? Brady *is* at the root of my problems and he has been ever since he crashed my wedding."

"So rude," Rose said, sitting opposite J.C. "You should've let your father have him escorted off the premises."

"I didn't want a scene," she insisted, pouring syrup over her pancakes though her appetite was quickly disappearing.

"You really don't see what you're doing, do you?" J.C. asked. "The reason Brady is a problem for you and Carter at all is because of you. You put him between you and your husband because you haven't let Brady go yet."

Liz set her fork down so no one would notice her hands trembling. "That's not true. Just because I don't want my sister and my ex-fiancé to be together doesn't mean I'm holding on to Brady."

"No." J.C. stood and tossed the blanket over the back of

her chair. "It means you can't stand the idea of Brady moving on. Of him wanting to be with someone besides you."

"But he doesn't want to be with anyone else, does he?" she snapped, immediately wishing she could take her words back when she saw J.C.'s stunned expression. The hurt in her eyes.

"You're right," J.C. said faintly, her face white. "I'll always be second choice to him." She rubbed at her temples. "Want to know the worst part? Up until this morning, that would've been enough for me."

Liz's chest burned. "J.C., I didn't mean—"

"Not now, okay? I...I can't handle much more this morning and I..." She brought her hand to her mouth, her fingers trembling. "I'm not feeling very well."

"Let me get you some ginger ale," Rose said, going around the table to the refrigerator.

J.C. was already backing out of the room. "No. Thank you. It's just a headache. I'll lie down until it goes away."

A moment later, they heard the front door close. Liz went to the sink and watched J.C. make her way up to her apartment, her steps slow, her shoulders shaking.

"She's crying," Liz said, pressing her fingers against her eyes. "I didn't mean to make her cry." She sighed and dropped her hands. "How did everything get so messed up?"

Rose set the dishes in the sink. "It got messed up because life is messy. People are fallible. They make mistakes, say things they shouldn't. And sometimes, they even hold on to a relationship, not because they still want to be with that person, but because there's unfinished business, unresolved feelings."

"My feelings for Brady are firmly resolved." *Liar,* a tiny voice inside her head whispered. She filled a glass with water and drank deeply, hoping to dislodge what felt like a pebble in her throat. "I love Carter, not Brady."

Rose smiled and patted Liz's cheek. "I believe you. And once you realize what's holding you back from fully committing to your husband, heart and soul, everyone else will believe you, too. Including yourself."

HIS MOTHER WAS getting married.

And instead of celebrating with her, her fiancé and their respective families, Brady was hiding upstairs in his father's office—in Aidan's office— where he could drink a few beers in peace.

Lying on the leather sofa, he stared out the window at the starry sky. Bing Crosby singing "White Christmas" floated upstairs, as did the muted sounds of laughter, conversation and general revelry.

He tipped his bottle of beer at the sky in a mock toast. Welcome to the Sheppards' annual Christmas Eve party, where more than one hundred of his mother's closest friends mingled downstairs. After his mother and Al had announced their engagement to wild applause, Brady had done his familial duty for about fifteen minutes before the press of bodies, the noise and smells— floral perfumes, musky colognes and rich, buttery desserts—forced him to find some solitude.

Sensory overload, he thought, drinking his beer.

But up here, with the lights off and no one asking him how his physical therapy was going or if he planned on sticking around Jewell now that his options were limited, he could breathe.

I'm in love with you.

The bottle slipped from his fingers, dropping with a thud. It rolled, spilling beer over the carpet before he could grab it. Damn it. Damn it! Why couldn't J.C. leave him alone? Every time he'd shut his eyes last night, he'd relived their lovemaking, the dreams so vivid he'd woken up reaching for her. Only to remember the look on her face when she overheard him claiming he didn't want the baby. That he couldn't love her because she wasn't Liz.

He tipped his head side to side until his neck popped. But he could still hear her voice in his head.

My son and I will be just fine without you. But I wonder, Brady, how do you think you'll be without us?

My son, she'd said, claiming their baby as effectively as if she'd said straight out she was keeping him. And he didn't doubt they'd be fine. J.C. was far more resilient than people gave her credit for. She'd be a terrific mother. And someday, she'd meet someone without so much baggage. A guy smart enough not to screw up what a good thing he had with her.

Sitting up, he finished his beer. He needed another one. Or twelve.

But to get one, he had to venture yet again into the party. This time he was bringing a six-pack out with him instead of one bottle.

He got to his feet as the office door opened and someone flipped the lights on.

"I thought you might be in here," Matt said from the doorway. He looked at the beer bottle in Brady's hand, his eyes narrowing slightly. "There's a pretty brunette out on the porch to see you." Jane.

"Why didn't you bring her up?" Brady asked roughly, already on his way toward the door.

"I tried. She said she didn't want to interrupt the party."

Brady brushed past Matt and was down the stairs in a

210

few minutes. In the living room next to the foyer, the party was in full swing. Avoiding eye contact, he paused at the front door to comb his fingers through his hair and realized as he raised his hand he still held the empty beer bottle. He stuck it under the skinny fake tree in the corner his mother had decorated all in red.

He stepped outside. Between the porch light and the white Christmas lights his mother had wound around every available surface, the porch fairly glowed, making it easy for Brady to see her sitting on the wooden swing.

Just not the woman he'd hoped it'd be.

"Hello, Brady," Liz said, stopping the motion of the swing and standing.

He exhaled. Mouth tight, he nodded.

"I'm sorry to barge in on you this way," she said, hunching her shoulders against the cold. "I forgot about your mom's holiday party until I pulled in and saw all the cars."

"Is J.C. okay?"

Liz looked at him speculatively. "As far as I know, she's fine."

"Good. That's...good." He shoved his hands into his pockets. "Do you want to come inside?"

"I'd rather stay out here if you don't mind. This won't take long."

He lifted a shoulder, then leaned back against the porch rail while she retook her seat on the swing. She cleared her throat. "Brady, I owe you an apology."

"Mind telling me what, exactly, you're apologizing for?"

Tipping her head back, she searched his face. "I'm sorry I wrote you that letter."

Out of all the reasons he could think of for Liz to show up at his mother's house on Christmas Eve, her apologizing for writing him a Dear John letter hadn't made the list.

"After everything we'd been through," she continued when he remained silent, "you deserved more than that."

It didn't matter. No apology could change what happened or bring him back what he'd lost. But maybe he could get some answers to the questions that had plagued him for so long.

"Why'd you write it?" he asked. "Why not break off things when I was home for leave that summer instead of letting me go overseas thinking nothing had changed between us?"

She clasped her gloved hands together on her lap. "I should have. But I'd convinced myself my feelings for Carter weren't serious." She lowered her head, her gaze on the porch floor. "But the biggest reason I didn't end our engagement face-to-face or even over the phone was because I knew you'd try to talk me out of it. I was afraid if you did," she said thickly, "I'd let you. And then things would go on between us the way they always had."

"That would've been so bad?"

"Not bad," she said with a shaky breath, "but not what I wanted, either." She raised her head, tears sparkling in her eyes. "I loved you, Brady. I loved you for half of my life but I...I didn't want to marry you," she whispered.

"What the hell does that mean?" he growled, not giving a rat's ass that she winced at his harsh tone. "You accepted my proposal. You wore my ring. Now you tell me you never planned on marrying me?"

"It wasn't like that," she said, getting to her feet. "I didn't even realize it myself until after I met Carter."

Brady stared at Liz as if he'd never seen her before. "All those times you pushed the wedding date back," he said, "because you wanted to finish college first, then med school and your residency, those were excuses not to marry me?"

"I kept thinking, hoping, something would change." She pulled a tissue from her pocket and wiped her eyes then blew her nose. "I held on to you because I loved you too much to let you go."

"You loved me," he said in a monotone. "Just not enough to commit to making a life with me."

"I was wrong. That's why I'm here. It's time I let you go for good, for both our sakes." She reached past him and he stiffened. But she didn't touch him, just set the blue jeweler's box containing the ring he'd bought her on the porch rail. "Goodbye, Brady."

He watched Liz walk away and stood staring out over the driveway long after she left. But instead of thinking of Liz and what she'd confessed, one thought consumed him.

J.C. had been right.

He wiped a shaky hand over his mouth. He'd been holding on to his past because he couldn't imagine loving any other woman but Liz. He'd thought they had the perfect love, but it had been a lie. All those years of waiting for Liz to set a wedding date, to be ready to marry him, he'd pretended everything was great because he wanted to hold on to the fantasy rather than face reality.

While he'd been focused on what he'd lost, he'd ignored what he'd gained.

A chance for the life he'd always dreamed of with a beautiful, warm, funny woman. A woman who'd give him a child. A woman who loved him. And he'd pushed her away.

16

"YOU'RE LATE."

With a gasp, Liz whirled toward the sound of her husband's voice. "Carter. You scared me."

"Sorry."

Frowning, she shut the front door and walked into their living room. Carter was slouched in an armchair staring at the flames in the fireplace. Other than the fire and the colorful lights on their Christmas tree, the room was dark.

"I thought you were going to Mitch and Kelly's for dinner," she said, taking her coat off and laying it on the back of the sofa before switching on a floor lamp.

Carter's shirtsleeves were rolled up, the top three buttons of his collar undone. His pale hair stuck up at odd angles, as if he'd repeatedly run his hands through it. "I didn't want to go without you. I wanted to spend our first Christmas Eve as a married couple together."

She crossed to him. "I'm glad. I want that, too."

"How was work?" he asked, sipping red wine as he regarded her over the glass. "You must've been busy."

Sitting on the arm of the chair, she slipped off her shoes

and wiggled her toes. "You know how it is during the holidays. The E.R. was a madhouse."

"Is that why you're late?" he asked in that calm way of his. "Why you've been crying?"

She rubbed at the aching arch of her foot. Though she'd done a quick repair job on her makeup in the car, she knew there were still traces of smudged mascara under her red-rimmed eyes. And the tip of her nose was still pink.

She helped herself to his wine, took a long drink and prayed she'd done the right thing for her marriage. "I went to see Brady."

His fingers dug into the arm of the chair by her leg. "Why?"

"To apologize." She tucked a strand of hair behind her ear. "And because we both needed closure."

She just hadn't realized how badly they'd needed it until yesterday after J.C. had left their grandmother's house.

Carter sat up. "You apologized for breaking up with him?"

"No. For how I handled it. How I handled everything." She stood and wandered to the tree. Traced a fingertip over a red ball before facing her husband. "He needed to know the truth about why I wrote that letter. And I had to return his ring."

"Did he take it back this time?"

"I didn't give him a choice." She clasped her hands. "I left it there. What he does with it isn't my concern. Not anymore."

"Why?" he asked quietly.

"I...I don't understand."

He rested his elbows on his knees. "Why worry about closure now, after all this time?"

She rubbed her hands over her suddenly chilled arms.

"For you," she told him simply. "For us. I want us to get back to how we used to be. And because..."

When she'd seen Brady leave J.C.'s apartment, Liz hadn't just been angry, hadn't just felt betrayed. For one awful moment, she'd hated them both.

Her throat burned with tears. "Because yesterday I realized I couldn't move on with my life until I'd settled my past. Neither could Brady."

Carter watched her, his expression unreadable. "What if we can't go back?"

Fear immobilized her for one heartbeat. Two. Then she shook her head.

"I'm not going to lose you," she told him fiercely.

Kneeling in front of him, she gripped his hands. Relief made her lightheaded when he linked his fingers with hers. "Thanksgiving, when we argued about Brady, you...you asked me if I still loved him and I didn't answer." She drew in a breath, then said in a rush, "Ask me now."

Dropping his gaze, he rubbed his thumbs over the backs of her hands. "I'm afraid to hear the answer," he whispered.

She brought his hands to her mouth, kissed both in turn and waited until he met her eyes. "I don't love Brady. I made a mistake, a huge one, in not telling you that before. You are the only man I love. And that is never going to change."

Carter searched her eyes and this time, instead of feeling guilty, as if she was hiding something from him, she let him see the truth.

He pressed a soft kiss against her forehead, then on each closed eye before wrapping his arms around her and dragging her onto his lap. She curled into him and rested her head on his shoulder.

"I love you so much, Liz," he told her. "I never want to lose you."

"You won't," she promised, stroking her fingers through his hair. She took his wonderfully handsome face in her hands. "I love you," she told him again.

Then she tugged on his hand and pulled him to the floor. And in the flickering glow of the fire, she showed him just how much.

WELL AFTER 1:00 A.M., when all the guests had gone and most of the cleanup was completed, Brady sat back in a recliner in his mother's family room, staring at her tree so long, the lights began to dance and blur in front of his eyes. He shook his head and blinked several times until his vision cleared.

The only reason he was still here was because Matt was freaking out about their mother's engagement. And because he wasn't in any hurry to go back to the cottage where he'd spend a restless night dreaming of J.C. Wondering if there was any way he could make things right between them again.

Yeah, even listening to Matt bitch and moan was better than that.

"You think Al would mind if I call him Daddy?" Matt asked from his spot on the sofa, his head propped up on his bent arm as he stared at the ceiling.

Aidan was on the floor, his back resting against an armchair, his dog lying next to him, her head in his lap. He stared at his youngest brother. "You're an idiot."

"Me? Hey, I'm not the one in this family who's taking the marital plunge with a guy who looks like a horse when he smiles. All those teeth can't be real. And if a man lies about his teeth, who knows what else he'll lie about."

Aidan pinched the bridge of his nose. "He's not that bad."

"He's a politician," Matt pointed out. "There's nothing *but* bad about that."

"He's retired," Aidan said. "Trust me, he's a decent guy."

"How do we know he's not after Mom's money?"

"He could buy the Diamond Dust outright—twice—in cash, and still have money left over."

Matt raised his head and looked at Brady. "What about you? Do you think Mom's making a mistake?"

As if Brady had any right to judge someone else's choices. "If she is, it's her mistake to make."

"That's such a cop-out. You don't think it's risky for a woman Mom's age to jump into marriage with the first guy who asks her?"

"He might not be the first guy to ask," Brady said, lifting his bottle of beer to his mouth. Feeling Aidan watch his every move. "For all we know, it's just the first time she's said yes."

Scowling, Matt got to his feet. "If you two aren't going to take this seriously, I'm going to bed."

"Merry Christmas," Brady murmured as his brother left the room, adding to Aidan, "I would've thought out of the three of us, you'd be the one having the hardest time with Mom getting remarried."

While Tom Sheppard had loved his boys equally, he and Aidan had had a special bond. Probably because they were so much alike.

"I like Al. More importantly, he makes Mom happy." Aidan leaned his head back on the chair cushion. "Besides, Dad would want Mom to move on."

Seemed to be the theme in Jewell. His mother getting remarried. Liz moving on with her new husband. And eventually, J.C. would move on, as well. She'd give birth to their baby, raise their son.

I'm in love with you.

Even that would change.

And that thought turned his blood to ice. He finished his beer and stood.

"Want another?"

"I'm good."

Brady tossed his empty into the recycling bin and grabbed a full bottle from the fridge. He flipped the cap into the garbage and then sat back down.

"You have something you want to say?

"Do you hear me talking?" Aidan asked.

"No. But I can feel all those waves of disapproval."

Aidan stroked Lily's head, her eyes squinting in pleasure. "I'm wondering what happened to send you back to the bottle."

"Maybe I'm just thirsty."

"I thought Jane would be at the party," Aidan mentioned way too casually for the comment to actually be casual. "Did she have other plans?"

He scowled. "How the hell would I know?"

"Thought you two were friends."

Cold sweat broke out on his forehead. Friends. Jeez. "We're not," he said.

Aidan bent one leg, resting his arm on his knee. "You blew it, huh?"

"There was nothing to blow. She wasn't what I wanted."

"Why not?"

He froze in the act of raising his beer to his mouth. "She's Liz's sister."

"You don't want her because she's Liz's sister? Or because she's not Liz?"

"Both. Neither." Hell. He carefully set the bottle on the table. "It would never work out."

Aidan raised an eyebrow. "Your crystal ball tell you that?"

"This isn't how my life was supposed to be," he said, feeling as if the words were being ripped from his throat. "Liz and me breaking up. My knee..." The nightmares. The drinking. J.C. and the baby. "None of it's what I wanted."

"And all this time I thought Matt was the idiot in the family," Aidan muttered as he stood. "You think you're the only person whose life is one hundred and eighty degrees from where you thought it'd be? If things went according to plan, Dad would still be alive and I'd be working my way up to partner at some high-end law firm in D.C."

"You could've still had that law career," Brady said, feeling as if he were backed into a corner and the only way out was to start swinging. "No one forced you to take over the winery after Dad died. The only thing you didn't choose was Yvonne leaving."

At the mention of his ex-wife, Aidan's expression hardened. "Why don't you take responsibility for yourself, for your decisions? It's not as if your life turned out the way it has through no fault or conscious choice of your own."

Brady wanted to deny it. He hadn't wanted Liz to end their engagement and he sure as hell hadn't asked for his vehicle to run over that bomb. But, damn it, he had stayed with Liz despite her repeatedly pushing their wedding date back. He'd joined the Marines, stayed in the Corps despite the risks involved.

He chose to spend time with J.C. even though his feelings for her grew more tangled, more confused with every one of her smiles. With every casual touch or soft kiss.

He'd let himself fall completely for Jane Cleo Montgomery.

Shaken, he rubbed the heel of his hand over his heart. "You were right the first time. I definitely blew it with J.C."

"So fix it."

If you ever start thinking you'd like to be a part of our lives after all— don't bother. My son and I will be fine without you. We don't need you.

His pulse pounded in his ears. "I don't think I can," he admitted.

"Want my advice?"

"No."

"Don't let her go. Do whatever you have to do or say to convince her to give you a second chance."

Brady brought his head up at the urgency in his brother's voice. "Is that the voice of experience talking?"

"It's the voice of a man whose wife walked out on him." Aidan's expression was grim. "A man who didn't stop her. Who chose not to go after her."

CHRISTMAS MORNING, J.C. and most of the other congregation joined in as the First Presbyterian's choir sang "Joy to the World" at the end of the church service. She snuck a glance down the wooden pew, past her parents and Grandma Rose, to where Liz and Carter stood sharing a songbook. They'd arrived just before services started, harried, windblown and flushed. And obviously very much together.

As J.C. watched, Carter bent his head and whispered in Liz's ear. She smiled, then caressed her husband's cheek with her fingertips.

J.C. jerked her gaze back to the songbook in her hand but the words blurred. Maybe this loneliness was her penance for coveting her sister's ex.

Or maybe she'd just been simply foolish to fall in love with someone as lost and damaged as Brady Sheppard.

The song ended and as usual, her family was one of the last to leave, thanks to Grandma Rose being in no particular hurry to get out of the pew. How it could possibly take someone so long to put on a coat, button it, pull on some gloves and dig her house keys out of her purse—because God forbid she'd have to stand outside her own front door searching for her keys—J.C. had no idea. All she knew was that by the time her grandmother was ready to go, the church was half-empty.

J.C. followed her family out of the pew. Her parents walked down the aisle with their closest friends, Sandy and Dan O'Brien, while Carter escorted Grandma Rose.

Leaving Liz standing in the aisle waiting for her. J.C. considered exiting from the other end of the pew, even took a step in that direction before sliding her purse strap over her shoulder and moving forward.

Liz's smile was bright, her eyes uncertain. "Merry Christmas," she said, hugging J.C.

Though it was petty—petty and immature and not in the Christmas spirit at all—J.C. kept her arms at her sides. "Merry Christmas."

Liz's smile faltered. She cleared her throat then swept her gaze over her sister. "Wow, you look really…"

So help her, if Liz said *tired* or commented on the dark circles under her eyes or the pallor of her skin, J.C. was going to hit her with a hymnbook.

"Pretty," Liz decided.

"Thank you." The baby moved—he'd been rolling

around like mad in there all morning—and J.C. rubbed her stomach. "I take it everything's all right with you and Carter?"

Liz glanced over at her husband, who was waiting patiently for Grandma Rose to finish her conversation with the minister. "I wouldn't go that far, but we're trying. We..." Fidgeting with the buttons on her coat, Liz lowered her voice. "We're going to look into couples' counseling after the holidays."

"That's good," J.C. said, meaning it. She stepped into the aisle, forcing Liz to hastily move out of the way. "I hope you two work things out."

She walked toward the double doors. The church had cleared out quickly. The kids were itching to change out of their fancy clothes and play with the toys they'd unwrapped earlier. The adults were either hurrying from one relative's house to another's or racing home to start Christmas dinner. Her parents were probably speeding home themselves to host their annual Christmas brunch at noon.

She'd planned to attend. Had told herself she was tough enough to survive a couple hours surrounded by family and friends. But now she was panicked at just the thought of acting as if everything were okay.

She'd go back to her apartment. Once there, she'd call and tell her parents she wasn't feeling well and wouldn't make it to their party.

"Jane, wait," Liz called, stopping J.C. before she reached the doors. "I...I want to apologize for what happened the other day. For the things I said."

"It doesn't matter."

Liz's eyes filled with tears. "How can you say that? I was horrible. What I said about Brady..." She swallowed convulsively. "About him not wanting anyone but me..."

"All you said was the truth."

Liz opened her mouth. Then shut it as she looked over J.C.'s shoulder, her eyes widening slightly. "No," she said, "I don't think that was the truth at all."

A ripple of awareness washed over J.C. Holding her breath, she turned slowly. And there he was—Brady Sheppard, leaning against the door, looking as sullen and dangerous and lost as he had on the day of Liz's wedding.

Except he wasn't looking at Liz. No, he was looking at her. Even when Liz brushed past him and walked out the door.

J.C.'s mouth went dry. Shock held her immobile as he straightened and strode toward her, his step purposeful despite his limp. He looked...well...he looked awful. As if he'd slept in his clothes—or hadn't gone to bed yet. His hair waved in disarray, his eyes were bloodshot and the thick stubble on his cheeks and chin did nothing to soften the harsh lines of his face.

He didn't stop until he was so close she had to tip her head back to meet his eyes.

"You're not at your apartment," he rumbled.

She blinked. Blinked again. "No. I'm not."

"You didn't stay there last night."

She gaped at him. "How do you—"

"I waited for you."

She remembered the other times he'd waited. Thanksgiving night. At the doctor's office for her appointment. "You waited all night?" He nodded curtly. "I stayed over at my parents' house. They didn't want me to be alone."

"When you didn't come home I thought..." He looked away. "I thought I'd lost you. For good. Tell me I haven't. Tell me I'm not too late."

Shaking her head slowly, she backed away. But for each step she took, he followed.

"I'm not doing this," she said, her voice trembling when she'd meant to sound confident. Angry. Damn it, she was angry. And way too raw to give him even the slightest opportunity to hurt her again.

"Please." He reached out as if to touch her face but she jerked her head back. "Please," he repeated, curling his fingers into a fist. "Just let me explain—"

"Explain what, Brady? You've made it perfectly clear you don't anything to do with me or our baby. Oh, or maybe you'd like to tell me how you'd rather be with Liz, but hey, I'll do in a pinch, right? And if it's dark enough and you pretend real hard," she said, her voice cracking, "you can convince yourself you're really with her."

"Jane...no...God, I didn't..." He looked stunned. "You know that's not true. I made love to *you* that night. You're who I want."

"It's too late."

She started to walk away. "I love you, Jane."

She stumbled and turned around, her eyes wide. "Don't say that," she snapped.

"It's the truth. I love you."

"You love Liz." She hugged her arms around herself. "You're always going to love Liz."

"I'm always going to care about her, but I don't love her. I'm not in love with her. Not anymore." He stepped toward J.C. "You were right. I couldn't see what had gone right in my life." Another step. "You, Jane. You and our baby are what's right."

She began to shake. "No."

He regarded her gravely. "What I said that morning after we made love...what you heard..." He blew out a shaky breath. "I was scared. Afraid of my feelings for you. I didn't know what to do with them. They were...too much. Too soon. I wanted to control them because so many parts of my life were out of my control."

"Stop. Please..." Her voice was raw. Her breathing shallow. "I can't do this again."

"You said you and the baby didn't need me," he said, relentlessly, stubbornly, as he closed the remaining distance between them. He gently lifted her chin. "You may not need me, but I need you. Both of you."

Afraid to believe, she searched his eyes. Joy and love, so much love for him, welled inside her and the tears she'd tried to hold back rolled down her cheeks.

"Don't cry," he said raggedly, wiping her face, his touch unsteady. "It rips me apart when you cry."

Throwing her arms around him, she pressed her face into his neck. She inhaled his familiar, comforting scent. He stilled for a moment, then with a groan, wrapped his arms around her, pulling her close, holding her so tightly, she couldn't breathe. She clung to him harder.

"Thank you," he murmured. "Thank you."

He pulled back and kissed her, his lips warm, his mouth coaxing. When he straightened, he cupped her face in one hand, his thumb caressing her jaw. His other hand went to the soft swell of her stomach, his fingers spread wide. "Tell me."

Because he still seemed so unsure, so nervous, she kissed him. Then smiled. "I love you, Brady."

He nodded and she felt some of his tension drain away. "I love you, Jane Cleo," he said, his voice husky.

And then—disheveled, contented and, if she wasn't mistaken, mended— Brady Sheppard smiled. At her.

EPILOGUE

ONE MONTH LATER

ABOUT A MILE AWAY from the turn to the Diamond Dust, Brady took a right down a narrow lane.

"Where are we going?" J.C. asked from the passenger seat as he passed two houses—one on each side of the road—and pulled to a stop in front of a large, well-maintained farmhouse where the street ended. "Brady, what's going on? You know how your mom gets if we're late for lunch."

Lunch with his mom, Al and Aidan had become a weekly Sunday event. Things were still tense with J.C.'s family, and he doubted he and Carter would ever be more than stiffly polite to each other, but J.C. and Liz seemed to be making inroads.

He unclenched his hands from around the steering wheel. "We'll be there on time. I..." His throat was dry. "I want to show you something."

Grinning, she rolled her eyes. "Like I haven't heard that line before." When he couldn't return her smile, hers slid away.

"You okay?" she asked, laying a hand on his arm. "Do you need to do some breathing exercises?"

"I'm fine." He squeezed her hand. "I'm not having an episode."

He'd been seeing a therapist for the past three weeks who'd officially diagnosed him with PTSD—post-traumatic stress disorder. And while he couldn't say he was thrilled with the diagnosis or having to spill his guts every week in his therapy session, the techniques he'd learned for dealing with his memories, stress and flashbacks were helping.

"Come on," he said, then hurried around the car, opened her door and pulled her to her feet.

She laughed but followed him to the wooden porch. He dug a set of keys out of his pocket. Her eyes widened. "What are you doing? Who lives here?"

"It's empty," he said, pushing open the door and tugging her into the wide foyer. He swallowed. "Want to look around?"

"Uh...sure."

Holding her hand, he led her up the stairs, turned left and walked into a large room with deep burgundy walls and white trim. "Master bedroom," he said, repeating the information the Realtor had given him, "complete with walk-in closets, bath and a balcony."

"It's very...pretty," she said, looking at him as if he'd recently suffered a head injury.

"Two more bedrooms up here." Spinning her around, he walked down the hall and into the room on the right—this one smaller and painted a sunny yellow—only to walk right out again and into the third bedroom at the back of the house. He opened the door at the end of the hall. "Closet." Gestured toward the final door. "Bathroom."

By the time he'd gotten her back down the stairs she was silent and his knee was aching.

"Foyer," he said as they passed the tiled entryway again. "That's the family room." He pointed to the large room off the foyer, then, knowing where he wanted the tour to end, he went the way they came, pointing at rooms as they walked. "Another bedroom or office, half bath, dining room."

Finally, his heart pounding, they reached the last room. "This is the kitchen."

"Yes," J.C. said, tugging free of his hold, her brow furrowed. "I can see that."

He waited as she slowly walked around, checking out the stainless-steel appliances, granite counters and built-in pantry.

"Well?" he asked, his voice a low growl when she remained silent.

She leaned back against the sink and crossed her arms. "Well what?"

He ground his teeth together. "Do you like it?"

"The kitchen?"

"The house."

She shrugged. "Yes."

He narrowed his eyes. Yes? That was it? "The asking price is for the house plus ten acres. And since it's been on the market for over a year, the owners are ready to make a deal."

"Well, if I was in the market to buy a house, that would all be good to know." Smiling, she straightened. "You ready to go? I'm starving," she added as she walked toward the door. "Do you think your mom made that potato soup I like?"

"I'm in the market."

229

Almost to the door, she turned slowly. "Excuse me?"

He shoved his hands into his pockets. "I'm in the market to buy a house. To buy this house." She regarded him steadily. Sweat formed at the nape of his neck, a bead of it sliding down between his shoulder blades. "I want to buy this house for you and the baby. For us."

"Why?"

"Because I love you," he ground out, crossing to her. "And you love me."

"Yes, I do." She tipped her head to the side, looking so serene and so damn beautiful, he caught his breath. "I want you to ask me," she said softly.

His chest tight, he pulled a ring box out of his pocket and opened it. "It was my great-grandmother's," he said of the round diamond set in a platinum scrolled band.

"It's beautiful." She kept her hands clasped in front of her. She met his eyes. "But I'm still waiting for you to ask me."

"I can't kneel."

"No." Her eyes glistened. "I don't want you to. I just want the words."

"Jane Cleo Montgomery," he said quietly, taking her left hand and sliding the ring onto her finger, "I love you. I want to make a life with you and our baby." He kissed her hand, then looked into her eyes. "Will you marry me?"

"Yes," she whispered, linking her fingers through his. She cleared her throat. "Yes, Brady. I'll marry you."

Humbled, grateful, he pressed his lips against hers. Her mouth softened. He lifted his head and grinned. "I know you're anxious to get to lunch, but what do you think about christening the house before we go?"

She laughed and linked her arms around his neck. "I think that's the second-best proposal I've had today."

The End

If you enjoyed A Marine for Christmas I hope you'll consider leaving a review!

Let's keep in touch!

Want all the updates, sneak peeks of upcoming releases, cover reveals, exclusive excerpts, giveaways and more? Sign up for my newsletter at www.bethandrews.net/newsletter. And keep reading for a sneak peek at Matt's story, The Prodigal Son.

Thank you so much for reading! I first wrote A Marine for Christmas back in 2010 and I had so much fun revisiting Brady and J.C. as I updated their story.

As we're all well aware, life does not follow a set road map—no matter how much we'd like it to. There are bumps that leave you flat and broken down. Turns that lead to wonderful new destinations. You may find yourself at the top of a high hill, joyous and certain that if you reach up, you'll touch the stars. Or in a valley so low you wonder how you'll ever climb out.

Ex-marine Brady Sheppard is in one of those valleys. The woman he loves has married another man. He's drinking too much and is also suffering post traumatic stress disorder. Too full of pride and anger to ask for help, he spends his days bitter and alone. Until he finds out he's going to be a father. Too bad the mother of his child, Jane Cleo (JC) Montgomery, is his ex's kid sister.

Let me just confess right here and now that Brady was no walk in the park to write. He was harsh and angry and dealing with some very big, very real issues. But somehow, he finds a way to deal with those issues and as I wrote him, I fell for him in a huge way. I hope you did, too!

Hugs!

Beth

Let's keep in touch!

Check out my website - www.bethandrews.net
Sign up for my newsletter -
www.bethandrews.net/newsletter.
Facebook - www.facebook.com/bethandrewsauthor
Instagram - www.instagram.com/bethandrewsauthor

OTHER TITLES

Written as Beth Andrews

Counting Flowers (Contemporary
Young Adult Romance)

Serenity Springs series

Not Without Her Family (Jack and Kelsey)
A Not-So-Perfect Past (Dillon and Nina)
His Secret Agenda (Dean and Allie)

The Diamond Dust trilogy

A Marine for Christmas (Brady and J.C)
The Prodigal Son (Matt and Connie)
Feels Like Home (Aidan and Yvonne)

The Truth about the Sullivans trilogy

Unraveling the Past (Ross and Layne)
On Her Side (Griffin and Nora)
In This Town (Walker and Tori)

In Shady Grove series

Talk of the Town (Neil and Maddie)
What Happens Between Friends (James and Sadie)
Caught Up in You (Eddie and Harper)
Small-Town Redemption (Kane and Charlotte)
Charming the Firefighter (Leo and Penelope)

Written as Bebe Marks

Once Tempted Series

Hyde's Return (Hyde and Everly)

For a complete list of all my available books, please check
out my website - www.bethandrews.net/books

THE PRODIGAL SON SNEAK PEEK

When the prodigal Shepard son returns, life at The Diamond Dust will never be the same.

HE WAS GOING HOME.

Not to stay, Matt assured himself as he steered the four-wheeled ATV down a row between thick, leafy vines in the eastern section of Queen's Valley's vineyards. He shut off the ignition. Never to stay.

The worst part about going back to Jewell? This wouldn't be the first time. No, he'd visited his hometown plenty of times since making his impassioned vow never to return ten years ago. He smiled ruefully. That was the problem with making dramatic, heartfelt declarations. They were hard to stick to.

Especially ones made in the heat of anger.

Lesson learned.

Which was why he rarely made promises. They were too hard to keep.

Shaking his hair back, he got off the ATV and unhooked

the bungee cords holding his equipment bag to the rack behind the seat. He took out his refractometer and slid it into the front pocket of his loose cargo shorts before grabbing a heavy plastic bag. Going down the row, he picked samplings of the Chardonnay grapes, tossing them into the bag.

Queen's Valley was forty acres of vineyards nestled along the Murray River in South Australia. The grapes thrived in the warm, temperate climate. All around him the vines reached well above his head with heavy clusters of healthy grapes and a well-maintained canopy, the leaves lush and green. He'd worked at wineries in Napa, France and Italy and could honestly say Queen's Valley was one of the best vineyards he'd seen.

And for the next three years, it was all his.

But first he had to return to where he'd begun. Oh, he'd tried to keep the vow he'd made graduation night. The next day he'd flown out of Virginia and told himself he'd never look back. For over a year he'd kept his distance from his family, the only contact with them an occasional email from one of his brothers, a weekly phone call to his mother. During that time he'd worked two jobs while going to school. Though it'd been a struggle, he'd managed to juggle everything and had put himself through college.

He'd figured out how to take care of himself. And as much as he hated to admit it, his father had been right about one thing. He'd had to grow up. He'd also discovered that he liked being on his own. That he didn't need his family.

Knowing that made it a lot easier to rip up the checks his mother sent like clockwork at the beginning of each month. It also let him swallow his pride and go home for Christmas during his sophomore year. Three days where, for his mother's sake, he'd tried his best to act as if everything was all right. As if all was forgiven.

But during his stay, he remembered his graduation night. His hurt and anger and resentment that his father couldn't appreciate him for who he was.

Couldn't support him in what he wanted for himself.

Then, less than a year after that awkward, tension-filled Christmas, the unthinkable happened. His father had been diagnosed with pancreatic cancer. Six months later, he was dead.

And he and Matt had never discussed that night or the many issues between them, never came to terms with each other. There were no apologies. No heart-to-heart talks. No closure.

Matt gave his head one sharp shake. That was in the past now. All in the past. He was more interested, more vested in the future. And his future was right here in Queen's Valley. Continuing to pick grapes, he walked down the row, taking samples from different vines and tasting an occasional grape.

For over twenty-five years, Queen's Valley had provided top quality fruit to local wineries. Now the owner, Joan Campbell, had decided to branch out and start making the vineyard's own wines. She'd spared no expense building a state-of-the-art facility and she'd hired Matt to run it all. He had final say in every decision from the variety of grapes to what type of oak barrels to purchase to the shape of the wine bottles. And everyone, save Joan and her daughter, Suzanne, were to report to him.

Total control.

Whistling, he repeated his picking process on the other side of the row. It was like a dream come true. He got to work for a winery that had everything at its disposal to produce the finest wines. A chance to build on his growing reputation, to be known for putting Queen's Valley on the map as one of the finest wineries in Australia.

The best part? It was halfway across the world from Jewell, Virginia.

As he made his way back to where he'd started, he heard the sound of another ATV approaching. A moment later, Joan came into view, her chubby body leaning over the handlebars. Her straw hat, tied around her throat with a string, sailed behind her as she sped down the row at twice the speed Matt would consider safe.

She came closer, and closer still. There was no room for her to get by his ATV without plowing through the trellised vines, but she showed no signs of slowing. Matt's heart thumped heavily in his chest. Instead of running him over, she stopped quickly, her rear wheels sliding. Clumps of grass and dirt shot out from the spinning tires and Matt jumped back to avoid getting sideswiped.

He wiped the back of his free hand over his forehead. Knew the sweat there wasn't just from the heat. "You are hell on wheels," he muttered when Joan shut off the vehicle.

"I'll take that as a compliment."

"Believe me. It wasn't meant as one."

"Now, Matthew, is that any way to speak to your employer?" Her words were like machine-gun fire—short, choppy bursts that came at a man fast and furiously. Combined with her raspy, smoker's voice and heavy Australian accent, he hadn't understood half of what she said the entire first month he'd worked for her.

And no matter how many times he'd asked her to call him Matt, she still insisted on using his full name.

Joan combed both hands through her windblown gray hair before putting her hat on. She tipped her head up so she could see him from under the wide brim. "I thought you had a plane to catch."

"Not for a few hours." He squeezed the grapes through the bag, crushing them and releasing their juice. "I wanted to check before I leave."

Chardonnay, along with Pinot Noir, were early ripening grapes. He wanted to make sure they weren't set to ripen while he was gone, since it would be impossible for him to decide they needed harvesting when he was on the other side of the world.

"Suzanne was just asking about you. Why don't you stop by and tell her goodbye?" Joan climbed off the ATV, her shrewd gaze on him. "I'm sure she'd appreciate it."

The nape of his neck tingled. "I'll be sure to do that," he lied.

He ducked his head and pretended dipping the slide of his refractometer into the juice took all of his concentration. At the previous wineries where he'd worked, he'd had to deal with long hours, early frosts, drought, blight... but never a matchmaking boss.

Not that he had anything against the pretty Suzanne. In fact, if the situation was different, he'd have done his best to charm her into his bed. But he preferred to keep his personal life separate from his career. No mixing business with pleasure. No ties. No commitments to hold him to a place other than a legal contract. And when that contract was fulfilled? He was free to go.

No hard feelings. No repercussions.

No one trying to guilt him into staying.

Looking through the refractometer, he noted the grapes' sugar content— twenty-four and a half Brix. The higher the Brix in the grapes, the higher the alcohol content in the wine. But the best winemakers didn't go just by the numbers. They took into account everything from the color of the skins and seeds, to the taste of the fruit, and the health of the vines and leaves.

He picked a plump, green grape and tossed it into his mouth. The sun rose over majestic, copper-colored limestone cliffs. It was the middle of February and he was sweating, his shirt sticking to his back. Even his scalp was burning. The breeze brought with it the scent of the river.

God, he loved it here. For now. And when his time at Queen's Valley was up, he'd be more than ready to move on to the next place. To the next challenge.

"You going to tell me your verdict," Joan groused, "or stand there and eat all of my fruit?"

"Skin's thick," he said, still chewing. "They're fairly sweet and fruity but still acidic." He swallowed. "They need more time on the vine."

She narrowed her eyes until they practically disappeared in her round face. "You sure you're not just saying that, not delaying our harvest so your plans don't get interrupted?"

He didn't bat an eye at her accusation. He'd quickly learned over the past few months that if he took offense at every brusque, argumentative word Joan said, he'd be pissed off all the time. Besides, he'd had tough bosses before.

The most demanding being his father.

And the most important lesson he'd ever learned from Tom Sheppard?

Never let them see you sweat.

"You hired me because you wanted someone knowledgeable," he told her, handing her the refractometer and the mashed grapes. "But if you don't believe me, see for yourself."

"Cutting it close," she said after checking the sugar content. "What if they turn while you're gone?"

"They won't. The next few weeks will be cool in the mornings. We have time."

Ripe wine grapes were at their best for only a few days, which made the decision of when to harvest important, but also risky. Matt wasn't worried, though. They'd had a colder than average summer and were experiencing a late harvest year. And the cool, foggy mornings would ensure the grapes finished ripening slowly.

Too bad Joan didn't seem convinced.

"Look," he said, "if they were ready or if there was the slightest chance at all that they could ripen during the next eight days, I'd stay."

"You'd miss your own brother's wedding?"

Miss a chance to spend over twenty-four hours of travel —most of them on planes—followed by a week of living in his family's pockets? Of dealing with his brothers. Trying not to feel guilty because he rarely came home, and when he did, he couldn't wait to be gone again.

Gladly.

"It wouldn't be the first wedding I've missed," he admitted, dumping the mashed grapes onto the ground and wiping the refractometer on the bottom of his shirt before putting it back into his equipment bag. "I was in France when my eldest brother got hitched. Couldn't make it home in time for the ceremony."

Not that he considered that a great loss. Especially since he and Aidan had a personality conflict.

The conflict being that Matt had a personality and Aidan was a humorless robot.

Besides, the marriage hadn't lasted.

Joan crossed her arms. "So if we get a heat wave and the grapes are ready before you're due back..."

"I'll get on the first flight out of the country." He checked his watch. Saw his cushion of two hours before he had to leave for the airport was now down to an hour and a half. And he still had to pack. "Don't worry," he told her as he sat on the ATV and turned the key. "I'll be back before the harvest. You can count on that."

———

OVER SIXTY HOURS LATER, Matt stood in his brother's cramped kitchen trying to make something edible out of eggs approaching their expiration date and half a loaf of slightly stale white bread.

He was in hell. Or, as everyone else called it, Jewell, Virginia.

Luckily, it was easy to keep his usual good cheer, thanks to the fact that his time in Jewell would be brief—six days, four hours and fifty-three minutes.

Give or take a second or two.

Whistling along with the classic Jackson Browne song playing on the radio, he transferred a soggy slice of bread from the egg and milk mixture in a large bowl to the hot skillet. It sizzled in the greased pan, the scent of cinnamon mingling with that of melted butter. He added a second slice to the pan and took a drink of coffee as a movement to his right caught his attention.

Sporting a seriously bad case of bedhead and wearing a pair of flannel pants with characters from *Family Guy* on them, Brady stood in the open doorway separating the kitchen from the hall.

Matt saluted his brother with his coffee cup. "Morning, Sparky. Nice pj's."

"I'm going to kill you," Brady said in a sleep-roughened voice. His scowl shifted into a thoughtful frown as he sniffed the air. "I'm going to kill you," he repeated, "right after I've had some coffee."

"Can't wait."

Eloquent as usual, Brady grunted and headed toward the coffeemaker, his limp less pronounced than it'd been two months ago when Matt had been home for Christmas.

Matt flipped the French toast with a fork. "You have any syrup? I didn't see any in the fridge." When he didn't get an answer, he turned to find Brady staring into his coffee cup, his eyes glazed. "If I'm not mistaken—and let's face it, I'm never mistaken—that's the look of a man who recently got laid. And based on the monkey sounds coming from your room when I got here, I'd say it happened...oh...about twenty minutes ago."

Brady pulled out a chair and sat at the table. "What's the rule about my sex life?"

"It's boring and pathetic?"

"It's not up for discussion."

"Who's discussing it? I was making a simple observation. It's not like I need a play-by-play of whatever it was J.C. did that put that sappy grin on your face."

Brady gave one of his patented *I was a Marine and yes, I will rip your head off and shove that fork down your throat if you say another word* looks.

"Fine." Matt glanced down the hallway to Brady's closed bedroom door. "Uh...you were with J.C., weren't you?"

Hey, it was a good question considering that at one time, Brady had been engaged to J.C.'s older sister, Liz.

Brady pinched the bridge of his nose. "Why are you here?"

"Aidan left a message on my cell phone yesterday about a top secret Sheppard brother meeting at eight."

"That's thirty minutes from now. And you're never on time anyway. Especially in the morning."

Matt transferred the cooked French toast to a paper plate and added more to the pan. "It's ten at night in South Australia."

"You're not in Australia."

No shit. In Australia—and everywhere outside of Jewell —he was a highly respected, highly sought-after vintner.

Here he was the family black sheep.

His fingers tightened around the fork. Too bad his old man hadn't lived long enough to see his youngest son amount to something despite his predictions. Matt forced his fingers to relax. Good thing he'd long ago stopped caring what his family thought of him.

"I'm not in Australia," he said, "but my body thinks I am. And since I was up, I figured I might as well come on over. Once I realized you were otherwise occupied, I decided to make myself at home."

Brady stood and held his hand out. "Give it to me." Matt handed him the plate but his brother shook his head. "No. Give me the spare key."

The spare key their mother kept at her house in case she needed to get into the cottage that sat on the Sheppards' property. The cottage Brady currently occupied.

"You're moving out after the wedding," Matt noted, tossing the plate onto the table. "What's the problem?"

"You let yourself into my house when I was still in bed," Brady said as if Matt was a few grapes shy of a cluster. "You're in my kitchen, blaring music—"

"Only so I couldn't hear all that moaning and groaning coming from your bedroom."

"—making breakfast—"

"For which you should be grateful, seeing as how I made plenty for all of us. That includes J.C."

"Where is it?" Brady asked, his tone low and dangerous.

Matt grinned and patted the front pocket of his jeans. "Right where it's going to stay."

Turning, he flipped the bread. A vise closed around his neck, choking off his amusement. No, not a vise, he realized as Brady yanked him away from the stove, but his brother's forearm. Before Matt could escape, Brady pivoted, clasping his hands together to tighten the headlock.

"The key. Now."

Matt pulled on his brother's arm but it didn't budge. "You want it?" he asked, unable to hide the challenge—or the glee—in his voice. "Go ahead and get it."

Brady squeezed, cutting off the last of Matt's words along with his breath. "I get the key," he said, dragging Matt toward the table, "and you get to walk upright once again. And save what's left of your dignity for getting your ass kicked by a guy with a bum knee."

"Ass kicked?" Matt muttered, doing his damnedest to shake his brother's hold. "I'm taking it easy so I don't hurt you."

"You keep telling yourself that." Then, in a move reminiscent of when they were kids, Brady gave him a quick, rough noogie.

Bum knee or not, the bastard was going down.

Matt grabbed Brady's hip with his right hand while shifting his body to the left. Pushing him off balance, he reached underneath Brady's left leg—conscious of the fact it was his bad leg—and lifted it off the ground.

Brady's arm constricted, cutting into Matt's windpipe. "If I'm going to hit the floor," he warned, "I'm taking you with me."

"Is something burning?"

They froze. J. C. Montgomery padded into the kitchen wearing a pair of pink sweatpants and a long-sleeved brown top stretched to its limit over her pregnant stomach. She wrinkled her nose at what Matt now recognized as the scent of burned French toast, her big brown eyes widening.

"Sorry," Brady said, hopping to maintain his balance. "Did we wake you?"

"That's all right," she said absently, tilting her head to the side to study them. "I hate to ask a stupid question but... is this one of those male bonding things? Because if you two pull out the bongo drums and start chanting, I'll get my phone so I can record it. I'm sure it'll be a huge hit on YouTube."

"We're not bonding," Matt said. "We're fighting. I was just about to drop your fiancé on his head."

"Oh. Well, that makes perfect sense. But since the wedding's in five days, I'd really prefer if he didn't suffer any head injuries. At least until after the ceremony. Besides," she added, "the physical therapist swore Brady will be able to dance with me at our wedding. As long as he doesn't do anything to strain his knee."

She stared at the knee in question—the one in Matt's hands.

Sighing, he let go of his brother. "Killjoy."

"That's me," she said. "A giant fun-suck. How about we arrange a wrestling match for the reception? Maybe one of those cage matches? That is, if I can find a company that rents..." She frowned. "Brady. The fight's over. You can let go of Matt." When he hesitated, she raised her eyebrows. "Now."

He mumbled under his breath, something about dead bolts, alarm systems and idiot brothers, before the pressure around Matt's neck eased.

Slipping out of Brady's hold, Matt smiled at J.C. then took the few steps necessary to cross to her. He gripped her arms. "Good morning, gorgeous." Then he gave her a smacking kiss on the cheek.

As he eased back, Brady growled. It made Matt want to kiss J.C. again.

"Uh...good morning to you, too." She peeked around his shoulder at Brady. "You never told me your family was so affectionate in the morning."

"He just did that to piss me off," Brady said.

"Not true," Matt claimed. "Though that's a nice side benefit. But the truth is," he continued, lowering his voice and leaning closer to J.C., "I'm weak. I have a hard time resisting a beautiful woman."

She blushed and attempted to smooth her wildly curling mane of dark hair. Damn, but she was a sweetheart. Brady had somehow hit the jackpot. That is, if you considered being tied to one woman for the rest of your life winning big.

Brady cleared his throat. "If you're done flirting with my fiancé, you might want to check your breakfast. It's on fire."

With a wink at J.C., Matt went back to the stove. There weren't any flames, just a lot of thick smoke. Matt flipped the burner to low while Brady opened the small window over the sink.

After he dumped the burned food into the garbage can, Matt unwound several paper towels from the roll, balled them up and wiped out the pan before setting it back on the burner.

"How about some French toast?" he asked J.C., adding fresh butter to the pan.

She looked up from pouring herself a large glass of orange juice. "You don't have to cook for me. I can fix some—"

"It's the least I can do."

"He's got that right," Brady muttered.

"Well," J.C. said as she picked the fork Matt had dropped earlier off the floor, "if you really don't mind..."

"Honey, I never mind cooking breakfast for a woman."

She smiled. "In that case, I'd love some."

In less than ten minutes, Matt made what he considered enough French toast to feed a family of five. Or at least two grown men and one pregnant lady. By the time the food was ready, Brady had donned a shirt and he and J.C. had paper plates, forks, an unopened container of syrup and a stick of butter still in its wrapper on the table.

They'd just started eating when Aidan came into the kitchen, his blond hair neatly trimmed, his dark slacks crisply pleated. "Morning," he said to the room at large as he went to the coffeepot and poured himself a cup. He took a sip, his eyes on Matt. "I didn't think you'd bother showing up until at least eight-thirty."

Giving himself time to hide a quick burst of irritation, Matt swallowed the food in his mouth. Just like their father, Aidan always thought the worst of him.

"Hey, you know I'm happy to obey your orders."

"Why, what time is it?" J.C. asked, sounding panicked. Before any of them could reply, she grabbed Matt's hand and twisted it so she could read his watch. "Crap. I'm late."

Leaping to her feet, she finished her juice. "I'm supposed to meet Mrs. Wertz in ten minutes for my last dress fitting."

"Don't you have the day off?" Brady asked.

"Yes, but she doesn't, and I asked her to squeeze me in before she goes to work. Thanks for breakfast," she called before rushing out of the room. A moment later, the front door banged shut.

Matt scratched his cheek. "Does she realize it's barely thirty degrees out and she's not wearing any shoes or a coat?"

Brady held his forefinger up. Two seconds later, the front door opened and J.C. sped past them. When she came back through a minute later, her sweatpants were tucked into a pair of boots and she was zipping up a bulky, shapeless coat, her purse hanging off her elbow.

And once again, the door slammed shut.

"One thing's for sure," Matt said as he snagged the last piece of French toast. "Your life isn't going to be boring."

Aidan sat in the seat J.C. had vacated. "Since we're all here, let's get right to it."

Matt snorted as he doused his toast with syrup. Right. Wouldn't want to waste time with small talk even if he hadn't spoken to either of his brothers for over two months. His mother being the only family he'd seen since he'd gotten into town.

"If this is about Brady's stag party," he said, "I've already hired the strippers."

"We want to talk to you about the Diamond Dust," Aidan said, sliding the remnants of J.C.'s breakfast aside before setting his cup down. He wrapped his hands around the mug. "We want you with us."

"I'm right here, aren't I?"

"We want you working with us at the winery. We want you to be our partner."

Matt stilled, his fork halfway to his mouth. His throat constricted.

Partners? With his brothers? "Why would I want to do that?"

"Told you," Brady said, leaning back in his chair, his hands linked on his stomach.

Aidan kept his hooded eyes on Matt. "Why wouldn't you?"

He slowly lowered his fork back to his plate. "I already have a career."

A damned good one, too, not that his brothers ever bothered to mention it. His reputation as a winemaker and consultant was growing and, after he led Queen's Valley to success, so would the number of wineries who wanted to hire him. He'd have his pick of jobs all over the world. And his brothers thought he'd give that up to stay in tiny Jewell to work at his father's business?

"Instead of making wine for other people," Aidan said, "you'd be making it for your own company. Your own label. And you'd have a chance to put down roots."

Put down roots? The back of his neck grew hot and clammy. "Thanks but when I do decide to settle in one place —" if he ever decided to settle in one place— "I'd rather it be Italy or France or Napa Valley."

"Dad's dream was to pass the Diamond Dust down to his sons," Aidan said quietly. "All three of us."

Matt tipped his chair back until it balanced on two legs. His father had hated when he did that. "Dad's gone. And like you said, that was his dream. Not mine. And as far as I can remember, it wasn't either one of your dreams, either."

"Things change."

True. But Matt hadn't changed. He'd never wanted to be stuck in Jewell working at the Diamond Dust. Working for his overly critical, rigid father.

And while Tom Sheppard might be gone, the worst parts of his personality lived on in his eldest son. The tight leash his dad had tried to keep him on when he was growing up had almost choked Matt to death. He wasn't about to put on another one.

"Sorry," he said as he stood, "but I'm not interested."

"Tell him," Brady murmured to Aidan.

His scalp tingled. His pulse pounded in his ears. "Tell me what?"

Jaw tight, Aidan slowly got to his feet. "You have to partner with us, move back to Jewell and help run the winery. If you don't, Mom's going to sell the Diamond Dust to someone else."

ABOUT THE AUTHOR

Romance Writers of America RITA® Award winner Beth Andrews loves Christmas, wine and chocolate—though not necessarily in that order. During the writing of this book she listened to hours of Christmas carols, visited a local winery (several times) and made many, *many* homemade chocolate truffles. All for research purposes, of course.

Sign up for Beth's newsletter -
www.bethandrews.net/newsletter
Visit Beth's website - www.bethandrews.net
Email Beth - beth@bethandrews.net

COPYRIGHT

A Marine For Christmas
© Copyright 2010 Beth Burgoon
ISBN: 9780692981320